Praise for Pulitzer Priz[...]
Fabiola Santiago and her poign[...]
RECLAIMING PARIS

"Like Miami, Santiago's writing is lush and crackles with a sophisticated sensuality. The prose casts a seductive spell on readers by transporting them to each of the cities that Marisol temporarily calls home."

—*The Boston Globe*

"Cuban and Latino readers will find much to identify with in this richly nuanced novel, and others will find it a fascinating inside look at a culture that is too often viewed as monolithic and alien. A true rarity—an erotic yet intelligent tale."

—*Kirkus Reviews*

"Santiago elevates this seemingly merely glamorous and romantic tale above the usual chick-lit fare by smoothly integrating immigration issues and a dash of mystery into the plot.

—*Booklist*

"Alone, in a hotel room in sultry Miami, sheets covering her quivering body, Marisol, the protagonist of this riveting book, weeps for her lost love. The scene will pierce the heart of every woman I know. For Marisol is us: defiant, romantic and, ultimately, our only true saviors."

—Mirta Ojito, Pulitzer Prize–winning author of *Finding Mañana*

"*Reclaiming Paris* is one woman's passionate odyssey through the shadows of tragic history and her own tumultuous past in search of her soul. Fabiola Santiago's heartbreakingly beautiful first novel throbs with sweet-scented poetry and the lusty heartbeats of Cuba, Miami, Barcelona, and Paris. She is a poet to die for."

—Edna [...] *Legally Dead*

"Santiago has cre[...] [...]derable disillusionments and [...] [...]r own heart into a reality she [...] [...]ust at some point in our lives, [...] [...]ny other."

—Cecilia Samartin, author of *Vigil*

This title is also available as an eBook

RECLAIMING PARIS

A Novel

FABIOLA SANTIAGO

WASHINGTON SQUARE PRESS
New York London Toronto Sydney

Washington Square Press
A Division of Simon & Schuster, Inc.
1230 Avenue of the Americas
New York, NY 10020

First Washington Square Press trade paperback edition August 2009

Designed by Jaime Putorti

Manufactured in the United States of America

10 9 8 7 6 5 4 3 2 1

The Library of Congress has cataloged the hardcover edition as follows:

Santiago, Fabiola.
Reclaiming Paris : a novel / Fabiola Santiago. — 1st Atria Books hardcover ed.
p. cm.
1. Women poets—Fiction. 2. Cubans—Florida—Miami—Fiction. 3. Exiles—Florida—Miami—Fiction. 4. Nostalgia—Fiction. 5. Loss (Psychology)—Fiction. 6. Place (Philosophy)—Fiction. 7. Memory (Philosophy)—Fiction. 8. Miami (Fla.)—Fiction. 9. Paris (France)—Fiction. I. Title.
PS3619.A578R43 2008
813'.6—dc22 2007052190

ISBN 978-1-4165-5112-6
ISBN 978-1-4165-5113-3 (pbk)
ISBN 978-1-4165-7964-9 (ebook)

To my forever loves,
Tanya, Marissa, and Erica

Ah, blue horizon
Ashimmer in the breeze!
Memories of childhood,
Recall my native shore!
Green were my mountains,
Fragrant in florid beauty.
Land of my fathers,
You I shall see no more.
Never, no, no, not evermore!

—FROM *AIDA* BY VERDI,
LIBRETTO BY ANTONIO GHISLANZONI

. . . Y pasó el tiempo, y pasó
un águila por el mar.

—JOSÉ MARTÍ, *LOS ZAPATICOS DE ROSA*

. . . And time flew by, and by flew
an eagle over the sea.

—JOSÉ MARTÍ, *THE PINK SHOES*

RECLAIMING PARIS

PROLOGUE

Men are like perfumes. In an instant, with nothing but a whiff of judgment, I either love them or discard them. When I love them, I fall blindly in lust with their scent, and for a while I can think of no other. I fancy that our match will last forever, and convince myself that I have discovered the most wonderful man (perfume) in the world. I wear it with gusto (both the man and the perfume).

Alas, I have the same problem with men as I do with my perfumes. As time goes by, the potion dwindles and it becomes necessary to find a replacement. It is then my senses awaken to new smells, and sometimes, as I am mourning the end of a beloved fragrance, I am no doubt already yearning for another.

I grew up on the island of Cuba smelling of Russian Violets, the signature perfume of pampered babies in the seaside town of Matanzas. It's a strong scent. The overabundance of spring in the formula takes some getting used to and lingers in your soul well beyond childhood. It's a useful scent. If you want to see a man run, splash your bedroom with *violetas rusas*. Makes them head for the door, claim forgetfulness, take up a cause. I use my shelved bottle of Russian Violets sparingly, sprinkling a few drops of the purple tonic in bathwater when love fades and nobody wants to do the slovenly job of saying *adiós*. It always works.

I like my men the way I like my perfumes, with a lot of poetry. I lost my virginity to Wind Song, built a career on White Linen, saved myself with Miracle. I prefer the complicated scents, the ones that are hard to find, like Habanita. As onerous as my bottled Habanita turned out to be, that will always be my favorite perfume. I remember how I treasured every last drop, and at the end, I wanted to smash the bottle to force the aroma to last longer, to make it linger in my bedroom.

But I've moved on now. I always move on. I've become a connoisseur of discovery, skilled at choosing new scents, choosing new men.

Now I am wearing Pleasures, and that too has its charms.

PLEASURES

1

Miami Riverfront Hotel
New Year's Eve, 2004

Miami is a city of unruly passions and transplanted ghosts. I have only to look through the panoramic windows of Room 1701 at the Miami Riverfront Hotel, and in the freeze-frame of a vista I find my place among the city's rhythms. The broken seas usher in the mouth of the Miami River, a coveted stretch of water and land that was sacred ground to the Tequestas of Florida until a chain of usurpers—Spanish conquistadores and missionaries, shipwrecked adventurers, and invading Creeks from the north loyal to the English—drove the few hundred who survived disease and warfare into deadly exile in Cuba. I also have made this city mine, and the Riverfront Hotel a place of veneration, the altar where José Antonio and I come to love every Friday afternoon. We are a perfect fit, this cauldron of a city and I, one of its denizens, a woman named after the sea and the sun.

"Marisol," I hear José Antonio call as he wakes up, startled to find emptiness where he remembers a blissful embrace.

"At the window," I answer, and he quickly turns around. "There's a beautiful sunset in the making. The orange sun is turning the river purple."

"Come back to bed, my poet, and tell me all about it here."

I obey and his kiss tastes of the tart *albariño* on the night table where three coconut-scented candles flicker as they did the afternoon José Antonio brought them in amber crystal holders to our first encounter. For three months, we have never made love in our hideout without the light and aroma of these candles and a respectable bottle of wine to toast our union. For three months, our lovemaking has been followed by our narration of enchanting stories of conquest and heartbreak, his and mine. For three months, except for our memorable weekend in the Mexican Riviera among Mayan ruins and deserted beaches, we have not missed a Friday at the Riverfront. The comfort José Antonio finds in our routine and our fledgling rituals is still foreign to me. I prefer the unscripted text of adventure, the illusion of discovery, but for now my free spirit has surrendered to José Antonio's deftly choreographed dance.

A little after three o'clock on Fridays, José Antonio calls me when he has finished checking on his moribund patients at Our Sisters of Charity Hospital. I can hear him through the cellular phone in the hospital parking lot straining to shed his white doctor's coat and talk to me at the same time.

"*Mariposa*, see you in fifteen minutes," he says, toying with my name, calling me "butterfly" as he opens the door to his silver Mercedes. "Twenty if there's traffic. God, I hate the traffic in this city when it stands between you and me."

I laugh.

"Here comes the *cubanazo* sweet talk."

"Let yourself be loved, woman."

I laugh again.

"That's exactly what I'm doing. Hurry."

I hang up and sprint to the bathroom to touch up the only makeup I ever wear, smoky eyeliner and mascara to enhance the almond shape of my black eyes, and I spray a subtle dose of Pleasures in strategic places. With the finesse of a diplomat, I leave my day job collecting Cuban-exile history for the Miami Museum of History using another inauspicious excuse, and I drive, darting from one lane to another, through the clogged downtown streets to the Riverfront, beating the approaching yacht or freighter du jour across the bridge in worse traffic than José Antonio will have on his drive north for a handful of miles along the skyscrapers of Brickell Avenue's financial district. I pass by a bearded homeless man holding up a cardboard sign that says, "Why lie? I need a beer," and I roll down my window to drop the change in my ashtray into his paper cup. He thanks and blesses me. No need, he has earned his pay with his wit.

José Antonio chose the Riverfront for its accessible location between our jobs and the privacy rendered by its architecture and landscape. The rectangular, nondescript ivory building with covered parking, the thick tropical foliage wrapped around the entrance, the river and the waters of Biscayne Bay behind it, camouflage the sin of our encounters. I like the setting for its history and the hotel for its impeccable white linens and Art Deco posters on the walls. After the Riverfront became our refuge, I entertained myself for days researching how the Tequestas weathered the humid subtropical environment, fished sea cows with their rudimentary spears, and struggled to survive the interlopers on the same riverbank where I now intend to bury whatever is left in my heart of Gabriel, that fraud of an *habanero* I once loved.

When I arrive at the Riverfront, I head for the garage to park my puny red Echo, which I bought from a repossessed car lot, and call José Antonio's cell. He gives me a room number. I write all the room numbers down in my calendar, as if chronicling this mattered: 1215, 1440, 1136, 1536, 1406, 1439, 1634, 1415, 1032. Today, it is 1701. I sprint inside through the back door, just as José Antonio instructed me to do the afternoon he plotted our first rendezvous. I suspect the cloak-and-dagger is artifice, as electronic surveillance cameras must be taping my every move, and the thought makes my heart race with fear. José Antonio is a respected cardiologist, a fixture on the social circuit of the bohemian and wealthy alike, a patron of the fine arts and of the recently arrived, which he once was. I am a free woman, but he is not a free man. I know that José Antonio has arrived at the Riverfront minutes before me, checked in, paid in cash, received the frequent customer discount and a wink of complicity from the front desk manager. *Why am I doing this?* I question myself all the time, during the frenzy of my drives to meet him whenever he has a moment, during the wanting nights in my own bed, on days like today when the what-ifs of history haunt me and I confuse the residual scent of losses with the fragrance of new desire.

I ride up to our suite in an elevator full of airline pilots and flight attendants who spend their off-hours here too. During those brief moments that we remain hostage to the bright brass accents of the enclosed space, I feel as if everyone knows what I'm up to. *Why am I doing this?* I'm choked by the guilt and for a moment, as the elevator stops on the third floor, I consider getting off, running down the stairs, and disappearing from José Antonio's life. But I can't. I won't. It is too late to let go. I inhale the trace of Pleasures on my wrist and the perfume becomes an amulet that turns fear into appetite.

The elevator doors close again and I think about the night José Antonio and I met. If only I had dismissed his attentions like I have those of so many others, I wouldn't be in a hotel elevator riding up to a rented suite to meet a married man. Swatting the undesirable men around me is part of living in this city, and the price I pay for letting my soul soar at the nightclub Dos Gardenias, the closest thing in Miami to the legendary watering holes in the Cuban capital, when that sad gray lady called Havana was in its heyday and nicknamed the Paris of the Caribbean.

Early into the night at Dos Gardenias, before the latest Cuban musician to defect takes the stage, commanding a hefty cover charge at the door, I perform my poetry in a duo with Alejo, who belts out boleros with the gut-stripping pain of one who has loved and lost. We sit close to each other on stools, and as a circle of soft white light envelops us, my poetry serves as an introduction to his songs.

He sings boleros. He pierces my heart.
No one escapes from love, the crooner mourns.
But that's only a song.
I will save myself.
Oh, yes, I will.
Yo sí. Yo sí.

On cue, accompanied by a pianist in the background, Alejo croons a sultry version of "Lágrimas negras," stopping midsong to smoothly chat up the crowd, getting them to agree that we've all shed those dark tears the lyrics speak of. As he does this, Alejo holds my hand, kisses my knuckles with flair, and returns to his song. At the end of "Lágrimas," I plunge into another poem as if it were an extension of the melody.

Once,
only once more,
do I want to see The Island.
And then
I will come Home.
Because the sea is the sea is the sea.

As my last word fades, Alejo begins to serenade the crowd with "Volver," the Argentine cult tango that has become the international anthem to the nostalgia of those who dream of a return to one's birthplace. And so it goes for the forty-five-minute set, poetry and song, song and poetry, and by the end there is not a dry eye in the house. Everyone is remembering lost loves, lost homelands, lost souls, and the dark, cavernous nightclub bursts into a cacophony of whistles and shouts of "Bravo!" and at least one "*¡Viva Cuba libre!*"

If only I weren't one of the scarred, if only mine were not a city forever nursing a sentiment that keeps us foolishly searching for an island forfeited so long ago, a mythical place that exists only in our yearning, then maybe I would have been able to overlook the gallantries of Dr. José Antonio Castellón the first night he saw me perform. But José Antonio is a heart doctor, with the manners of a gentleman from the golden era of Spanish letters and the history of a jaded hero, a healer who couldn't mend his own fatal wounds but instantly soothed mine.

That night in November when we first meet, a total eclipse of the moon is forecast, and after Alejo and I bask in applause and thank our audience, we rush outside to the dim parking lot we call backstage to see if we can catch the moon's passing through the darkest part of Earth's shadow.

The second we step out, I look up, catch a sliver of the reddish moon, and without thinking twice, I pray, "Send me true love."

"Send me money," Alejo says.

The celestial show lasts but an instant. We are only able to see the last seconds of the moon's exit. Alejo lights a Marlboro, and just as I'm about to chastise him for it, José Antonio strolls up to us in a crisp white linen *guayabera*, the uniform of Cuban nights in Miami. He extends his hand, first to Alejo and then to me.

"I want to thank you both for making us all relive the most wonderful years of our youth," he says, after introducing himself, without any medical references, as José Antonio Castellón. "Your performance was like a vision of what we once were, and we cannot help but mourn what we lost on our dear island, those endless Havana nights."

Then José Antonio looks at me with a warmth I was not expecting.

"Blessed is your pen, sensitive and melancholy," he says.

He keeps holding my hand.

"You are a poem yourself."

I am caught off guard by the over-the-top elegance of his praise, and I am left without anything to say but obligatory pleasantries.

"I will come again soon," he promises.

"Please do," I say. "We may not have Havana, but we have Miami—and the night."

He smiles and disappears back into the club.

"You flirt!" Alejo punches me in the arm the minute we are alone. "Do you know who that is?"

"Who cares?" I tell him. "One more melancholic Cuban."

The owner of the club comes out with a couple of beers and the conversation turns to the mysterious power of lunar eclipses. He too lights up and when the smoke between those two gets unbearable, I go back inside the club. José Antonio and his table of guests are gone. I do not see him again for many months, until one day I am at the museum working on an exhibit of antique prints depicting the flora and fauna of Cuba, when an e-mail flashes onto my computer screen.

Dear Marisol,
I hope you remember me from Dos Gardenias. Your number one fan. Common friends gave me your address. I want to hire you and Alejo to perform at an event in my home. I would be honored if you would send me your phone number so that we may discuss details.

Saludos,
José Antonio.

I give him my number and he calls that evening to invite me to lunch to discuss what he calls "a sensitive issue." He wants us to participate in a *tertulia* in his home with Cuban musicians visiting from the island, the kind of underground get-together where booze and rhythms flow, and before night's end, so does truth on both sides of the political divide. I have to consult Alejo, I say, but José Antonio insists that he prefers a one-on-one with me first so that we can discuss the preliminaries, and then we can bring in Alejo. I agree because the gig he's offering requires strategic finesse, and Alejo can be, as he likes to remind me, "more *gusano* than a worm." The musical exchange never happens, but I end up with a new man, a complicated man drowning in his own history, a man who doesn't belong to me.

Why am I doing this? The seconds in the elevator seem endless. I am being smothered by my thoughts. I will ruin the afternoon. I stop myself by reading the name tags of the flight crew on this ride: Desiree, Giovani, Donna, Marc. *Why am I doing this?*

Gabriel.

Maldito Gabriel. That's why.

I want to erase his cursed name from my life, his narcissistic caresses from my face. I want to forget the things he made me yearn for, the fury he planted in my heart with his betrayal, the door to the past he opened like a blinding spray of sunlight. I should have never, ever loved an *habanero*. The men from Havana are arrogant conspirators and schemers, not naïve, like most of us who hail from the parts of Cuba where nature softens the soul. *Guajiros*, they call us, hicks, as if it were a stain to be born in the womb of a country. We may be peasants, but we have hearts—humble, vulnerable hearts.

Gabriel.

Damned Gabriel.

I am almost in tears when the elevator opens. The seventeenth floor. I am safe. Just a few steps to 1701 and I am safe.

I knock on the door, and I don't have to wait long before José Antonio greets me in his black Gucci underwear and eyes the color of sweet *dulce de leche*. He embraces me, oblivious to the mess that I am at this moment, and I lose myself in the familiar scent of his Bulgari and my sobs. He kisses my tears. "I love you, I love you," he whispers. "We are together now, my butterfly."

"I want you," I say, and he leads the way to bed.

2

In José Antonio's bed, I always find deliverance. After we make love with the synchronicity of long-term partners and the carnal appetite of fresh lovers, José Antonio asks me to recite one of my poems, and although I don't feel like performing this afternoon, I try to please him. Sitting up in bed with nothing but the white sheets draped around my lap, I close my eyes and conjure the gods of inspiration. I summon images of José Antonio's seductive dance—a heady mix of honed Casanova skills and a disarmingly roguish, dated execution—and the images of our affair flow like a radiant shooting star in the dark night.

Our first lunch at a trendy bistro under the shady oak canopy of Coral Way, the two of us in smart, tailored suits, as if we were another set of professionals from the nearby banking district discussing our ambitious business agenda over wild salmon. We talk about poetry and my ongoing project at the museum piecing together biographies of Cuban exiles who are key players in the city's history. He quizzes me like a journalist and only at my insistence that I get equal time does he talk about his medical career. He has become bored with the routine of it all, he says, and could we, please, move on to more interesting topics like, "What does a lovely woman like you do for fun besides perform poetry?" I smile and he says he loves the way I smile. "You have an honest smile," he says. I tell him I did not know there was another kind. He is so charming I forget why we are having lunch in the first place. Only when he pays the valet attendant for both of our cars, and the young man runs off to fetch his Mercedes and my Echo, does José Antonio bring up the Cuban musicians' visit. Their trip to Miami is in jeopardy, he says. They haven't been able to get permission to travel, but he'll keep me posted.

Next, José Antonio invites me to follow-up drinks at the swanky Four Seasons, where Botero's *Sitting Woman* in the seventh-floor lobby becomes a meeting spot and, many pinot noirs later, where he springs on me a first kiss. We are reveling in the sculpture's sensuality and voluptuousness—"Doesn't she seem to be thinking, '*¡Qué buena estoy!*' " I quip in Spanglish—when José Antonio leans into me, pecks my neck, and whispers, "What I'd give to dive in there."

I pretend that his lips have not electrified me, that his words have not installed themselves in my imagination. But my eyes, and the undeniable fact that I look forward to his increasingly frequent calls, speak for me. He delights me with his repertoire of topics and I readily jump into the conversation. A provocative installation by a Cuban conceptual artist new to exile, a García Lorca production at a local theater, a panel discussion on the dying sugar industry on the island, and after I prod him, the story of another exiled luminary whose faulty heart valve he has repaired, whose life has been saved by his keen diagnosis. "The stethoscope tells you everything," José

Antonio says. "You have to be a good listener, like a musician, and know the rhythms of the heart."

He seems to easily predict mine. Somewhere along the journey to friendship and familiarity, he nicknames me "*mariposa*," a reference to the fierceness with which I cling to my freedom, he explains.

"Good morning, *mariposa*," he greets me with a phone call in the mornings on his way to the office. Or, "How's my *mariposa* today?"

At the end of the day, his cheer sounds depleted.

"I envy your wings, *mariposa*," José Antonio signs off one night, and the sadness in his voice inspires me to write a poem, "Flight," which I incorporate into the Dos Gardenias show. José Antonio never sees me perform it. By then, I have already asked him to stop coming to the club with his wife and their ever-present clan of life-long friends. By then, José Antonio has come clean about his intentions. It happens on a soothing night at the Four Seasons' rooftop terrace, a brilliant half-moon above us. As he speaks, I can hear the sound of potted palms swaying in the breeze, as if they were accompaniments to his swan song.

There were never any Cuban musicians from the island coming to his house, he confesses. His wife, whose politics are staunchly hard-line and conservative, never would have allowed friendly relations with people who have not broken publicly with the regime. But he needed an excuse to get to know me, he says, and he knew he had to come up with a topic that would keep the door open. With the penitent look of the lead man in a *telenovela*, he begs for forgiveness. He does not wait for my reply, and begins to draw a picture on a napkin.

"If someone were to paint my life, *mariposa*, it would be a giant web, like this, coming out of a man's ass and trapping him in it," he says. "I am trapped in a web of my own making."

"A golden web," I add to his fantasy.

"Yes, that's it, the story of my life."

"Or maybe it's a flimsy web, like a real spider's web," I probe, "and all you have to do is brush it aside, and it comes crumbling down, and you're free."

"I wish," is all José Antonio says.

Then he looks into my eyes and pronounces with an enviable dose of confidence the words that forever change our friendship.

"I am falling in love with you, *mariposa*. You are the most fascinating woman I have ever met, and I have been with many women."

I feel my heart flip, but I remain outwardly steady, my hands underneath the table gripping my chair. I remind José Antonio of his unavailability, of the image of entanglement he has so eloquently described, and I remind him of his place in the pantheon of Cuban Miami's Hall of Fame among its impressive benefactors and pillars of success. I emphasize the worth of friendship over the perils of romantic relationships that begin with betrayal and are doomed from the start. But I only seem to be encouraging him.

"All I want is a small space in your life," he says. "All I want is for you to allow me to love you."

I never agree with words, nor do I fly into his arms that night. But I do not deny him the opportunity to see me, and the more I do, the more I realize how big the spaces are in my life, how empty they feel. José Antonio fills the voids with laughter, with flattery, with generous words and gifts, and even if he doesn't mean to, with hopes ever so foolish. "You've had my heart in a frying pan since the day I met you," he says one afternoon, and I laugh for days every time I remember the silliness of his compliment. I hop on his roller coaster and I ride it way up to the moon, leaving all painful thoughts of Gabriel below on planet Earth. I do not have to speak a word of confirmation. José Antonio speaks them all for me.

"You will never shed a tear for me. I am yours," he promises on another date, sealing the words with a long sultry kiss. We are huddled next to each other at Bond St., a newly opened upscale sushi lounge in South Beach, an outpost of the Manhattan restaurant, incarnated here in a splash of pristine Deco white and black lacquer in the basement of the renovated TownHouse Hotel. As our kiss lingers, I feel as if all eyes are on us, but when I come up for air from the wetness and look around, it's obvious that we have competition. A famous rapper is indulging in his own pleasures on a papaya-toned love seat in another corner of the lounge. All eyes are on him, not us. Having also made that observation, José Antonio proceeds to feed me spicy tuna rolls with chili mayonnaise and crispy lobster wontons roasted in garlic mustard sauce, washed down with throat-warming sake, more delicious kisses, and under-the-table moves.

One weekday afternoon, instead of escaping to one of our trendy hideaways, José Antonio calls to invite me to happy hour at the oldest watering hole in town, a throwback to 1912 when it was opened as a bakery but was a front for a speakeasy, and today a funky bar with the reputation of packing in journalists from the *Miami Standard* and their Deep Throats from county government for the two-for-one specials. I think our meeting there would be dangerous, but José Antonio says he is not as well known among the mainstream as I think. "I am a blank to them," he says. "Sometimes *los americanos* come to my office because they have no choice. Their doctors refer them to me, and when they see the Spanish name and hear the accent, they feel closer to death immediately."

"And what do you do to break through their prejudice?" I ask.

"I don't give a shit what they think," he says. "If they don't like me they can find some other doctor."

"I think you're missing an opportunity—" I start to say.

He cuts me off.

"*Mariposa*, let's make a deal right now. I don't tell you how to do your job, and you don't tell me how to do mine. I am here to enjoy myself, to escape from the stupidity and monotony of my days, not to be lectured on community relations or on how to improve my bedside manner."

He has never been rude to me before. His comment stings, but I'm not sure how I want to react.

"Well, let's hit Tobacco Road, then. See you there," I say, and hang up.

It's a short drive to the bar, past shuttered fresh seafood restaurants on the river and high-rises under construction, but long enough that I run through our conversation a few times. I arrive at the bar with a deliciously vengeful streak in my soul. He is already there, a wide grin on his face. I order a Corona and it comes with a lime wedge on the rim. I bring the lime to my mouth, suck its flesh with all intention of unsettling him, then chase the bitterness with the beer, working the bottle like a man, thirsty, fast, long. It works. José Antonio cannot keep his eyes off me. The house band plays Bob Seger's "Against the Wind," and I am back in the carefree days of my bell-bottom youth. I boast about singing this song at the top of my lungs at a concert in a cloud of marijuana smoke, one of my many adventures while at college in the Midwest. From our table, I start singing along with the band, high on chugging beer too fast for my five-foot-three frame, secretly indulging in too many remembrances of night moves I would never share.

After the song ends and the singer announces a break, José Antonio seems to be in a better mood, directing his applause at both the three-man band and me. Then he inches closer. "I apologize for my stupid, insensitive words earlier," he says. "You had the best of intentions. I am a clod."

In the pacifying fog of beer and rock-and-roll, his words no longer bother me that much, but I don't get to say a word. He goes on, as usual, unstoppable in his monologue, and I, like a patient therapist, simply listen. "It's just that I am so tired of it all, Marisol, but I will take your advice and do better by the people of this great country, who, after all, opened their arms to us all. I am grateful, truly I am."

I reach for his flushed cheeks and run my hands along the puffy surface, working my way down to his goatee, then I let my fingers caress the overgrown curls showing some gray. A devil-made-me-do-it smile appears on his face.

"I have a surprise," he says, pulling me closer, and, like a tattletale, whispering his scheme in my ear. He wants to take me to the Mexican Riviera in a couple of weeks, a Thursday-to-Sunday adventure along the Caribbean coast of Mexico, a place blessed with graceful palms and flame trees in copious bloom, a mirror of my beloved Matanzas. But first, he says, we should consummate our love. He has found the perfect place, the Miami Riverfront Hotel, not too far from here.

"It is time," he says, and it is not a question.

The Riverfront will become our oasis, he promises, and the Riviera Maya the magical stage for our "honeymoon." I ask for time to think about it, but in my heart, I know that I cannot resist the prospect of an escapade with a man with so much to reveal. José Antonio, indeed, had come to discern me well.

"Let's toast to America the beautiful," I say a little too loudly, hoping to distract him from the overwhelming desire he has planted in my soul. When I see that it's the waiter's attention I have attracted, I point to my bottle and signal him to bring me another beer. José Antonio declines another; his bottle is still half full.

"And a toast to us," he chimes in, "together until the cirrhosis of the liver separates us."

I write a poem entitled "The Rescue" the night before José Antonio and I agree to our first encounter at the Riverfront, and in the afterglow of sex I read it to him, not yet having memorized it. More than an ode to our fortuitous meeting the night of the eclipse, the poem is a warning about my haunted heart, and I tell him so.

"I'm a broken woman," I say. "I don't do relationships well. I'm a good Cuban—lots of talk, music, and bravado—but when things get tough, what I'm really good at is leaving."

José Antonio remains silent. He kisses the page, pronounces the poem the most genuine gift he has ever received, asks if he can keep it, then hops out of bed and slips it into the inside pocket of the pinstriped Italian jacket he had carefully folded over an armchair. I watch him, still woozy from the effort of the performance and the sex. He's overcome by sniffles. They are short sniffs, and if he's aware of them, he doesn't show it. He turns his attention to his buzzing cellular phone, excuses himself, and heads to the bathroom. I am glad to be alone for a few minutes. I stretch on the white bed with pleasure. I cannot deny the pleasure.

José Antonio returns, places his cellular phone back on the dresser, and joins me in bed.

"I want you in my life forever," he says, kissing my neck, my lips, my nipples so delicately that I, indeed, want to stay forever. From that day on, he nicknames me *mi Gabriela Mistral*, adding the name of the great Chilean poet to his endearing repertoire of pet names, and when he calls me in the morning as soon as he leaves his waterfront Key Biscayne estate, he wants to hear all about my literary production. Fueled by his encouragement, I write and write and write, noticing less my loneliness and the still-empty spaces.

3

The Friday night after José Antonio and I first make love, I perform "The Rescue" at Dos Gardenias after Alejo sings the bolero about the lover who wants to be adored with the same fervor of twenty years past, "Veinte años," composed by the grand dame of Cuban *trova* music, María Teresa Vera. We're told that there's a large Mexican contingent in our audience, and between songs Alejo delights them with tidbits about the joint musical history of Cuba and Mexico, soul sisters during the golden age of boleros in the 1940s. We keep our act breezier than usual, not an easy shift given my wretched poetry, but "The Rescue" helps me upgrade the sexy meter and set aside the nostalgia, and at the Mexicans' request, Alejo sings "Bésame mucho," composed by the grand dame of Mexican ballads, the beautiful Consuelo Velázquez.

Our improvisation works as smoothly as if we had rehearsed it, and Alejo and I are riding high on our chemistry. After the show, as we share an overly minty *mojito* at the bar, I confess to Alejo what I did that afternoon with José Antonio.

It doesn't alarm him.

"Fuck him without mercy," Alejo advises, swinging his head in diva fashion. "Enjoy yourself, honey."

Alejo's antics, accented by the survivalist lingo of the Cuban streets he endured into his forties, always have the capacity to entertain me. And if his colorful vocabulary doesn't do it, then his unrelenting loyalty moves me like few things can. He is perennially on my side. If I love a guy, he loves the guy. If I hate a guy, he hates the guy. In his view, I can do no wrong. From our shared childhood in our paradise of Matanzas's bayside neighborhood of La Playa, when he was the only male friend I was allowed to have, to our emotional reconnection three decades later in Miami's Little Havana, Alejo has been my guardian angel, my confidant, my accomplice. He is the only person in this world I consider family.

It was only destiny, that illusive trajectory from which we cannot escape, that shepherded our friendship to an unassuming stage surrounded by walls packed with black and white pictures of a legendary musical past. There they all are, showering us with generous doses of Yoruban *aché* while we are performing: Beny Moré, the uncontested king of rhythm; Celia Cruz, the salacious salsa queen; Olga Guillot, who begs in her trademark song, "*Miénteme más, que me hace tu maldad, feliz,*" lie to me more, your wickedness makes me happy, the hymn of betrayed Cuban housewives who play possum. I never could have imagined I would share this stage, let alone that this little piece of nostalgic Miami would become the podium for my flight. But Alejo had it all planned out, as only people who have escaped from hell with nothing but their lives know how to do.

One night at my house, we were both reeling from broken

hearts when Alejo began singing the vintage ballads of our parents' generation. He recalled how much my mother loved to sing. She was a tropical beauty like the ones depicted on American travel posters from the 1950s, and her moment of glory came when she got to sing "Nosotros," in a talent show at Matanzas's famed Teatro Sauto. I remembered Abuela telling me this story, but I had long forgotten my mother's face. Alejo remembered everything, but most of all her sultry voice. His being one year older than me seemed to have made all the difference. What he didn't remember, I suspected, he smoothly invented as the situation required, sometimes to feed my nostalgia, sometimes to assuage my pain. And that particular night required some spin. I was mourning the end of my long relationship with Gabriel and Alejo was steaming over a New Yorker he met on South Beach who only wanted to sample the legendary Cuban lover, not take him home to Mother. Alejo wanted me to sing with him.

"Try it, live a little," he said. "You must have it in you, it's in your gene pool." But I have no voice to speak of, no swing to carry a melody, and so I began reciting poetry I had written under the spell of heartbreak.

If the pens of this world could cry,
mine would overflow the Yumurí.

As I moved from short verses to longer pieces, the rebound mood of the night called for theatrics to go with my words. More than reciting, I was acting out the role of femme fatale. And thus, our show was born.

We called ourselves Nosotros, The Two of Us, after my mother's favorite ballad about lovers who are forced to part, and Alejo and I indulged in fantasizing about what it would be like to perform onstage. What I didn't know then was that on and off Alejo had been seeing the owner of Dos Gardenias, who was in the middle of a breakup as well, and it wasn't long before Gustavo auditioned us, without my knowing what was happening. Alejo was wise enough to keep his intentions a secret from me. He knew my insecurities well. I never would have agreed to make a public spectacle of myself. I hated the limelight, having come off the fast track to a career in government because of it, and in historical research had found a quiet passion.

But Alejo, who in a country saddled with perennial food shortages had been forced into a career in nutrition, had ended up earning dollars singing in Varadero's tourist-only hotels and nightclubs. In his Miami exile a physician's assistant in a clinic, he was itching for an opportunity to return to the nightlife. Alejo invited Gustavo over for dinner at my house, and after Alejo cleverly saw to it that I downed a bottle of pinot grigio almost by myself, he began to croon "Nosotros" and to embrace me, egging me on to follow his lead. I was drunk enough to indulge him. Gustavo fell for our lovers' chemistry and offered to help smooth the rough edges and mature the concept of a duo. He brought in a pianist, became our producer, and, before I had the opportunity to think through what I was doing, booked us as an opening act of sorts to entertain the early crowd fresh from an elegant dinner in nearby Coral Gables. Dos Gardenias became my second home. I was growing more and more comfortable in my theatrical role and we were getting gigs to perform at private parties when José Antonio came that night of the eclipse with his wife and friends, as I would later learn, to celebrate his sixtieth birthday.

Now when I confess to Alejo, somewhat repentant, that José

Antonio and I have become lovers, he doesn't think the revelation all that important.

"I've had plenty of affairs," Alejo says, dismissing my concerns. "But you know what, honey? It was a lot easier in Cuba. Everyone on the island is fucking somebody they are not supposed to fuck, literally and figuratively. Nobody worries about it. We were all in that forgotten pit of the earth together, and sex was all we had to pass the time."

Alejo's words do not comfort or amuse me. I start to feel sorry and embarrassed at myself for trespassing into another woman's territory, a capital sin in my American feminist handbook. I regret the confession. If anything, I want José Antonio to be my secret. He is not only married, but he is fifteen years my senior. Alejo does think José Antonio is too old and complicated for me, and he's right, but I am strangely attracted to the depth that history brings to his personality. In his presence, I feel a connection to something intangible. He has become a strange refuge, dangerous and safe at the same time.

I try to explain some of my ambivalence to Alejo, as if having second thoughts makes me a better person.

"And what do I do with the guilt?" I ask. "He's a good guy. I don't want to hurt him or get him into trouble. Imagine the scandal if people knew."

He is still unimpressed.

"Scandal? In this town? P-l-e-e-a-se, *corazón*, on what planet do you dwell? Affairs are more common than a cold here. Plus, don't you know the code? It's not happening. You pretend it's not happening and everyone lives happily ever after. Deny, deny, deny."

"Funny," I tell him, "that's what José Antonio said the other day. He told me that his credo is deny, deny, deny. He even used those words. He says his wife has always known about his affairs, but when she asks, he denies them all. You men are all the same; gay or straight, you're all scoundrels."

Alejo takes a long sip of his *mojito*, then spits out a piece of the bitter leaf of *yerbabuena* that had made it up the straw. We don't speak for a while, and I know by the look on his face that he is lost in his own thoughts about the men he has loved and now detests.

"I tell you what the downside is: He won't be there when you need him," Alejo says. "Don't fool yourself thinking he's going to change his life for you. Those people are so used to living a lie that they wouldn't know what to do with truth."

I challenge him. "Are we talking about me or are we talking about you?"

"Listen, my friend, you go ahead and do what your heart tells you to do. Enjoy this for a while. Me, I am done being people's Eleguá," he sighs, evoking the *santería* deity who is said to clear the roads of life. "No more opening closet doors for others. You show them the way out, and then, when they're free, they kick you in the ass. But you, you've got a lot to learn, my sweet Marisol. A little affair with Dr. Castellón might do you some good. I know about doctors, had one myself. They know their anatomy and that's what you need right now to heal your heart. Just don't take it too seriously. File it in that little head of yours under 'education,' the Education of Marisol."

"He says he loves me," I say, feeling instantly foolish. "But I'm only using him to assuage my pain. How fair is that?"

"My little darling, I know you, and that heart of yours already has a spot with that man's name scribbled on it. You're the one who has to be careful. You're using him to fill that empty space with the name of that *cubano mal nacido* who does not deserve your tears, and he's using you to assuage his boredom. It's a wash. Just keep the fantasies in the bedroom. In this country, it's all about the millions at stake, and that man is never going to leave all his glory for anyone. Ugh, sometimes I hate capitalism. Sex to escape oppression is a lot more poetic."

With that, Alejo rests his head on my shoulder.

"Hmm, you sure smell sexy," he says.

"You're drunk," I say, and kiss his head.

4

My heart. Alejo is right about my heart. Once I dig like an archaeologist into the terrain of José Antonio's soul, all I want to do is love and protect him, as if he were a mischievous child without a place to call home, and as if in the cocoon of my embrace he could find redemption.

My heart. José Antonio earns the rights to my heart in Mexico, as he probes every corner of me, kisses the scars, finds the spaces of joy in the turquoise sea, on the soft white sands, under the mosquito-netting canopy of our bed in that luxuriously rustic resort aptly named, in Mayan, Poetry of the Sea. From the moment I arrive at Miami International Airport on the day of our trip, I have no doubt that this man loves me. In the way that he is able to love, in the way he knows how to love, he loves me.

When I reach the gate for the Miami-Cancún flight, José Antonio is already waiting for me. He kisses my right cheek and immediately turns his attention to help with my carry-on luggage.

"What is that?" he asks, pointing to a yellow plastic bundle sticking out of the side pocket of my black and beige Kipling backpack.

"Oh, I didn't have time to read the newspaper this morning with all the business of packing and the appointment with the manicurist, all the girl stuff," I say. "I thought we could both read it on the plane."

José Antonio reaches into the backpack, pulls out the yellow package, walks over to a garbage can, and dumps my *Miami Standard* in it. "Not on my time, *mariposa*," he says. "You are all mine this weekend."

And so begins the most intense three days of my life.

Following good sex, José Antonio becomes a spirited storyteller. He loves to talk about his lies and his conquests—his lies to his wife and his conquests of other women. He has quite a repertoire of tales that span the hemisphere, a revolution, a counterrevolution, and his forty-one year marriage. When he starts looking back and reminiscing about "the small little thorns of life," as he calls his failed romances and botched friendships, he has my full attention. I am addicted to the narrative of his life and I listen with as much eagerness as love.

What fascinates me about José Antonio is what I loathe most, the double track of his history. He is an admirable survivor, the quintessential wounded exile whose work ethic and overabundance of hope raised Miami to international prominence. He also is a chronic philanderer who thrives on the rapture of erotic adventures, executing the most wrenching betrayals on his loved ones and then boasting about them to his closest friends. As we work on generous portions of shrimp ceviche at a beach shack in Playa del Carmen, our bare feet playfully submerged in sand, and later, as we walk hand-in-hand along miles of secluded beachfront paths, José Antonio tells me his life story.

He married at nineteen in 1963, on the second anniversary of the failed Bay of Pigs invasion, in which he had participated, trained by the U.S. government and assigned to an aquatic landing party that never got close enough to the island to see any action. His bride, Magdalena, was equally young, a teen sent alone into exile by parents who feared her Communist indoctrination and the threatened assignment of parental rights to the state. Magdalena, a beauty with dark waist-long hair and enchanting cat eyes, was staying with friends of José Antonio's parents in Miami. Her parents remained on the island, trying to decide whether to leave everything behind and join their daughter in exile, or await a miraculous fall of the new regime. From the day they met, José Antonio felt it was his patriotic duty to protect the petite girl with generous breasts.

"*Hijo, no te cases,*" José Antonio's father had pleaded. "Don't marry when you're on a downward slide."

The early 1960s were years of consecutive downturns, as though the disastrous invasion had set José Antonio and his compatriots on a cursed streak. A precocious student in Havana's Belén Jesuit, at sixteen he had passed the necessary exams to become a pre-med student at the University of Havana before he left Cuba in 1960 with his parents on a tourist visa. But later in Florida, José Antonio failed the English-language test to get into the university system. He enrolled at the English Center in downtown Miami and, as soon as he mastered the basics, joined the U.S. Army. He quickly discovered that he made a miserable soldier, scoring in the bottom tenth of his class on all physical challenges except swimming. He married Magdalena while on a weekend leave and by the time he returned to the military base in the Carolinas felt somewhat accomplished. He was a married man with traditional ideas about what a good wife should do (blindly trust her man) and should not do (work outside the home). He was building his life's pyramid based on Jesuit values of sacrifice and devotion, and marrying the pious, virginal Magdalena would be at its foundation.

His vows, however, didn't make it to their first anniversary. A knee injury landed José Antonio in the infirmary, into the arms of the night nurse, and back on track for a career in medicine when his orthopedist, impressed by the young man's precocious self-diagnosis, became his mentor. For the rest of his life, the dual morality of his ways would become José Antonio's winning formula. His wife ran the household and oversaw his administrative affairs at the office with exceptional efficiency, and a slate of lovers conveniently anchored close to the hospitals where he made his rounds fed his erotic pining. Throughout it all, his intellect remained sharply focused on being the best in his field. In this heady equation, there was room for only one tragedy—the sadness and bitterness of being an exile, of rebuilding a life truncated from all that had been familiar—and it bound José Antonio and Magdalena forever.

"She made a lot of sacrifices for me," José Antonio tells me as we rest on a hammock after a long walk, the afternoon breezes cooling our sunned bodies. He does not expound on what those sacrifices were, nor do I probe, but he does issue what I grasp as a subtle warning, which for a moment makes me uncomfortable. "I will never leave her. I cannot leave her. I do not want to leave her. She is family, and you never leave family."

What José Antonio did leave was *la lucha,* the decades-long struggle by many of his contemporaries to overthrow one of the world's longest-lasting dictators. "The Bay of Pigs incursion," José

Antonio says, "was my one and only sacrifice in the name of patriotism." I disagree, as I know that the longevity of his showcase marriage is also part of the patriotic equation, but I stay silent. The breezes are too calming for scrutiny, and if there's one thing that can't be debated with exiles of José Antonio's generation, it is the depth of their devotion to the cause, no matter how subtle the hues, no matter how ill-informed their history, no matter how misguided their missiles.

After he tells me all this, I only feel remorse and sadness for Magdalena, and for all she might have become had she not remained tied to a man who did not love her. I suspect that fear, more than love, inspired her choices. Magdalena never saw her father again. Her last memory of him was the look of dread on his face as she walked up the stairs of the Pan Am propeller plane that was purportedly taking her to study in New York. Feeling awkward in a wool suit on a steamy May morning, she turned around to wave good-bye one more time. It would be her last image of her father and, for a long time, of her mother, who with one hand tightly clutched her husband's arm, and with the other, a red polka-dot umbrella to shelter herself from the Caribbean sun. In *el norte*, Magdalena stayed with an aunt who, years before the triumph of the revolution, settled in Union City after marrying a Cuban trumpeter, a regular in the Latin clubs of Manhattan. Magdalena had been warned that winters would be hard on a girl accustomed to the tropics, but that would not be the worst of her exile. A year after she left the island, Magdalena's father suffered a massive heart attack and died without ever speaking again to his only daughter. Magdalena learned about his death in a yellow telegram from Western Union. "Your father is dead," was all it said, and it was signed, "Your mother who misses you."

Magdalena hated the winters. They turned her mourning into

depression, and when she was offered the opportunity to live and work with friends of her parents in the Miami grocery store they had just opened, she did not hesitate to move south. She remained separated from her widowed mother for a decade. Her mother remarried, and that complicated her exit papers. When she arrived on one of the last Freedom Flights of 1971 with her new husband and briefly joined the Castellón household, Magdalena was raising two toddlers born a year apart from each other, and doing so almost alone, as her husband was busy day and night tending to his career and love life. José Antonio's residency at Miami's public hospital had been stellar, but as soon as he could, he set up his own practice. He wanted independence and control. He was making more money than anyone in his struggling immigrant family had ever seen, even in Cuba, for his father had gambled away everything the family owned, including the house in Miramar.

His relative wealth turned José Antonio into an instant benefactor, as well as the cardiologist of preference for the newly exiled. He treated refugees for free, and gave them a hand getting started, obtaining jobs for them through his vast network of contacts. He hired some to work in his office and others on his house, which he then sold, turning a profit and buying a bigger one. He did this several times until he could afford the bayside estate of his dreams. His practice grew astronomically, a success mirrored by some of his patients, who became as wealthy as he—owners of expanding furniture empires, beer-brewing companies, packaged Latin food conglomerates, restaurant chains—and they rewarded him with their business and friendship for the rest of their lives.

From the outset, José Antonio was highly skilled at leading the double life. He carried on an affair that lasted more than a decade. He set up that woman in an apartment with a view of the city, which he considered his second home. José Antonio says little about her, as if she were a blank, and he only becomes slightly animated when he adds one detail about that time in his life: For most of those years, he also was cheating on the lover. Their relationship had become so marriagelike that she was as bothersome to him and uninspiring as his pretty but old-fashioned wife, who had become, with the passage of time, acrid and stern. When he finally left the lover, José Antonio points out, he decided to be honest. "I want to explore other emotions," he told her. The woman tried to kill him with her car, he adds, amused by the memory. She told Magdalena about the affair, but Magdalena preferred to believe José Antonio's tale that the troubled woman suffered from "an unrequited case of fatal attraction."

"I'm a prisoner of the flesh, a slave to lust," he confesses.

For a time, when he still subscribed to Jesuit values, he tried to quell his lust by flagellating himself—flogging his body with a whip until the pain burned red wounds into his skin. But he no longer even prays. In the last decades, he has only prayed once, when he was about to undergo an operation to remove kidney stones. And even then he only offered this prayer: "God, if I have ever offended you, forgive me."

"With this act of contrition," José Antonio explains, "I thought I could wriggle into a spot in heaven."

Only the tale of another of my lovers, Blas, can top the stories José Antonio tells me in the shared intimacy of our Mexican holiday. But Blas was an artist who grew up in the boiler of Centro Havana in the 1970s, when playing the Beatles was illegal. After getting tired of the oppressiveness, he literally pissed on the Revolution during a public art performance, and went to prison for it. No one else's stories can compare with his tales of avant-garde art exhibits and boring

Soviet Bloc movie premieres that ended in orgies on the moonlit rooftop of a crumbling tenement.

José Antonio is all about pleasures. It's a good thing I am so numbed by the tequila we consume at night, so exhausted from dancing until dawn in the salsa clubs of Playa del Carmen, so blissfully satisfied from making love as if we were teens on a deserted island, that I can sleep the sleep of the dead, and not feel the weight of him on my body or my soul. When I wake up, he feels so heavy that I have to make an effort to catch my breath. He encircles me with his arms and legs as if he, indeed, wants our connection to save his soul, to help him find the elusive gate to heaven that his belated prayers might not deliver.

I feel the weight both of his body and of his history, yet when José Antonio tells me his stories, he disarms any attempts by me to pass judgment by pointing out that he is accustomed to lying, but that with me, he finds it impossible not to tell the truth. "You are my best friend," he says. "I have never told anyone the things I have told you."

I don't believe him at first, but go along with his game to see how far he travels with his tales. And he travels far. I like the ride.

He tells me an old story about his sexual initiation in *el barrio de las putas* in Old Havana, followed by a tale of another calamitous adventure, four decades later, in an elegant gentlemen's club in Buenos Aires, a bargain after the economic crisis. At first I don't understand why he is telling me these two disparate stories back-to-back, but their common thread soon becomes obvious: his failure to perform.

"The only two times in my life," he says.

He seems a little annoyed when I laugh.

"Never a problem with me," I say, correcting course.

José Antonio was fifteen the year I was born, and by then he had been initiated into the thrills and disappointments of sex in the stuffy room of a ramshackle tenement in Havana's red light district, not far from where he was born to an elementary school teacher and her gambler dandy of a husband. So delighted and expectant was José Antonio about what would be his first romp that, unlike other initiates his age—he was thirteen—he wanted to take his time and make love like the leading man in his favorite movies.

He aspired to be a great lover like Jorge Negrete, the handsome Mexican actor who always got the girl. José Antonio did not have Negrete's dark looks, but ash-blond curls and light eyes, traits that made him popular with the stuffy society girls and the barrio beauties alike, and later helped him age better than his friends because the white in his goatee was barely visible. He also was taller than Negrete. José Antonio reminded himself of these facts as he walked up the stairwell of the prostitutes' tenement. His kind mother used to frequently note his increasing height, assuring him that he still had growing years ahead. Surely he would be the tallest man in the family. By the time José Antonio knocked on the door of the dingy room he had been assigned, he had committed to memory, as if it were a recipe for love, the gallant way Jorge Negrete used his hands to caress the shoulders of his leading lady María Felix, and the way he looked deeply into the eyes of Gloria Marín in *Una carta de amor*; a leading man can always aspire to hold many leading ladies.

And so, when José Antonio reached the third floor, he was ready for his debut. He had come to the *prostíbulo* with his clan from Belén, and with no small amount of pride, he had paid top price—five pesos—for the best girl in the house. When José Antonio studied the purchased woman who was to be his first, he was pleased to see that she was Chinese. *A porcelain doll*, he told himself.

When they were alone and the girl approached him, José Antonio brought his hands to her hair, thinking how it was as dark as night in the countryside. He looked deeply into her crescent-moon eyes, and she looked down, unzipping his navy blue pants before he could register that he would soon be naked, pulling the trousers around his feet so fast that she took down his boxers as well. Although he did not like the gesture, it wasn't enough to dampen José Antonio's ardent mood. He checked the girl's face for her reaction to his swollen condition and its size. If she was disappointed with what she saw, she did not show it. José Antonio had already learned that he was not as gifted as his friends, and being the smartest boy in his class, he had come to the conclusion that he would make up for nature's shortcomings with gentlemanly manners, expertise when it came to female anatomy, and loads of Latin lover charm. He tried to talk to the girl, who couldn't have been more than twenty years old, and he made a mental note to himself that he would bring her flowers next time.

"What's your name?" José Antonio asked, but instead of answering him, the girl pushed him onto the bed and straddled him in silence.

José Antonio surrendered to an intense wave of pleasure and searched for her eyes again, stroking her hair. The woman moved feverishly on top of him, and the more sensations he felt, the more José Antonio wanted to get to know her. He grabbed her face and forced her to look at him.

She met his look with annoyance and admonished him, "Hurry up. What are you waiting for?"

Instantly, José Antonio felt desire leave him as fast as it had arrived. Wilted and confused, he flung her from his body. As he stood up from the bed, he noticed the red velvet curtains on the windows, and they seemed a joke to him propped against the vintage green peeling walls of a slum.

"I'm done with you," José Antonio said, dressing faster than he had ever done in his life. He was still stuffing his blue-and-white-striped shirt into his tailored pants, the uniform of Belén Jesuit, when he walked out into the mercifully dark night.

His giggling adolescent friends were waiting for him, sharing the only cigarette they had left between them.

José Antonio faked a laugh and high-fived them.

"How was it?" Pedrito asked.

"*Cojonudo*, man. I slammed her good."

They went to celebrate at a nearby bar with one cold Hatuey after another.

"She was Chinese," José Antonio says to me again after he is done telling me the story. "A lot of Chinese emigrated to Cuba and there was a Chinatown in Havana. Did you know that?"

"Yes, everyone knows that," I say. "There are Asians all over Latin America. I don't find that so remarkable. Why do you think Peru has the best Chinese food in the Americas? Have you ever eaten at a Peruvian *chifa*? It's the best."

"Is there anything I can tell you that you don't already know?" José Antonio says, and he seems hurt and bothered.

"Everything," I say, embracing him to appease and comfort him. "You can teach me everything. I learn a great deal from everything you tell me."

My show of affection works.

"I never told anyone that story," he says, softening, and I believe him.

He hardly ever tells anyone the full truth, José Antonio says.

"And how do I know you're telling me the truth?" I ask.

"Trust your instincts," he advises.

He also lied to his friends about what happened at a different kind of *prostíbulo* he visited decades later, when he was already the famous Miami cardiologist, José Antonio Castellón, M.D.

"M.D., do you know what that stands for?" he asks, and answers without waiting for my reply. "Manic-depressive."

I don't find the joke very funny. I'm no psychologist, but it sounds too on point for comfort. It doesn't matter. José Antonio is in a world all his own when he indulges in truth-telling, and he has made a mental transition to another story, traveling far away to the land of tango in the southern hemisphere.

A few years ago, he was invited to lecture on the topic of congenital heart defects at a medical conference in Buenos Aires. His talk went so well that he felt "the sharpest of God's light inside of me" as he spoke to his colleagues. Afterward, he was surrounded by doctors from all over Latin America with interminable follow-up questions, when one of the organizers apologized for the interruption and pulled him aside. An excursion to a gentlemen's club had been organized for some of the visiting guests, the young man told him. Unofficial, of course. Would he be available that evening at six? José Antonio was riding so high on his performance that he readily agreed without giving the proposal or his wife a second thought. He made up a story about accompanying the city's leading heart surgeon on his rounds at the hospital and left Magdalena in the hotel room with excessive amounts of shopping money and the promise that he would return to take her to the best tango show in town.

The gentlemen's club in a restored eighteenth-century mansion in the Recoleta district was everything the young man had promised. Located on a narrow street packed with antique shops, art galleries, and a bakery one could smell from a block away even in the late afternoon, the street and the building had a Gothic French flair. At the entrance to the club, named El Imperial, flower boxes bursting with purple geraniums lined the stone stairwell. Inside, the rooms were accented in rich mahogany moldings; tear-drop chandeliers hung from the ceilings. The men were ushered into a large sitting room filled with antique furnishings, the seats covered in intricate patterns of navy blue and gold. As soon as they were invited to sit and relax with a glass of cognac, they were offered Cuban cigars. Being the romantic he is, José Antonio chose an aromatic Romeo y Julieta, although he probably would have enjoyed the pulpier Cohiba more. For a Cuban exile, smoking a Cuban stogie is a guilty pleasure and the pungent aroma made José Antonio feel invincible. But it would not be long before the elegant women milling about the room hijacked his attention from his exceptional cigar. The women glided across the room, from man to man, introducing themselves: Inés from Chile, Yeleny from Cuba, Katrina from Russia, Sherry *la americana*. They were a United Nations of pleasures, and José Antonio quickly fixed his desire on Consuelo, a *mulata* from Santo Domingo who had abundantly cascading brown hair and hips with the sultry promise of a Caribbean breeze. It would be the first time he would bed a black woman, he thought, and the idea filled him with anticipation and vigor.

Yet when his host came to take his order—as the most distinguished speaker at the conference he was given first dibs on the women—José Antonio chose Melania, the blond Argentine who had delighted him with her green eyes.

"Cowardice," José Antonio tells me at this point in the story.

The woman escorted him upstairs to a luxurious suite in a decorating scheme of dark green and gold and British hunting motifs. She poured a glass of champagne for him and one for herself. She wore a strapless baby-blue dress, long and clingy, and although her breasts were small, José Antonio could guess through the thin fabric that they were round and perfectly erect.

They toasted to good times. After taking a sip, Melania walked up to José Antonio, took off his coat, languidly hung it in a closet, and returned to undo his tie. José Antonio sat back on the bed and let her begin to unbutton his white shirt. She was quite beautiful, he decided, as he watched her manicured hands move down the buttons.

He gulped the last of his champagne.

"Another glass?" he asked, softly taking her hands off his chest.

"If you like," Melania said.

He detected a slight annoyance, but maybe it was all in his head. She poured two more glasses. He sipped his a bit too fast, coughed, and when Melania again glided over to him, José Antonio found himself saying, "Let's talk. I want to know more about you."

"I'd rather make love to you," Melania said.

"Well, I don't feel like it right now," José Antonio said.

"So what did we come here for?"

"I want to have a conversation with you," he said.

"I don't get paid to talk," she said.

José Antonio whipped out a wad of American dollars.

"How much?" he said.

"Two hundred for an hour," she said.

"Here," he said, handing her three hundred. "Can we talk now?"

Melania took the money, slipped it into her small silver night purse, and began a rabid rant about how no man had ever turned her down. The angrier she got, the more she made José Antonio laugh so hard that he began to weep as soon as she was finally, thankfully, and gloriously out of sight.

"*Tienes que ser maricón*," was the last thing he heard her say.

"I probably do have a bit of a faggot in me," José Antonio says to me. "When I was a boy, I made a friend of mine suck my dick. But the truth is that as beautiful as Melania was, all I could think about was the *mulata* I didn't choose, and I knew I would not be able to manage an erection with that woman no matter what."

"You don't seem to have a lot of luck with prostitutes," I say, sounding more like his analyst than his lover.

He seems perplexed, as if he had never thought of that himself until this moment.

I fill the silence.

"Cowardice," I say, "diminishes the quality of orgasms."

That night after we make love, José Antonio is still wrapped around me when he asks me to open my mouth.

"Now breathe in when I exhale into you."

Clumsily, I do.

"Now we are breathing the same air," he says. "We are one."

After the carnal confessions and the exchange of breaths, I believe José Antonio more than I ever doubt him, but on my lonely weekends following our trip to Mexico, I ruminate about how bizarre it is that I have come to value this man just because he tells me the truth about lying. It is not him that I question, but myself.

Yet José Antonio tugs at my heart, again and again, and our time together becomes more precious and bonding. We meet for *cafecito* in the mornings before work. In the late afternoon, we stroll through the city's parks holding hands. The Friday after our trip he brings to the Riverfront a file folder full of sepia-toned and black and white photographs of him as a child and as a teenager in the Havana of the 1950s. He asks me to take the photographs home, to study them so that I can get to know him better. "Keep them for me," he begs. I cannot believe he is entrusting me with such a precious batch of memories, as I would not do that with anyone.

Then, after we make love, José Antonio opens another chapter in our story.

"Now you tell me about your first time," he says after sex, his fingers playing with my newly styled hair.

I have never told anyone this story. Not even Gabriel, who had crawled into every inch of me and drained all the spaces. Something had kept me from sharing my secrets with Gabriel, and my other lovers never cared enough to ask.

José Antonio's truth-telling is contagious.

"It's a very long story, and it goes back, way back, two generations," I say. "In fact, my story is older than your story. It happened before you were born."

His sweet incredulous eyes tell me I have his full attention.

"I came into this world with a lot of baggage," I tell him. "It is not a complaint. I like my baggage."

5

People think of Miami as the poster of sun and fun, a day city. Or they remember it as the capital of vice and fast cars, a night city. But my Miami is most glorious when afternoon melds into evening in a stunning choreography of light. The sun grows to otherworldly proportions and brushes the sky in shades of lavender and pink before disappearing, ever so slowly, as if it were sinking into the Everglades, behind the endless rows of Mediterranean brick-tiled roofs in Western suburbia. Quite a spectacle.

I cannot see the sunsets in all their grandeur from the Riverfront, as the rooms either face north or south. I can only suspect the sunsets, from glimpsing a sliver of sky to the west, or better yet, from watching the way the river below mirrors the sky, spinning colors like a kaleidoscope. When this happens, I know that there's another blessed sunset out there, and so it is on this last Friday of the year.

Standing at the window while José Antonio naps, I wish we were outside, like any other couple planning their year-end celebration, not sequestered between these beige walls. But when he awakens and calls my name, I push aside thoughts of such unattainable desires. The river view of Room 1701 and the sleepy smile on his face are enough to fill me with gratitude for this most imperfect man who cradles my heart with such tenderness. As I softly kiss his pink eyelids, ushering him from sleep, I tell José Antonio how I love the rivers and the oceans at dusk. I have made it a point to document in photographs the sunsets of every city where I have traveled. One of my favorite photographs is of the first time I saw the Eiffel Tower. I was coming out of the Métro station on Place de la Concorde to take my first walk down the Champs-Élysées when I spotted the famous icon in the distance, and right above it, the setting sun, a small round ball in a dull yellow with a halo around it, darting in and out of clouds. It was not a distinguished sunset, but it is a lovely photograph. Paris is so grand a city that it can even upstage a sunset.

José Antonio repeats his vow to love me forever. I don't see the connection between my comments and his reaction. Perhaps he is not moved enough by nature and thinks me silly. Perhaps he is lamenting, like I am secretly in my heart, that we will never have Paris. I don't return the vow. Then he requests that I perform "The Rescue," and I confess that days like today, when the world is engaged in transitions and celebrations, are exacting on inspiration. Every New Year's Eve, history has a way of haunting me with a vicious grip, and I descend into mourning my loves and losses, the island and the men, and an anguish that I cannot kiss away begins to envelop all of me.

"It happens to all of us Cubans," José Antonio says. "Life as we knew it changed forever on a day like this. I hate New Year's Eve too. We all put up a good front, but the anxiety is always there, like a curse."

"But I wasn't even born then," I remind him. "I wasn't born until that spring."

"But you inherited it all," he says. "It is your legacy, your history."

I nod in agreement, but also remind him that there are more urgent tragedies in the world than a fumbled revolution: the attacks on the World Trade Center, the war in Iraq, and now the tsunamis. Nature, wise and beautiful, also unleashes devastating fury, and only five days ago, the tsunamis caused by the Indian Ocean earthquake washed away entire villages in twelve countries and swallowed hundreds of thousands of people. For many, this will be one of the most tragic year-ends in world history. José Antonio hardly needs reminding; he tells me that he has already made a donation to the relief efforts.

"Your generosity is only one of the reasons why I've come to love you so much," I say, and peck his lips. I want to say more, but I don't. More than ever, I feel the need for the refuge of his arms, yet I dare not ask for it. I don't need to. He embraces me tightly, and once again I want to lose myself in the earthy fragrance of his cologne and its potent mix with sex. More than ever, I detest the swift passage of our time together, the buzzing of his cellular phone on the dresser intruding on our intimacy, reminding me that he will not mark the symbolic passage of time with me at midnight, but with the people who really matter in his life. It is not a good day for poetry. Instead of reciting verses, I would prefer the escape of José Antonio's quixotic stories, tales that have the power to drown out my woes and tickle my imagination. But in his most caressing voice José Antonio insists that I recite his favorite poem as a New Year's gift, and I cannot deny him. Our time together becomes the well from which I draw my inspiration, and I let my feelings of gratitude win me over once more.

After a false start for which I blame a raspy throat, I finally deliver; and as always he is generous with his praise. He claps—"Bravo!"—kisses me on the lips, reaches for our empty glasses on the night table, refills them with the aromatic *albariño* cooling in the ice bucket, and, handing one glass to me, proposes a toast to the New Year.

"May we live many more afternoons of love like this one," he says, bringing his glass close to mine.

But before our glasses meet, José Antonio suddenly withdraws his, and his expression turns somber.

I know instantly and instinctively that all is about to change between us. His toast stings my soul in a way I was not expecting, and I cannot erase from my face the disappointment, the pain that has washed over like a tropical storm, unrelenting and erasing all that is not strong enough to withstand the cleansing.

"I'm done pretending," José Antonio says, putting back his glass on the night table. "I've known something was wrong with you from the moment you walked in the door. What is it?"

I try to take back my part of what is being unleashed.

"Nothing," I lie, inching closer to him and trying desperately to smile.

He pushes me away.

"I know you better than that," he insists.

The anguish is smothering me, and the more I try to search my mind for an adequate explanation of why I am becoming undone, the deeper the pain I feel. I grapple to get back to another script, any script: the state of the world, the betrayed revolution that stripped us of our homeland, the sunsets. But my lips refuse to speak words that are only stand-ins.

"The toast, my love, come on, pick up your glass," I wrestle with fake words. "Yes, let's toast to many more . . ."

I cannot finish. He takes the glass away from me. He places it next to his own and scoops my face into his hands. I am awash in tears, and then in sobs so strong I do not recognize them. José Antonio presses me against his chest and whispers, "*Mariposa, mariposa*, everything is going to be okay," but it is me now who pushes him away. The words roll off my lips and I cannot stop them. I am not in charge of them. They are being said by another version of me.

"I cannot do this anymore," I hear myself say. "I do not want my life to begin and end on Friday afternoons."

José Antonio's face turns a shade of sheer red and his *dulce de leche* eyes burst with a fury I have never seen him display. He does not move from his place at the edge of the bed. He only stares at me. Then he starts to sweat.

He doesn't speak and neither do I, but streaks of sweat are pouring down his face, running down his side, and I can hear the air-conditioning humming at full blast. The quieter José Antonio remains, the more he sweats, and the more I feel the need to fill the silence.

"I would have wanted to be with you forever," I say. "No one has ever filled so many spaces in my life so quickly, but I don't have what it takes to do this."

"I never lied to you. I explained my life to you," he says so softly I can hardly hear him. "I am trapped in a web . . ."

"You are not trapped by the web," I say. "You cling to it."

I don't have time to check his face for signs of emotion. He hops from the bed, walks to the bathroom, and returns to tower before me, patting his face with a hand towel. As soon as he dries the scraggly lines of sweat dripping down his forehead and under his arms, the wetness returns. I have never seen him sweat like this, not even when we baked our bodies under the spell of the Mayan sun. He looks at me, the sting in his eyes devoid of any desire, only of the saddest anger I've ever seen.

I am scared but feel no mercy. I cannot stop the train wreck spilling from my lips.

"Call me when you are a free man," I say.

As soon as I say the words, I become aware of my nakedness. I am still sitting in bed with nothing but the bedsheets around me, and I remain there like a statue. He returns to the bathroom, and on the way there turns the air-conditioning to an even lower temperature. He comes back with a bigger towel, and begins to pat his entire body dry.

I'm freezing and I want to cover up, but I don't. I find strength in my nakedness, in my hardened nipples, in my body's renewed desire for this man, in the decision I have made, despite myself, to gamble, knowing well that these are all-or-nothing stakes.

He turns to the armchair and begins collecting his clothes.

"You had to be born on a Wednesday," he says in Spanish.

I ask him why he would say such an odd thing at this moment, but he has paused to dress. "*Porque eres una atravesada,*" he finally blurts out again in Spanish. Because I am an interrupter, a breaker-upper, a midweek nuisance. Slowly, José Antonio slips on his transparent black Gucci underpants, then angrily he takes them off and flings them at me. "Here, you keep them," he says, "a souvenir." Without taking his eyes off me, he slides into his brown slacks and the brown silk shirt he had folded, as always, neatly on the armchair. When he is done with the last button, he turns to the wall with the Art Deco poster of a Miami Beach building.

He leans in and kisses the wall.

"I spent the happiest hours of my life here," I hear him mumble to the wall, his voice breaking. "It will never be like this again."

Then he walks out without saying good-bye, all six feet of him, slamming the door hard enough for the room to shake. I bury my head in the white pillows and weep. The bed linens smell of cool lavender and satisfying sex and that makes me cry even harder.

THE RESCUE

When I prayed to the veiled moon
to send you to me
I didn't know
you were already there,
watching me,
relishing me,
the way I want you
to watch me,
relish me,
penetrate my soul
naked before your mischievous intentions.

When I prayed to the hidden moon
to challenge me
to feel,
you had already dreamed,
predicted,
concocted
the dance of our indiscreet passion
and the efficiency of your kisses
on my heart.

And now, conquered, kissed, surrendered,
I ask the New Moon for another encounter.
Come, lover and friend,
rescue me from my demons,
make them yours.

WIND SONG

6

Matanzas, Cuba

Abuela warned us about Cuban men. She ranted about their wicked ways, their ill intentions, their one-track minds with pretty young women, virgins like my fifteen-year-old cousin María Isabel and I would be until our wedding night. "Beware of sweet-talking men," my grandmother said. "They will love you and leave you. *Mueleros*, all of them. Liars and cheats." Back then, Abuela's lectures were not aimed at me, but at María Isabel, who was seven years older and had crossed the threshold of womanhood by becoming a *quinceañera*. I was too young for such man talk, but I was always around the two of them, and my eager ears picked up every detail of my beloved grandmother's warnings, which were like hopeless prayers. María Isabel's heart had already set its course and her body could only follow the mandate.

As if the turn of the calendar were a fairy godmother's magic wand, on María Isabel's birthday, Eduardo, a sixteen-year-old boy who lived in the city center near El Parque de la Libertad, the one with the statue of José Martí looking as if he were still leading the

War of Independence, came to her house to ask for permission to court her. It was very difficult to deny a *quinceañera* anything on her big day. María Isabel's parents allowed the couple to get to know each other, but only under the strictest rules of supervision: No time alone. Too busy working at their government office jobs and volunteering as fatigue-clad *milicianos* to ensure the success of La Revolución, María Isabel's parents assigned Abuela Rosario the title of official chaperone.

My parents were busy waging their own little war—arguing, spying on each other, locking themselves up in their bedroom for days—and I too was left in Abuela's care whenever I was not in school. When they married, my mother and father set up house half a block from Abuela's, and two of my aunts, one of them María Isabel's mother, lived on the same block as well. I became Abuela's shadow, her favorite grandchild, the one who got to help her in the kitchen mashing the garlic for her famous black beans. I was the one who got to clean her cherrywood china cabinet, where she kept the porcelain cake tops from all of the weddings of her married children. Best of all, I was the grandchild who got to venture out early in the morning with Abuela to the backyard behind the backyard, to feed corn and table scraps to her spirited brood of chickens, and to the goat she kept tethered to the trunk of her bountiful *guanabana* tree. I named the white goat Laika after I learned in school about the first dog in space, a Russian dog. Like her namesake, my Laika also mysteriously disappeared one day, leaving me broken, and my loss unspoken, without a word of acknowledgment from my otherwise kind grandmother. It would always be that way between us, the silences and the losses, one after another.

When it came to María Isabel's status as the newly minted "*novia de Eduardo*," Abuela Rosario assigned me the all-important job of assisting her in chaperoning María Isabel and the smooth-talking Eduardo whenever Abuela had to step away from the couple to do any of her chores.

I hated it at first. I was forced to sit in the small living room, sometimes for hours, on Abuela's old rocking chair, which had a rip in the cane panel right at the spot where I rested my head. María Isabel and her boyfriend sat on the sofa in front of me. There was no place for my eyes to go but straight to them. It was that or looking out the window, and there was nothing to see outside except for the same sliver of empty street and Cuquita's shuttered window, which had been that way since the *milicianos* came to search her house and took away her husband and a boxful of papers. Without knowing why, I did not want to be looking at Cuquita's house any more than I wanted to look at María Isabel and Eduardo, even if most of the time they acted like I wasn't even there, and after a while I convinced myself that I was see-through, like a ghost. It was on this sofa that María Isabel and Eduardo spent most of their courtship night after night, far apart enough from each other to satisfy the neighborhood's evil tongues and Abuela's archaic traditions.

On some days, the scene at the sofa gave me a stomachache. As soon as Abuela was out of sight, Eduardo would inch closer and closer to María Isabel, and start sliding one hand up her arm and the other up and down her cheek.

"Give me a little kiss," he'd whisper in her ear, loud enough for me to hear it too.

"No, no kisses," María Isabel would say even louder, pushing him away. "Abuela will hear us and come back."

"Come on, *chica,* don't be such a prude. If you don't give me at least one kiss, I'll leave and never come back."

"Marisol," María Isabel would say to me, finally acknowledging my presence. "Turn your head a minute."

"But Abuela said—"

"If you turn your head, we'll take you to El Bar de Yiya for ice cream," Eduardo would then promise.

I'd grudgingly turn my head, and after Abuela returned from her chores, Eduardo would make the generous offer of taking us all out for ice cream. If anyone liked ice cream more than me, it was Abuela, and Eduardo was well aware of the fact that he was romancing more than one woman in our family.

From María Isabel's courtship of hastily stolen kisses and from my stint as its witness and first-base chaperone, I learned little about the ways of love. The tale that forever shaped my rebel soul was Abuela's own love story, which became a legend in our hilly slice of Matanzas, a city of crossing rivers and peasant poets, aptly named "slaughter." Everyone knew Abuela's story, yet no one dared to talk about it, lest they risk the wrath of Rosario del Carmen Sánchez, once known as Rosario del Carmen Sánchez de San Martín. "Of Martín," an attachment that told the world she belonged to the dashing José Manuel San Martín, dubbed by his friends "Machito," literally, Little Macho Man. It was an attachment Abuela wore on her name until a day of fateful revelations and treachery.

Abuela was a beautiful brown woman. She wore her pride waist-long—flowing strands of what I used to call Indian hair, imagining her as an exotic descendant of the island's Tainos that I had learned about in school. In her youth, Abuela's hair was as dark as an *azabache*, the tiny ebony stone Cuban mothers pin on their children's clothes for good luck. Through old age, Abuela wore her thin graying strands like a crown, tucking them into a soft, more-white-than-pepper bun, and she let me—only me, her favorite *nieta*—unravel it and comb through it until she nodded off to sleep, right there in the squeaky cane-backed rocking chair.

While a teenager, Abuela married the man she ardently loved, an adventurous stowaway who arrived in Matanzas harbor from the Canary Islands seeking, like the Spanish conquistadores, to make his fortune in Cuba. In their first twelve years of marriage, she bore Abuelo José Manuel six children, four girls and two boys, one of them my father.

It took almost a lifetime for me to piece together Abuela's story, prying bits and pieces from the women in our family, eavesdropping on conversations I wasn't supposed to hear; first as a child, pretending to be aloof and immersed in a game of jacks, sprawled on the cold gray-tiled floor of Abuela's front porch; then in exile, when it was just the two of us, and it became harder for her to keep her secrets.

Her story went like this:

One day close to the end of the sugar harvest, the neighborhood *chismosa*, a gossip who couldn't control her urge to spit out tales of other people's business, came to tell Abuela that Abuelo was seeing a woman up the hill. "Of course, I would only do this for you, Rosario," she told my speechless, stoic Abuela. "I wasn't sure if I should tell you this, but I want to do the right thing."

Abuela thanked her and continued her chores.

She slowly soaked Abuelo's sweaty white cotton work shirts, scrubbed them hard, one at a time, on her corrugated wooden washboard out in the patio. Then she hung the shirts to dry on the clothesline, forming one straight line of nothing but the whitest of white shirts. Next she thoroughly dusted the cherrywood cabinet, the one displaying the beginnings of what would grow into the collection of figurines of married couples I would clean a quarter of a century later. They were precious to her, these porcelain couples in wedding attire. No one would have suspected that this silly insistence that the two of us, and only the two of us, clean the cherry cabinet was like an omen of what would come, our solo flight into the perpetual uncertainty of exile.

That day the winds would brew another kind of revolution.

Abuelo came home as the sun set behind the lush green hills I believed to be haunted by ghosts on horseback, dressed in white sheets, because I once saw them in the distance with my very own eyes when I was walking home from school. Abuela heard him open the kitchen door from the patio behind the house, and when Abuelo approached her, she kissed him sweetly.

"*Hola, cariño,*" he greeted her as usual.

Today she noticed his good mood. She noticed his hands clean, also his ears. The sweet smell of the harvest and brown print of the earth were only on his clothes.

"The children?" he asked.

"They went to the river to fish with Alberto."

"Did the girls go too?"

"Yes, I didn't want to let them go, but your sister Rosa was going too, and they begged, and she promised to watch over them . . ."

Before she had finished, he started to walk away. He often did this and it unnerved her. But she never thought much about it until now. It was as if her words did not matter, as if he were so accustomed to the singsong of her voice that it held no magic, no surprise, no promise. She was thinking this as she fixed his bath, boiling the water to force the steam to rise, the way he liked it. She planned to feed him next and she went to the kitchen as he bathed, but when she heard the splash of his body coming out of the washtub, she rushed to meet him with a thick, clean white towel. She started to dry him softly, studying every inch of his soaked skin with her small hands and her ebony eyes. She memorized every dark freckle on his wide, tanned shoulders. He was short enough for her to reach, the perfect height for a petite Cuban woman, and he was gifted in size in a way more pleasurable to her.

He responded to her unwitting touch, her lost caress. At first she did not notice, so lost was she in her study, hands and towel wrapped around his legs and making their way to dry each and every toe. But when he grabbed her briskly and she rose, all of him grew taller, larger, and now more desirable to her than ever, in a crazed way she had never experienced before. At the sight of him aroused, she was filled with anger and a painful love that choked her, but what moved her more was a lust so intense that it had been long forgotten, the lust of the new.

He threw her on the floor and mounted her, but she did not let him stay there, as he always did until he was finished, smothering her with his clumsiness. A strangely delicious fever made her want to move in other ways and it gave her a will to come out from under him. Before he could protest, she was guiding him to take her place below. That night Abuela made love to Abuelo with the kind of passion that had only been of his making for so many years in their bed. She was surprised that she was better at it than he. Perhaps it was the practice of watching their sessions aloof, sometimes as if suspended from the ceiling, other times fixing her eyes on the frenzied lovemaking playing out in the blurred mirror on the wall.

This time it was all so different. Abuelo, drunk with this unexpected vision of his woman, completely surrendered to her spell. She taught him how to use his hands for the first time in their long marriage. She moved at will, guided by the sweetest of rushes, in a wild chase of something she did not know. And as the tips of her long black hair brushed against her buttocks and his thighs, his hands tightly squeezing her thick nipples, life flowed in and out of her, in gusts, and out of him in a jolting rush. They fell tired and silent.

It was the first and last time Abuela made love.

The next day, after the younger children went to school and the oldest to their jobs in the bodega that the Sánchez and the San Martín families had opened together, Abuela went up the hill. She sat under a sacred *ceiba* most of the day looking at the house that came to her by way of a wicked, loose tongue.

As afternoon fell, she saw Abuelo approach the other woman's door.

By the time Abuelo came home that evening, Abuela had ironed his white shirts, mended all of his socks, and neatly folded all of his pants, packaging the stack of clothes into two potato sacks she tied at the ends with rope. She placed the bundles by the doorway, and after that, she sat in her old rocking chair in the living room wearing the black dress she donned for all the funerals in the family and the neighborhood, her hair tightly combed back and wrapped into what became her trademark bun, as she never again wore her long hair down. She waited for Abuelo with no rush in her heart.

When Abuelo walked in, it was close to dinnertime and the house was empty, except for the dark figure that did not let him continue past her rocking chair. When Abuela stood up, he went to kiss her, but she jerked her face away, and it was then that he fixed on her steely eyes. He was about to ask her who died when she pointed to the bags by the doorway and, without showing any emotion, said one word: "Leave."

He was confused, suddenly afraid, as if something lurking in the shadows had spooked him. He looked all around, and, not gaining any understanding from what he saw, all he could manage to do was stare at his wife and the darkness consuming her. She returned the look, telling herself that he was nothing but a blank wall, and not her beloved husband.

"Leave this house, leave this city," Abuela said. "I do not want to see you ever again."

"Rosario, I don't understand," Abuelo muttered.

"I saw you this afternoon. And now I want you not only out of my house but out of my city. Leave."

"What did you see?"

She did not answer. She took out a bundle of bills from her pocket, grabbed his hand, and forced them into his palm.

"Get out of here. There is enough there for train fare. All of your clothes are in those bags. Leave."

He did not look at the bags. He did not need to; stunned as he was, he now understood what she knew.

"Rosario, I can explain."

"We have nothing more to say to each other. As long as I am alive, don't come back to this city."

Abuelo did what cowards do. He did not fight for the woman he loved. He stuffed the money in his pocket, grabbed both bags with one hand, and walked back out the door. As he turned to grab the doorknob, Abuela allowed herself one last look at the man she loved. She contemplated his arms, the muscles shaped by working the land inherited from her father, his hands callused but elegant, and it almost choked her with grief. Then she noticed his hastily buttoned white shirt, the ends mismatched, and she hung on to that vision to get through the night. Abuelo spent his night at the train station, and in the morning he took the first train to Havana. The woman he had visited that afternoon, and many afternoons before the fateful one, was Abuela's best friend.

My grandfather's betrayal and my grandmother's drastic punishment happened way before I was born. I never knew Abuelo, but I met him the day before Abuela and I left Cuba on a Freedom Flight in 1969. I had already been living in Abuela's house for years. Papi had been dead for two years, killed in circumstances that were never explained to me, Mami was crazy and confined in Mazorra, the mental hospital in Havana, and Abuela and I were flying to the United States. I was ten years old, and was not fully aware of all that was going on as relatives filed in and out of our house day and night to say good-bye. In the middle of the day, my cousin María Isabel, the only person who spoke to me with frankness, said we would be going to El Bar Yiya to say good-bye to a special man.

"This time, we're not going for ice cream, Marisol. We are going to meet our grandfather."

I thought this was another prank orchestrated by María Isabel to see Eduardo, but on the way there she was very serious and did not speak a single word about Eduardo. Instead, María Isabel told me Abuela's story, adding that Abuela had become famous in Matanzas after she had banished our grandfather from the city. Abuela had raised the younger children all on her own, and she was the envy of all the women who put up with cheating husbands, although for a while, as her story spread, there was absolute fidelity in Matanzas and the tiny towns beyond the great Yumurí Valley.

"Don't tell Abuela I told you," she warned.

I didn't. I had heard snippets of Abuela's story, always told in the frame of "*el carácter de Rosario*," her stalwart personality, but María Isabel's details were what I needed to make it mine, to see Abuela's life in full color, like in a movie. Of Abuelo, I remember little. We had to meet him at Bar Yiya, across from the seawall that wrapped our Matanzas Bay like an embrace. This was as near her house as Abuela had agreed to allow him to wander. Our meeting was arranged through an intermediary, their merchant son Ramiro, the eldest, who had married and moved to Havana to expand his food distribution business.

Abuelo seemed a sad old man, as if he were still carrying those two sacks around with him. He was bald, except for tiny white hairs in the shape of a half-moon in the back of his head, and he had round, knobby fingers. I do not connect any feelings to our meeting. All I remember is that he gave me five pesos, that I thanked him, and asked María Isabel if we could buy vanilla ice cream with the money. Abuelo said to keep the money for my trip and he bought us both ice cream with the rest of the pesos in his pocket. No one knows if he ever built up the nerve to see Abuela that day, to say good-bye to her once more, and in our long years of exile, I never had the courage to ask her.

Abuelo's exile from Matanzas was the first in our family. Mine and Abuela's from the island was the second, and mine from Miami, the third. I am the third generation of wandering souls, and I am real good at leaving.

7

Miami

Abuela may have warned us about Cuban men, but I did not heed her warning. Instead of scaring me away from men, her rants lured me to them. I would conquer men, beat them at their game. To play well, I had to start strong. They would not seduce and leave this virgin. This virgin would seduce and leave *them*. And so I went on a search for the man who would slip into me and rip away that which stood in the way of freedom. I picked him, the policeman, to be the one to draw the blood of innocence. Innocence dressed in red, but not the color of love. Red, the congratulatory color of victory, of a job well done, red as in the scarlet hue of a ribbon won at the county fair, second place, but demonstrating a lot of promise.

And this is how it came to be:

I cannot remember the date exactly, but spring was surely turning into summer. The flame trees all around us were bursting with orange flowers and the bougainvillea were shedding their gaudy paper leaves, turning the ground into a purple and pink carpet. I was working after school at El Palacio de Delicias on Flagler Street, peddling produce, serving *jugos naturales* at the juice bar, running dishes of spicy oxtail and garlicky morsels of pork to the picnic tables out back, when Clarita, the owner, called the police. A strange man, disheveled and mumbling, had been sitting on a bench for hours scaring the customers away. The man refused to talk to any of us and we left him alone for a while, hoping he would leave on his own. But when he started opening and closing the back door, then sitting down again, Clarita lost her patience.

Arturo walked in wearing a pressed navy blue uniform, so dark it looked black, and right away I noticed the .38-caliber tightly packed on his right side. He had big brown eyes, and although he looked to be in his mid-twenties, he was already losing his thin light brown hair. The early baldness, more than the uniform, gave him an air of authority I liked as he walked over to me.

I was behind the pastry counter.

"*Hola*," he spoke first, looking straight into me unlike most customers, who immediately lost themselves in the rows of guava, meat, and cheese pastries that conjure smells of home and the warmth of a grandmother's embrace.

"*Hola*." I smiled automatically.

"What's the trouble?"

I pointed to the man, whose gaze was fixed on the gray cement floor.

"He has been sitting there for hours and won't talk to anybody. We don't know who he is or what he's doing here."

"This must be my lucky day," the cop said, never taking his eyes off me.

I didn't understand.

"Were you looking for him? Is he a fugitive or something?"

"You have bedroom eyes," Arturo said.

To my own surprise, I flirted back: "And what are we going to do about that?"

"Beautiful and sure of herself, I like that," he said.

So I was, but my instincts told me I shouldn't be so easy a catch. This was the moment to change the conversation.

"Didn't you come here for something?" I said.

"Beauty first." He smiled and his full, thick lips came into focus. I could not help looking at them and wondering how they would feel on my neck. But as I was thinking this Arturo left me and walked over to the man sitting there as if this world weren't his kind of place.

I watched as Arturo approached him. He spoke to the man softly, and after the minutes ticked away and an hour passed, the two of them just sitting there like lost souls, Arturo wrapped an arm around him. The man got up, walked with Arturo to his police cruiser, and eased himself into the backseat. Just like that it was over, and that's when the idea that he was the one popped into my head. Arturo, the man who could penetrate the darkness of a faraway spirit, would be awarded the prize of my virginity.

But first I let Arturo romance me. I let it happen slowly, never quite fully giving in to his advances. The fence is a great place for a woman to be. I knew this early on in life, as if this knowledge were my birthright, an inheritance, a silver spoon that came with the linen *canastilla* my mother had hand-embroidered to usher me into my first months in this world.

After that day when he became Clarita's hero and my object of lust, Arturo started coming by the market almost every afternoon. I began wearing Wind Song, the perfume Clarita had given me for my eighteenth birthday.

"A woman should never be without a memorable fragrance that identifies her," Clarita had ceremoniously declared when she presented me the gift, which I loved from the moment I saw the quaint wrapping in pink paper and ribbon. Clarita was a woman of exceptional taste, and it did not escape me that the box proclaimed that the perfume was created by a prince. She may have run a culinary haven where the thick, garlicky smell of sizzling Cuban dishes ruled, but Clarita dressed and smelled as if she worked at the beauty counter in Jordan Marsh.

From the moment I sprayed the first drop of Wind Song just below my left ear, I felt a tingle. The flowery fragrance made me feel sensual and sophisticated, and suited me well, as I was born on the first day of spring. Arturo noticed my perfume the first day I wore it. He was ordering a mango shake and I was taking the order behind the counter.

"Hmmm, you smell delicious," he said, inching forward. "Bet you taste even better."

Then he asked me for a first date.

Sipping his shake slowly, Arturo waited until we could escape the premises during my dinner break. I never ate anything but his kisses. His first kiss was as sweet as a creamy cheese flan. Then they got deeper, wetter, and silky, like coconut ice cream. One night when we were in his beige Monte Carlo and his lips brushed up and down against my neck with the softness of rose petals, I unzipped his pants. It was very late and we were supposed to be going out dancing to a discotheque by the airport. It was our first real date outside my dinner breaks, but I knew this would be the night for me to carry out my business. It was pitch-dark when we drove into a dark perimeter road by the airport to watch the landings by moonlight. On this night, only a sliver of a moon lit the sky and not one star blessed the universe. A dark canopy sheltered us and I let Arturo's kisses progress as if it were he, and not me, who was leading the seduction. I let his hands roam free. I let my hands roam free, caressing the strength of all I found.

"Are you sure?" he whispered in my ear.

"No," I said, touching him everywhere and swallowing his lips.

He led his hands up my baby-doll dress and pulled down my pink bikini panties in one fast move.

"I'm not sure what I am supposed to do," I confessed.

"Do what your instincts tell you to do," he said.

And I did. I dipped my hands into his pants and cupped all of him.

"Ay, Marisol," he softly groaned. "*Sí sabes*."

Yes, I knew. I was born knowing.

And so I straddled his hips with my knees, and gently guided him into me. The pain pierced me sharply, intensely. It disrupted my breathing and I had to pull back.

"You really are a virgin," he said.

I did not answer him. "I'm sorry," he said. "Take it gently. Let me make it good for you."

And he did. He kissed my lips, my neck, my breasts, and as he did this, he laid me down on the seat and gently pushed and pushed until blood gushed everywhere. I couldn't stand the pain and I pushed him away. He kissed my lips.

"Thank you," I said. "But I don't think I can keep going. It hurts too much. I'm sorry."

"It's okay," Arturo said, and pulled me to his chest, caressing my hair. The smell of him, sweaty and filled with desire, fed my own. I had chosen right. I kissed him again. Then he pulled me away, pointed to himself, and said, "What are we going to do about this?"

And what is a girl to do, but sweetly kiss that which is an awesome thing to behold, that which has set one free? From Arturo that night, I learned many things about how to please a man.

Over Arturo, I never shed a tear. I never asked about his life and he never told me anything that mattered. It was the simplest relationship I ever had. He was a gentle teacher and I was a grateful student. When it was time, Arturo and I said good-bye without any melodrama. I was going away to college, fleeing to the plains of Middle America and its dramatic change of seasons. He said he was happy that I was going to make something of myself, even if I didn't yet know what that would be. On our last date, he took me to dinner at the Denny's by the airport on LeJeune Road, and I had a turkey club sandwich with french fries and a Tab. I don't remember what he ordered. All I remember is that he was wearing his navy police uniform, a sweet puppy-dog look on his face, and those pouting lips with which he would kiss me over and over in the restaurant parking lot before delivering me a block from home so that I could arrive on my own and keep Abuela from asking more questions than usual.

The last I heard of Arturo came by way of a greeting card that arrived in my mailbox on my second week at the University of Iowa. It featured a bald guy getting a belly massage on the cover. "I certainly don't need this . . . ," the card said, delivering the punch after I opened it, "just thinking of you gets me all a-quiver!"

In the same small-cap script I had seen in his police reports, Arturo wrote in black pen:

Mari,
Believe it or not I miss you, but I guess I can always fly up and visit you. Don't hesitate to write. You´are always welcome in my box.

Love,
Art

P.S. *Don't let those Hawkeye guys take charge of your sexy* [he underlined this twice] *lips, face, eyes, nose, legs, etc., etc., etc., etc.*

I never wrote back. I was too busy building a new life in a fascinating and strange place, and Arturo never visited, but his card gave me the dose of confidence I would need for the next four years, the most transforming of my life. When I felt lonely or disappointed, I would reread Arturo's words, even though in Iowa I was happier than I was forlorn or discouraged. It was there that I learned to love fresh beginnings. When my Delta Airlines flight took off from Miami International Airport and I soared to freedom, my heart became a vagabond heart, enchanted with the possibilities of my new life. I was eighteen years old and high on the emancipation I had earned by graduating at the top of my class after pouring my grief, alienation, and energy into scholarship. I clung to that euphoric rush as if it were the secret to life, and it always got me through the rough parts.

8

Iowa

I was sad to leave Abuela behind, but not too sad. She had plenty of company, or so I told myself to quell the guilt creeping up on my joy. Abuela had her letters from Cuba to keep her company, never frequent enough but always a reminder that she had made the right decision to leave everything behind, to save me. The letters, written on slithery onionskin paper, were full of bad news and requests for goods that Abuela had no way of sending to the island. But the arrival of a letter was like a family visit. For years, when the isolation between the two countries was as hermetic as a cave in the wilderness, the letters were our only link to loved ones on the island, and as the years extended, they became a coveted treasure, oftentimes the only memory of our dead.

In Miami, if not family, Abuela had her neighbors, most of them Cuban exiles like us, and she had her friends at the *peluquería* on Coral Way, where, as the oldest employee both in age and longevity, and best friend to the beauty salon's owner, Abuela was receptionist/office manager/in-house psychiatrist. The beauticians and manicurists were like sisters, daughters, and best friends all rolled into one, and I knew that in my absence, they would keep Abuela company with that in-your-face camaraderie that someone who has worked at a Cuban beauty salon or lived in a Cuban neighborhood can come to appreciate—or, like me, loathe at the same time. I did not know it then, but my hyphenation had already begun. I had developed a strong distaste for various Cuban ills, especially the cultural rights to meddle in everyone's business, second only to all the talk about "preserving our honor." If there was something I took to right away, it was the Americans' healthy sense of personal space. But in Abuela's beauty parlor, boundaries melted like Swiss cheese on a burger. Everything was everybody's business, and every topic fair game. Reigning over this animated court of jesters was a new role for my grandmother, who had always advised me against partaking in the conspiracies of *las malas lenguas* of this world, the evil tongues skilled at spinning misery, but exile turned every life upside down, and Abuela's was no exception.

But more than once, the tongues and dullards of the beauty salon worked in my favor, inspiring my secret world of adolescent daydreams and plots to escape the dull confines of my life. It was at the beauty shop, of all places, that I first heard of the University of Iowa.

I was sixteen years old and dancing at the *quince* celebration of the daughter of one of Abuela's clients. One of the perks of being one of the fourteen couples who get to dance with the *quinceañera* princess and be part of her court was the trip to the beauty parlor for a fancy hairdo of *bucles* à la Marie Antoinette and a manicure with half-moon tips. Conchita was putting my hair in rollers when the woman next to me, who was getting her hair teased and shaped by Violeta into what looked to me like a football helmet, began to gossip about "the horror of what is happening with our children in this *exilio*."

She told a movielike tale of "a girl from a good Cuban family" named Ana Mendieta who had been sent to the United States alone with her sister in 1961 because the family was involved in subversive political activities. The girl was first sent to the Catholic home for unaccompanied Cuban children in Kendall, then shipped to a children's home in Iowa, from there to be shuttled from one family to another until she graduated from high school and went to college. Her father, who was an important man in Cuban politics, had been sent to prison, accused of collaborating with the CIA, and the girl's mother and brother were not able to get out of the country until many years later on a Freedom Flight. When the family was reunited in Cedar Rapids, the girl was already in college, making these pretty sculptures and studying painting. "She is at this University of Iowa and she has become crazy, crazy," the woman said. "She gets naked in front of all these people and pours chicken blood all over herself, takes pictures, and she says this is art. This would have never happened in Cuba, never."

My grandmother chimed in that she knew the Mendieta family well. The girl's mother was from a prominent family in Cárdenas, a stone's throw from our Matanzas, and it was where one of Abuela's daughters had settled with her family after she got married. The girl's great-great-uncle, a general during the Spanish-American War, had founded Cárdenas' famous museum of history and culture in 1900, Abuela said. On her father's side, her uncle, Carlos Mendieta, had been president of Cuba.

"We used to see them in Varadero all the time," Abuela said. "They had a fabulous house and all the family gathered there in the summers."

And from there the conversation turned to remembering life when the stretch of Vía Blanca from Havana to Matanzas to Varadero in a slick 1956 Buick packed with newlywed couples was the road to paradise, no matter which way you took it, to the city or to the beach. After that, it was my turn under the bulky hair dryer, which drowned out all conversation with its loud hum, the perfect place to dive into my thoughts. I wished I were Ana Mendieta, free enough to get naked, although I had to admit that the stuff about the chicken blood was pretty gross. "Artist" sounded like a great thing to be, and the University of Iowa, a kind of Eden for those yearning to cut loose from the stranglehold of family ties and burdensome heritage. As soon as I got to my room, I went to my desk and looked up Iowa in my school atlas. It was in the heart of the country and, being in the middle of America, seemed like a great place to be. All I needed to get there was a plane ticket and a scholarship, and for both of those things there was only one thing to do: work hard and save my money. Two years later, when it was time for me to choose a school, my National Merit Scholarship became the ticket, and there was only one school to which I applied for admission.

The day I got my acceptance letter from the University of Iowa, I walked to the *peluquería* after school to pick up Abuela and accompany her on her trip back home. I would not tell her at the beauty salon because I wanted Abuela to be in the best of moods when I delivered the news that I'd be moving fifteen hundred miles away. When I entered the beauty salon, everyone seemed to be in an exceptionally good mood for a lazy Wednesday, giggling and passing around Polaroid shots of the manicurist's firstborn grandson.

When the photos made their way to me, I couldn't believe what I was seeing: a plump eighteen-month-old in the middle of a diaper change grabbing his penis and, photo after photo, pulling on it with delight.

"Isn't it huge?" Yesenia, the proud new grandmother, beamed from her station as she filed a woman's nails. "The family stamp."

From the topic of the grandson, they transitioned to talking about the size of Yesenia's ex-husband's penis, and how that was what had made their breakup difficult for her. Yesenia detested all of him, but she liked his penis, which her son had inherited, and now her grandson as well. Yesenia, a bleached blonde, was as nonchalant as if she were discussing how to make the best arroz con pollo in Miami, not too soupy, not too dry. "I have to find a way to send the photos to Cuba so that his great-uncle can see him," Yesenia said. "Are any of you sending a package soon? We can share the cost."

Surely, among this brood, Abuela would be fine in my absence, not to mention entertained, and so she was. Our last days together were unusually good, as if Abuela wanted me to remember her as the progressive woman she was not. She even stood up to the new hairdresser who, after learning I would be studying away from home, warned her, "Don't let her leave. She'll come back to you with a big belly on her, you'll see."

"I have raised my granddaughter to know better," was all Abuela said to that.

She hadn't raised me to know better; we never spoke about the subject of sex. Telling me about the hairdresser's prediction was all the sex education Abuela could muster, but it was enough for me. I didn't respond to the commentary, as I had come to make Abuela's established silences my own. But I wouldn't disappoint her. I'd make sure the beautician would swallow her words, as wicked tongues should.

When I finally delivered the news of my acceptance the day Yesenia's grandson's penis made his public debut, Abuela tried her best to show that she was proud of me. She didn't fully understand why I could not go to a local university, but she accepted my explanation that they weren't good enough, and that the only one that was, was a private school, too expensive. Iowa had given me a full scholarship, I boasted. It became my mantra, and also Abuela's whenever she had to explain my absence. "Marisol is so smart that they are paying her to go to school in Iowa," she told everyone. But late at night, I could hear her weeping into her pillow.

A week before my trip, Abuela surprised me with a shopping spree for winter clothes at the cheap warehouse outlets in the blighted downtown district of Wynwood. Accessing bargain wool weaves, we made peace with the shortcomings of my adolescence, and she helped me pack for my new life the way a mother helps a daughter plan her wedding. For the four years I lived in Iowa, she wrote me a letter every week, egging me on to succeed, and she called once a month at an agreed-upon time, as she could not afford to make long-distance calls, and neither could I. Our exchanges in Spanish were my only ties to being Cuban. The beauteous drama of autumn colors eased my transition from the perpetual warmth of Matanzas and Miami, and by the first snowfall, I had wholeheartedly embraced Iowa and my Americanness.

In the fall of 1977, chablis was the wine of choice, vans were groovy, and so were denim overalls. I learned to drink wine, love in vans, and wear faded blue overalls and tan suede Earth shoes to class. Under the yellowing trees in the courtyard of my dormitory, the resident assistants held a get-to-know-each-other marshmallow roast. Sophomores Kevin and Jeannie played Dylan on their guitars. Carol, my roommate, knew the words by heart, and hers was the crispest voice singing along. I was the only one freezing and wearing gloves. With fall, there also came an outdoor Halloween Ball by the riverbank that the university's administration threatened to ban forever given the invading smells of illegal substances throughout the night, and the empty bottles of Southern Comfort and cheap vodka covering the lawn at sunrise. Carol used her red-and-white-striped pajamas to turn herself into a candy cane. I merged scattered pieces of my wardrobe, long necklaces and hoop earrings, my one and only long skirt, and a Mexican peasant shirt borrowed from one of the girls down the hall who had it as a vacation souvenir, to become a gypsy.

I took to Iowa City—dubbed "The Athens of the Midwest," just as my Matanzas was "The Athens of Cuba"—as if it had been waiting for me all of my life. There was something magical in knowing that two of my favorite writers, Flannery O'Connor and Tennessee Williams, had studied and written works there. But for months after I first arrived, I had a recurring dream about a faceless woman running through cornfields in a long white skirt. She was running away or running to someone or something, I wasn't quite sure. There was an urgency and vigor to her flight, but just as it was beginning to seem wondrous, I noticed that her naked torso was marked by bleeding red scratches. As she fled past the corn rows, her skin was being sliced by corn husks. I always woke up before her destination was revealed to me, and as I became more and more comfortable in Iowa, the dream disappeared. Perhaps it was what prompted me to become a fledgling explorer when, in the spring term, I saw a bulletin advertising the university's Earth Club. I joined and set out to hike Iowa's scenic trails, prairies, and woodlands surrounded by young people whose hearts were connected to the land. In the camaraderie formed by walking for miles on quiet trails, Cindy, Dale, Valerie, and Mary Anne became good friends with whom I shared my love for the great valley of Yumurí, and the natural beauty of my harbor city of rolling hills, Matanzas, bathed by the San Juan, the Yumurí, and the Canímar rivers. In the cradle of simple friendships, I could conjure the beauty of the past without resurrecting the stinging pain of loss. To my new friends, I was an exquisitely exotic creature, or so was the vibe I felt. And who could grieve when, after I finished one of my dreamy descriptions, Mary Anne chimed in, "Cuba, where's that?" And when I answered, "The Caribbean," she responded, completely serious, "Is that near Africa?" and Dale, who dreamed of being a pilot but was indulging his parents' expectations that he get an education, replied, "Wrong side of the world, Mary Anne. Scoot left over the ocean a little."

It was while camping at Old Man's Creek with the Earth Club that I learned one of the most valuable lessons of my college life. Our guide, Bill, a short-haired hippie with taut skin baked by the sun and who roared to our get-togethers on a Harley, had promised a night walk that we'd never forget. We left the camp as a group, ten of us with walking sticks in hand, and nothing but a new moon and the stars in the sky lighting the trail. It was so dark we could not see our own hands. After we had walked for about a mile in silence, as we'd been instructed to do, Bill said we would separate and return to camp alone, one by one.

"If you've listened carefully to your surroundings on your way here, you'll find your way back," Bill said. "Let the light of the moon, the stars, and your instincts guide you."

At first I felt an unspeakable fright, but one by one the men started walking the trail back, then the sportiest of the women among us, and it became obvious that I would have no choice but to return alone. Valerie, who grew up in a pool home in Southern California and, given her stories about her Christmas gifts (a trip to Paris, a motorcycle, an apartment in Iowa City to share with roommates), was clueless about how much wealthier she was than the rest of us, protested the assignment. I chimed in with halfhearted objections as well, more out of loyalty to her than anything else. If we had been told in advance, I told Bill, we would have been better prepared for the journey back. We would have paid more attention. Perhaps Valerie and I could team up, I suggested.

"You two can go together if you want to," Bill said in his most mellow hippie voice, "but you'll be robbing yourselves of this experience. Trust me when I tell you, you'll find your way back, and doing so alone will be important."

Valerie still refused to walk alone, but Bill's words inspired me. I left the two of them arguing, their voices fading as I made my way down the dark trail.

The moon is a fine traveling companion. She did not light the way, as I was expecting, from above, but she was behind me, and although at first I often looked back when I could not sense a clearing ahead, the walking stick helped me, like a compass, stay on the path. As soon as I was far enough from Bill and Valerie, I welcomed the silence. I could hear the rippling creek, the fluttering leaves on both sides of me. I learned to appreciate the solitude. But I also learned to dread too much of it. When I was most comfortable, I bumped into a branch and my heart began racing. My walking stick, once again, helped me correct course. It is so easy to misread spaces when it is dark.

After that, it was tough to quiet my heart. I was wondering if I was going to be walking in the night forever when I heard voices coming from our campsite, and then I saw flickers of light in the distance. With the campfire, my hands came into view, and then the narrow trail. The rest of the jaunt to camp became my definition of joy. I had learned something too precious to explain, to name. I slept well that night under a green communal tent, my tired body snuggled inside my burgundy sleeping bag. The next day we went swimming, clothing optional. I did not dare shed my bikini, although I wanted to. Valerie did, showing an equally naked Bill that, given the right circumstances, she could be the bravest among us.

9

Once the novelty of being free from Abuela's grip began to wear off, I started dreaming about the future, and part of my equation for happiness entailed finding my fantasy, an all-American knight in shining armor. I yearned for love with the same ardor that I craved straight golden American hair like my roommate Carol had. Both of my dreams came true. For a while, I had Andy, an *americano* who would stand beneath the third-floor window of my dorm and holler in a Southern twang for me to come down so that he could walk me to class. And one morning I woke up with straight golden hair. Carol and I produced the miracle overnight with a bottle of Nice 'n Easy in a shade of blond that turned out to be more dirty than blond, and an empty roll of toilet paper. I had seen the hairdressers at the beauty salon use oversized rollers to straighten hair, and Carol, an industrial engineering major, became a perfect partner for the project of straightening my soft waves. She helped me wrap my bleached and colored wet hair all around the cardboard roll, stretching it tightly as she went along and securing it with two rows of pins. I had to sleep all night with this contraption on my head, but when I woke up my natural wave had yielded, and I had my own peculiar shade of straight blond hair. I was thrilled, even if my American hair came with a stiff neck.

Reeling in Andy, my knight in tight blue jeans and flannel, was easier.

I met him at an off-campus party given by friends of Carol, who lived in an apartment on the west side of the river and, like Carol, were from tiny Muncie, Indiana. When Carol told me it was a potluck affair, I offered to make a staple Cuban dish, *picadillo*, and the memory of the aroma of Cuban cuisine gave my heart a tug. Carol was thrilled. Having no interest in cooking, she readily offered to pay for the ingredients in exchange for my labor. We sealed the deal with a high five. All we had in our cluttered dorm room was a refrigerator, so I ended up cooking at the party while everyone drank, smoked, and danced.

I was regretting my offer when Andy walked into the party late and alone. I was stirring my slow-cooking *picadillo* so that the ground beef wouldn't stick to the bottom, and from the opening above the kitchen counter to the crowded living space, I saw Andy making his way through the crowd, a little uncertain. Right away I knew he was the gringo of my adolescent diary dreams, with all that wispy blond-hair falling on his shoulders in layers and his eyes a deep shade of blue-green, the way I remembered the waters of the Caribbean. I watched him until he disappeared from view, then I went back to dipping a plastic spoon into the cheap ground beef to skim off the thick layer of orange fat building on top of the meat as it simmered. I was struggling to remember Abuela's recipe: onions, garlic, vinegar, dry wine, green peppers, tomato sauce, a handful of raisins. Neither the Spanish dry wine nor the Spanish olives stuffed with pimento required by the recipe were available in the supermarkets of Iowa City. Salt! I added more salt. Still, something else was missing. As we would say in Miami, this *picadillo* was not even "*la chancleta*" of Abuela's. It could never measure up. I wanted to call Abuela collect and consult her, but I dared not. Surely she would start asking me questions about where I was and why I was making this huge batch of *picadillo* out here in Gringoland. Then she would lecture me that I should be studying this late at night and not partying with strangers. The irony of it was that after Abuela scolded me, she would turn around and tell the story to her favorite neighbor, Rosita, in a totally different light, making me look like the perfect granddaughter. I could imagine Abuela telling Rosita, "Isn't it nice how Marisol is teaching all the Americans in Iowa [*Ay-yoga* to Abuela] to eat Cuban food? Wasn't it sweet of her to call me and ask for my special recipe? She misses my cooking." And surely the next day Abuela would repeat the story at the beauty salon, spiked with an even higher dose of grandmotherly pride. I had seen her do this before with my late-night arrivals during my last year of high school, boasting to Rosita about how hard I worked at El Palacio de Delicias, you know, just in case she was thinking something else when she peeked through her vertical blinds and saw me arrive past midnight.

No, it was better not to call home. Even this far away, Abuela and her admonishments haunted me, hung on my thoughts like weeping Spanish moss. Nor could I shake the ghosts of Mami and Papi, and the Cuban guilt that choked me when I least expected it. I wanted so badly to be carefree like my American friends, but it wasn't a slam dunk, as Carol liked to boast when she easily beat me at backgammon. My heart often ended up divided, half of it pining for a home that was somewhere between Iowa and Matanzas, half of it embracing the spirit of golden bumper stickers that claimed "It's Great to Be a Hawkeye!" Cooking *picadillo* had stirred my ghosts. I knew that no one at this beer, weed, and rock-and-roll party had such stupid thoughts. But I couldn't help mine. Abuela and my missing parents would have been appalled had they seen these people passing around one joint after another and pumping beer from a big silver keg. Or would they? I knew Abuela well, but I never really knew my parents. Abuela objected to everything I embraced, labeling my hunger to exercise my choices, from hippie fashion to dating without a chaperone, "*libertinaje*"—debauchery, licentiousness. The navy tank top I was wearing cut at the midriff with tight-fitting blue jeans hugging my hips would certainly qualify as that. The show of naked torso and belly button was absolutely prohibited back home. "Only those loose American girls wear such things," Abuela said when we went shopping for college clothes and I made a move for the rack of $2 tank tops. That day I made peace with her, however, knowing that her prohibitions wouldn't ruin my plans to modernize my wardrobe. The minute I landed in Iowa, checked into my dorm, unpacked my two suitcases, and found a spot on my dresser for my curvy bottle of Wind Song—without question, the happiest moment of my life—I headed for the nearest store and spent a secret stash of $50 in savings on tiny shirts, short shorts, a pair of hip-huggers, and a hot pink bikini with a string top. Only the Iowa winter would generate regret.

No, with all that history, I couldn't risk calling Abuela from the party. She'd ruin my night with her questions, reproaches, and summary judgments, which she could hand down from Miami as easily as if she were the Supreme Court of Cuban Motherhood, and I the

Renegade Daughter Defendant. And, more likely than not, these *americanos* wouldn't notice anything missing from the *picadillo*. How would they know any better? No one at this party had even heard of the word.

"Sure smells great in here," said a hunky voice that had snuck up behind me and my thoughts. Spooked, I turned around and instantly lost my sanity at the sight of the infinite blue of Andy's eyes searching for mine. I couldn't utter a word. It was as if all of a sudden I couldn't speak English.

"Love that smell! I'm starving," he said as if I had cooked for him all his life. "What is it?"

"It's called *picadillo*," I said, dipping in a small silver spoon and offering him a sample. "Here, have a taste."

He chewed, swallowed, and stuttered, "Pey-cawh-del-loo. Tastes like sloppy Joe to me!"

"Now, that's an insult! This is a Cuban dish and it doesn't taste one bit like that greasy stuff you put on a bun and call sloppy Joe," I said. "Now go away. I'm trying to remember my grandmother's recipe, and I can tell you're not going to help."

He didn't move.

"Tastes great to me," he said. "So, Ms. Julia Child, let me introduce myself: I'm Andy. Andy Nielsen."

"Trust me, I'm no Julia." I smiled and extended my hand. "I'm Marisol," I said, a little embarrassed at the foreignness of my name. If he couldn't say *picadillo*, what could I hope for with Marisol?

"Sounds like a song!"

"More like a poem," I corrected.

"What does it mean?

"Sea and sun, *mar y sol*."

"A name as pretty as you," he said, and I liked the quirky way the word "pur-r-r-tee" flew out of his lips.

I think it was precisely at that moment, his blue eyes glued to mine, the *picadillo* simmering without my attention, that I fell in love with Andy Nielsen, a country boy with a melodious twang and killer shoulders, homemade in the USA. I could extend the language lessons for a lifetime under his spell. Or so I thought then.

I was glad the lights were dim because I could feel myself blushing.

"Where are you from?"

"Miami, and you?"

"Asheville, North Carolina, home of the Blue Ridge Parkway, prettiest place you've ever seen. But tell me, pretty Marisol, where are you *really* from?"

"Miami, that's where I'm really from."

It was not the first time I had been asked the question twice in Iowa. I knew what he meant, but I didn't want to give an inch. Although at first I had enjoyed an otherness some people found attractive and dubbed exotic, it was as if when I was not in Miami, I had a sign on my forehead that read "I don't belong here, ask me."

The exchange turned my smile into a frown, but Andy was still all smiles.

"You're even prettier when you're annoyed. I like that thing you do with your right eyebrow."

"You don't want to see me mad," I said, turning my attention back to the *picadillo*, which had started to stick to the bottom, and plunging into a mental conversation with myself. *Okay, slow down, Marisol, the guy could turn out to be another jerk, and a slow jerk at that. You already told him the* picadillo *was a Cuban dish and he didn't get it.*

Maybe he wants to rub it in that I'm different, that I don't belong, like those bigots on the radio and on TV who never fail to make the point that you're only a guest in this country.

But moving closer to me and the stove, Andy asked, "Would you like to dance?" He towered over me. Too tall, six-plus, I figured.

"What about my *picadillo*?" I stalled him. I needed a chance to think. "Didn't you say you were starving, don't you want to eat first? And, before you say any more, I was born in Cuba. I'm Cuban, very Cuban, like the *picadillo*, and very American, like Iowa."

I scooped some *picadillo* on a spoon, blew on it, and brought it to my lips. Not quite the real thing, but it was as good as it was going to get. I turned off the fire and moved the pot to a cool burner.

"Have some and tell me this is the best you've ever had before you really get on my nerves and I start speaking Spanish," I said, looking for a paper plate to serve him.

"You're feisty. I like that. I'll have some of that pee-ca-what-chamacallit if you dance with me," he said. "I already know you can cook. Now I want to know if you can dance."

Sweet revenge that would be. I danced better than I cooked, and definitely better than any gringo from the mountains. Now I'd really show Andy Nielsen where I was from. We walked to the living room packed with sweaty college students drinking too much beer and inhaling too profoundly, and before we found a spot for ourselves, Andy held my hand. The Eagles blared their sexy "Hotel California," and I closed my eyes to let the music ease into me. I have always felt the music, any music, the same way, in an intimate, rousing rush, no matter who was singing, Joe Walsh or Beny Moré. I swayed slowly to catch the rhythm with my hips. (It's always the hips, that's the trick.) Andy let go of my hand.

When I opened my eyes, I saw Andy standing in front of me, not moving, his infinite eyes staring, his lanky body towering above me.

"Aren't you going to dance?" I said, moving still.

"I think I'll just watch you," Andy said. He looked fine in tight dark blue jeans and a green and black plaid shirt, sleeves rolled to his elbows.

"Come on, I don't want to dance alone," I said, taking his hand.

Just then, the song ended. I made a move to leave the dance floor but another Eagles tune immediately started to spin, "I Can't Tell You Why." Andy didn't waste any time. He wrapped his arms around me, and I felt as if I were hugging the Jolly Green Giant. He must have been thinking the same thing because he set out to correct the distance, bending down and bringing his lips close to my right ear.

"You're the most beautiful Cuban girl I've ever seen," he whispered.

"I'm probably the only Cuban girl you've ever seen," I said.

"True."

Andy turned out to be the easiest catch of my boy-chasing career, which dated back to first grade at a strict private school in Matanzas. Like everything else, that school was confiscated by the Revolution and declared a property of the state, becoming even more dogmatic. At age six, when most girls think boys are stupid, I was already deeply in love with Carlitos—and paying for my sin. Our teacher caught me writing a note telling Carlitos how much I liked him, how he was "the love of my life," words I no doubt copied from the enamored musings of my cousin María Isabel. The note never reached Carlitos.

Señora Martínez gave it to my mother, who spanked me right in front of the teacher, and forbade me from seeing my friends for a month, a penalty I endured quite comfortably thanks to Abuela, who came to my rescue telling Mami she needed my help with chores around the house. After a short session dusting the cherry cabinet, Abuela invited over her neighbor's granddaughter to play jacks with me on the cool floor, and that was the end of my penitence. Word of my whereabouts spread and my entire jacks club found its way to Abuela's house. Soon I was spending more time at her house than mine, which didn't matter much.

Although my love note didn't reach Carlitos, its declaration of love spread through the entire school as my girlfriends shared "the secret" of why I, the number one honor roll student, had been grounded. I became the sophisticated heroine of love, and Carlitos, who by all accounts of boys at this age should have been thoroughly disgusted, was thrilled to be the subject of such attention. He sent word through his friends that my love was returned. Carlitos was the second smartest kid in class—after me—and he vowed to like me forever if I played baseball with him and his friends during recess. But I chose to be with my girlfriends, and that was the end of that short and beleaguered love affair. We remained bitter competitive enemies for the rest of our school days until I left Cuba, vying neck-and-neck for first place on the honor roll. He eventually beat me after my parents refused to allow me to become a *pionera*, a member of the Young Communists Pioneers. Carlitos did become a *pionero*—which consisted of wearing a red scarf around your neck and participating in activities spiked with Communist ideology—and the teachers gave him extra points for revolutionary fervor, enabling him to beat my nearly perfect grade-point average.

After Carlitos's betrayal, I pledged not to like boys anymore, but in fourth grade I fell hard for Robertico, a boy from my neighborhood. He was Alejo's best friend, and we played together while my parents were working or socializing with Alejo's parents. Unlike Carlitos, Robertico was sweet-natured, a young Cuban Romeo who sang boleros with Alejo and wanted to be a crooner when he grew up. Thanks to Alejo's matchmaking powers, we were a couple—a secret couple, lest I be grounded for life by Mami and Papi, of course. Our romance lasted until I left with Abuela for exile in the summer of 1969, shortly after *el americano* Neil Armstrong became the first man to set foot on the moon. On the eve of my flight, Robertico and I said a tearful good-bye through my aunt's bedroom window. We promised to meet again in the new year, which the government had decreed to be *El Año de los Diez Millones*, the year Cubans would produce a ten-million-ton sugar harvest, the largest in the island's history. To us, the militant rhetoric of how the people's massive effort would achieve this great goal made it sound like it would be a magical year. Robertico and I decided it would be a good time to marry then, never mind that I would be barely eleven years old and he twelve. Or that we would be living in different countries forever. On the night before Abuela and I were driven to the airport in Varadero to board the plane that would whisk us from our beloved island, Robertico asked me for my hand in marriage through my aunt's window. When I extended my hand through the black iron bars and closed my eyes in a mix of romantic delight and gripping fear, he kissed it softly and ran away. Our engagement was sealed. When the plane took off into the clouds, and all I could see was the vast green and turquoise of my island, it was Robertico I was thinking about, it was for him that I was shedding the tears. It was for him that I sang my sadness away in Spanish with the bubblegum tunes of Roberto

Jordán, only to rediscover that in English they were the songs of Ohio Express and the 1910 Fruitgum Company.

For the first three months of exile, I vowed to love Robertico forever and prayed daily to *la virgencita del Cobre*, Cuba's patron saint, that his parents too would leave Cuba and bring Robertico to Miami and to me. But there was little chance of that. The sugar harvest was disastrous and, like our passionate puppy love, sent the Cuban economy on another tailspin. No sugar quota met, no wedding vows spoken, not even a letter arrived from Cuba that year. Robertico's parents never left the island. They were staunch party activists and neighborhood watchdogs, the ones who kept tabs on people's activities. My parents had maintained a love-hate relationship with his family because they were the nicest Communists anyone ever met, but as I once heard my father say before he died, "The only good Communist is a dead Communist."

After 1970 came and went without word from Robertico, I started to like the Cuban boys in my new school. I couldn't make up my mind which one of the four refugee boys in my class I liked the most, perhaps because the sweetness of Robertico's kiss lingered on my hand despite my survival instinct to forget him and move on. It didn't matter. The Cuban boys didn't want me or any other Cuban girl. All the Cuban boys wanted were the *americanitas* with their blond hair and blue eyes and their lack of inhibitions and prohibitions. The American girls in school, and the one or two left on our block, where every day it seemed a new Cuban family took up residence, were allowed to play baseball with the boys out on the street while most Cuban girls like me were expected to remain inside helping with chores in the house or playing with dolls. The *americanas* played a mean ball game, going out there in shorts and T-shirts and batting the ball sometimes farther than the boys. I envied their freedom.

"Your father, who is watching from heaven, doesn't want you out there playing with boys," Abuela would say to me whenever I insisted on going outside. "It's not proper for a young lady. We are not like them."

We are not like them. It became Abuela's battle cry throughout my first years of exile, and her way of saying no to everything that was the least bit fun for me. Her constant refusals to allow me to partake in virtually everything I wanted to do propelled me to develop a character trait I later found helpful in life—put on the spot, I oozed vast amounts of ingenuity to wriggle my way out of certain situations, as I had done to break free from Abuela's social dictatorship. Under Abuela's rule, I developed the necessary skill of lying with perfect pitch.

Her grip sometimes slipped a little, thanks to the many extracurricular activities at school to which I subscribed, and the complicity of teachers and counselors who felt sorry for the smart orphan girl under the tutelage of the tough-cookie *abuela*. I joined every club I could, the Civinettes, the French Club, the Pep Squad. When I was old enough, I added another layer to escape Abuela: my after-school job at El Palacio de Delicias, which extended to weekend hours as well. But I swore off Cuban boys for a while. Cuban boys were way too much like family, complicated and hurtful.

Until the night I met Andy in Iowa, I didn't believe the stuff about the way to a man's heart being through his stomach. I thought the penis was the way, as I had learned with Alejandro. But the pot of *picadillo* had cast a magical spell on the boy from the winding roads of North Carolina, and the music brought him even closer to me.

As the Eagles' leading man crooned, Andy pulled me tight. He smelled of spring in the forest after a cooling rain, and I gave in to his embrace, letting the music dictate our rhythm. We only let go when Carol's voice interrupted the bliss.

"Okay, everybody, come and get it!" she announced. While we danced, Carol and her host friends had set up the dining room table, buffet-style. Gobs of my *picadillo* had been plopped on buns and was being called "a Cuban sloppy Joe."

The dance floor emptied in a matter of seconds, except for the two of us.

"The munchies," I said, chuckling.

"Yeah," Andy mumbled and went back to rest his head on mine.

"We must look really silly being the only ones on the dance floor and me being so short and all," I said. I felt stupid for saying the obvious.

"Maybe it's not that you're too short, but that I'm too tall," he whispered again in my ear.

"Aha," I agreed, and closed my eyes for the rest of the song.

As the party wound down, Andy asked me if he could take me home.

"My dorm is far, on the other side of the river. I came with Carol, she's my roommate."

I had settled for the most modest dorm at the University of Iowa, an old brick building built in the 1920s. I loved the archways and columns, the rustic stairwell and the cracked walls. Maybe I loved it, in part, because Abuela nearly fainted when she came to visit me one Thanksgiving, and saw that the building had no air-conditioning and no elevator, and that I had been assigned to the top floor, the fourth.

But I loved my dorm and the ten pounds it had helped me shed. It was as bohemian as my blue jeans, and so liberated, just like the new me.

It was around three a.m. when Andy and I walked out of the party and bummed a ride to my dorm. Carol had decided to stay the night with her friends.

"Can I walk you upstairs?" Andy asked when we reached the old creaky wooden door of my building.

"No, it's past curfew. I'll get in trouble," I said, knowing it was an excuse. The curfew was real on paper, but most people broke it, and nothing ever came of it, as the resident assistants in charge were as guilty as the rest of us. Still, the no-boys-after-midnight curfew became a great excuse to say good-bye to a date outside when you didn't want it to go any further. In this case, I wanted it to go further, much further. But that was precisely what I feared. Every girl knew the golden international rule of dating that if you put out too early, he walked.

"I just want to leave you at your door, safe and sound," Andy pressed me.

"We are at my door," I said.

"Yes, but you told me you're up on the fourth floor. How do you know there's not some creep lurking on the stairs, waiting for your pretty face?"

"Now you sound like my grandmother. Okay, come on up. But be very quiet or you'll get me in big trouble," I said.

I maneuvered the bigger of my keys into the door and it opened without effort. I was starting the climb up the stairs when Andy, who followed close behind, pulled me against him and planted a wet kiss on my lips.

"You promised," I mumbled, but I offered no resistance.

We kissed passionately for a while in the darkness of the bottom of the stairs. But then we heard voices outside and, as if on cue, we both darted up the stairs. Two floors up and I was breathless. I knew it was the company. I was in great shape and easily made it to the top each day without losing an ounce of energy. Andy wasn't affected at all. He grabbed my waist and brought my lips to his again. I got away from him and ran up another flight. He bolted after me and caught up with me as I reached my door.

He kissed me softly, then hard, then softly again. I felt lost, like in a trance, swept away. He slipped a hand under my shirt. I let him, reveling in the trembling uncertainty of his hand, but as I longingly glanced past his shoulder, I swear I saw my grandmother standing at the end of the hallway.

I pulled away fast, rough.

"I'm sorry," Andy said. "I didn't mean to offend you. I got carried away. I really like you."

I kept staring at the hall, but now she wasn't there.

I felt faint.

"Marisol, what's wrong?"

"I'm okay, I'm just tired," I lied. "I think all that smoke we inhaled is getting to me now. I need to get to bed."

"Can I see you tomorrow? How about a movie at the Bijou? There's always something strange enough to be good there."

"Sounds fine to me," I said, and gave him a quick peck on the cheek. I needed to get Andy Nielsen out of my dormitory. All I wanted to do was look for my grandmother in the closets, under the bed, inside the black trunk Carol used as a night table, anywhere my Cuban grandmother might hide to spy on her *nieta*'s sins.

"Pick you up at six," Andy said, that smile still glued to his face.

"How about we grab a beer at the Fieldhouse, then head on over to the 'B'?"

"Cool," I said in my best American voice.

He kissed me softly on the lips and disappeared down the stairwell. I ran inside to inspect the room. After I made sure Abuela hadn't transferred to the University of Iowa, I vowed never again to smoke marijuana or make another awful batch of *picadillo* without the aroma of laurel leaves. The next day, I restored my Cuban hair with a new color kit, this time a deep shade of brown like the grooves on the trunk of a *ceiba* tree.

10

"Iowa City has the most beautiful women in the Midwest, but all of them have boyfriends," a fraternity brother was quoted as saying in the student newspaper, the *Daily Iowan*. "There are more boyfriends than Frisbees in Iowa."

It was a valid complaint. I met Andy halfway through my second year, and I never dated another boy there again. As we bonded over study sessions and exploratory sex, the vision of Abuela's ghost lurking in my dormitory dissipated. And after Andy kissed me in the shadow of the towering Black Angel in the city's cemetery, as Hawkeye tradition demands, I never again dreamt of murderous cornfields. Carol's high school sweetheart, Brian, transferred from Indiana University, and the chemistry between the four of us developed so naturally and instantaneously that the next semester, we all moved into a two-bedroom apartment off-campus. I felt sophisticated and grown up, but when it came to Abuela I was still an adolescent. I didn't tell her about my living arrangements, and whenever she came to visit for a special weekend, Mother's Day or Thanksgiving, Carol and I jammed

Andy's clothes into her closet, his toiletries into her bathroom, and the boys disappeared, using Abuela's trips to visit their own families or to go fishing. Andy did not understand all the effort behind the camouflage. "What is she going to do," he said on the eve of one of her arrivals, "whip out her machete and fight me?" My stories about Abuela and her infamous persona had left their mark on Andy, the latest being the machete she kept by her bedside in light of the crime wave sweeping Miami. I laughed so hard I could not take our lovemaking seriously that night. The thought of Abuela reaching for her machete to save my honor made me giggle every time Andy tried to touch me. I couldn't put my imagination to rest, and Andy was irked. He would not see me for four days and his intentions had been to spend the night making love, not talking about my grandmother. After he gave up trying to be serious and surrendered, we both learned about the potency of laughing our way to ecstasy.

"You are a strange breed but I so love you," he said.

"You're pretty strange yourself, and I love you too."

Andy was like a soothing balm. Under the steady rhythm of our relationship, a friendship I mistook for love, I settled on a major—political science with a minor in history—and I got the best grades of my college career. I aced subjects like urban planning, using Miami as the city for which I built my community development projects. Likewise, I sailed through Latin American politics, supplementing my academic research with the accounts of the region's history that I had read in the media about Miami's cadre of Latin American ex-senators, ex-mayors, and a deposed president or two. At the same time, I expanded my worldview with courses on world history, the Middle East, and the ancient Romans and Greeks, and I could not get enough of art and theater appreciation. Abuela seemed fascinated hearing about my subjects of study and she became my best ally in research, sending me clippings from the *Miami Standard* with every letter. The newspaper was full of stories about a Miami undergoing social upheaval and change: episodes of police brutality, racial tensions, a controversial "dialogue" between members of the exiled community and the Cuban government that pitted exiles against one another; the emotionally charged release of some political prisoners on the island, among them poets and aging ex-diplomats.

In one of her letters of 1979, Abuela delivered her own news, and her words filled me with fear. She was returning to Cuba to visit family. For the first time in exile history, the Cuban government was allowing those who fled to reunite with loved ones, if only temporarily and under the most chaotic travel conditions and restrictions. The country's economy needed an infusion of American dollars and who better to provide it than the prosperous exiled community yearning for a return? "We, the 'worms' who left," Abuela mused in her letter, "are now butterflies who return." She said that she had struggled with her decision, but couldn't give up the opportunity to see her surviving children and grandchildren "at least once more before I die." Her oldest son, Ramiro, had died of a massive heart attack, and she received the news in a Western Union telegram two weeks after it had been sent, long after her beloved Ramiro had been buried in the family tomb in Matanzas alongside my father. Abuela did not want to risk suffering any more losses without the promise of sharing another embrace. Sensing her uncertainty, the pain in her words, I called Abuela instead of writing her back, and I found myself offering to accompany her if she made the trip during my spring break.

She declined without hesitation.

"There is nothing for you on the island," Abuela said. "Your destiny is here, in this great land that has given us refuge. You must not risk your life by going back. For you, there is only the future, and it is here."

Lucky for me, Abuela was in Cuba only a week, and when she returned, I was so happy and relieved that I surprised her and came home for a long weekend. I found her forlorn and more introverted than usual. She would not offer many details of what she called her "odyssey," except to say that everyone was in good health, and that María Isabel, who had kept her house, still missed me. Eduardo had cheated on her and left her pregnant with their second son, which María Isabel had delivered while Abuela was there. Abuela had taken a suitcase full of gifts for the family—clothes, shampoo, soap, medicine, canned meats, and even toilet paper, basic goods that were nonexistent in Cuban stores. Abuela was happy to have brought the family some relief and joy, but she never again wanted to make the trip.

"There is no return," Abuela said. "Not anymore."

I did not understand her cryptic assessments, but after her trip, Abuela began to study English and accounting, and during my last two years at the University of Iowa, she came to visit me more frequently. She became fluent enough to carry on a conversation with Carol, although she had difficulty understanding Andy's twang. She liked Andy, although when she learned of our relationship, she tried to impose—albeit long-distance—her rule that Andy and I see each other with Carol as our chaperone. Eventually, she ended up accepting that she could not control what I did in her absence. But she would never acknowledge my freedom. As long as I wasn't married, Abuela said, she was my custodian, "even if you are forty years old." Her old-fashioned ways were not a problem fifteen hundred miles away, but kept me from bringing Andy home to Miami with me. When I asked Abuela in a letter if Andy could come spend a week's vacation with us in the summer of 1980, she politely refused.

"I have to go to work every day and it would not be proper for me to leave you two alone in the house," she wrote. "It's not that I don't trust you, but it wouldn't look right. What would people say?"

The new order that evolved between us was simply that what her eyes didn't see, didn't exist, and it solidified the silence. In my next letter, I informed her that I had decided to stay in Iowa City for the summer. I had a job at a restaurant waitressing, and I further supported my case adding that I would be taking a course that was too difficult for a non-art major to enroll in during the regular year, art history. I had imagined that she would still object, but her answer surprised me.

"It is best that you are not here," Abuela wrote. "This city is crazy, crazy."

Accompanying the letter, and all of her letters that summer, were newspaper clippings showing pictures of shrimpers packed with Cuban refugees arriving on the docks in Key West. In five months, the Mariel boatlift, named after their Cuban port of departure, brought one hundred and twenty-five thousand new Cuban refugees to U.S. shores. Also that summer, the city's neglected and predominantly African-American neighborhood of Liberty City erupted in deadly riots after police officers accused of beating a black man to death and covering it up were acquitted by an all-white jury in Tampa. Adding to the tumult, it seemed as if the city awoke every day to news of another dead body found in a car trunk or in the polluted river, floating along the sparkling waters of Biscayne Bay. The murderous enterprises of cocaine cowboys and the civic strife earned Miami the title of "the new Dodge City."

After the summer of 1980 Miami would never be the same, and although I didn't know it then, neither would I.

In Iowa, I was safe. Life was like the river that ran through the city, peaceful and clear. I observed and explored the landscape with child-like innocence, free-spirited, like the promise of the wind's song in my perfume. I adhered to the same study-work ethic that had gotten me there, settling on practical scholarship that could translate into a career. I did not dream of silly, impractical things like being a poet or an artist. When it came time to leave the life raft of college life, I wanted to remain free from Abuela's rules, and for that I had to ensure that my education would be the route to financial independence, and a job as far away from Miami as Iowa was.

I was not yet prepared to unearth deeper, impetuous passions. It would take me a decade, a great loss, and a great love to develop the courage to seek the forbidden. Even then, it would take what seemed like a lifetime to confront the ghosts fueling those passions and, harder still, to surrender to my destiny. All of that remained ahead, yet unscripted. In Iowa, there were only small moments of revelation, subtle hints of the heart, and I was not yet able to recognize their transformative power.

One of those moments came early, during that first fall of new beginnings and hope in 1977, when I toured the campus in my free time, dashing in and out of buildings and manicured lawns like a butterfly in a garden.

"Gallery of New Concepts," a sign above an open door promised, and I walked into a deserted space of white walls filled with photographs.

"*Silueta Series*," a group of the color photographs was labeled, and I began to examine them, one by one. On riverbanks, on mounds of grass, a woman's silhouette had been carved, as if she had intended to become one with the earth. In another labeled "*Untitled (Tumbas)*," hands, legs, and other body parts were carved into small mud tombs sculpted along Old Man's Creek. The last photograph showed a petite woman in a red bikini studying one of the tombs on a riverbank.

Her name: Ana Mendieta.

I stood before the photographs that autumn day when life for me was simply beginning, and I let the tears flow against my will.

There was so much to learn, so much to conquer in Iowa, that I never thought about what had so profoundly moved me that day, nor did I hear of Ana Mendieta again until many years later, when I was living another life. But I did think of her for no reason at all on a lovely spring day in 1981 when I borrowed Carol's old baby-blue Volkswagen and drove thirty miles north along Interstate 380 to the Cedar Rapids Airport to pick up Abuela, who was flying in for my graduation. Whenever I traveled to Miami from Cedar Rapids via Dallas, Atlanta, or Chicago, or vice versa when I returned to Iowa, I would take a Greyhound bus the last leg of the trip if Carol or Andy couldn't rescue me. But I would not let my aging Abuela go through all that trouble. She was well into her seventies, and although working at a beauty salon came with the perk of free makeovers, every time I saw her, she seemed inevitably frailer.

When Abuela emerged from the gate, she looked splendid in a new peach suit, and as I embraced her, I cupped her now-white bun in my hand as if it were a precious stone.

"*Mi hija*," she said, capturing all of me with a single glance, "you are so thin! Good thing I brought you a box of *pastelitos*!"

No sooner had she whipped out the white box with the gold "*El Palacio de las Delicias*" seal from her carry-on bag that I lunged for it and ripped the clear tape from the flaps with a hunger that was more a craving of memory than of need. I went for one of the flaky meat pastries first, gobbling it in four bites, then for a sweet one. If one could have an orgasm eating, mine would crest with the sweetness of a guava and cheese pastry fresh from the oven of a Cuban bakery in Miami. "It takes two planes to get here, Marisolita," Abuela said as if I did not know the route, "and the people on both planes wanted to kill me because of the smell of my carry-on." I had forgotten the proud lilt of her voice, the smallest of reproaches hidden in her phrases, and it made me both smile and cringe to think of the emotion-filled days ahead of us. "People kept asking me, 'What do you have there that smells so good?' I smiled and pretended I didn't speak any English so that I didn't have to share your *pastelitos*, but I really wanted to give everyone on the plane some. Don't you think it would help our image if we went around the country handing out *pastelitos* to all the Americans?"

In my absence, Abuela had added to her roster of abilities that of political ambassador for Miami Cubans.

"What's the matter with our image?"

"Ay, *hija*, those criminals you-know-who sent here when he emptied his jails into those boats have Miami on fire, and it is all over the news. *Imagínate*, they now work for the cocaine cowboys. Don't you watch the news?"

"I don't watch the news," I said. "I read books and I read your letters!"

With that, I embraced her again and guided her to the blue bug. We drove to Iowa City immersed in conversation about how all the Americans were leaving Miami, and the fact that there was not one left in our neighborhood. When I got home, Carol was dusting cobwebs from the top of the front door, lest Abuela think any less of her as a suitable friend for me. Under protest, Brian and Andy had moved in with friends for the weekend. Their families also were in town for the graduation ceremony but they were all staying at hotels. Abuela would have thought such a thing an insult. Having to stay in a hotel when your granddaughter has an apartment in the same city is a great offense in the Cuban Book of Sins Against the Family.

The next afternoon, Carol, Brian, Andy, and I graduated with bachelor's degrees in a long, dull ritual, made worse by our seating assignments far from each other and by thoughts of the impending breakup of our foursome. After the ceremony, Abuela and I were invited to celebrate with the other families at a steakhouse, and I had never seen my grandmother prouder. She was even happier when I told her I had sent my résumé to three cities in South Florida, one of them Miami. I did not tell her that I had no other choice. The recruiters who came to Iowa were unimpressed with the bilingual skills and degree of a Cuban woman from Miami. "You will make a great bilingual secretary in Miami," one of them advised. Most of them looked at their watches while they interviewed me, and I never heard from them again. I would return to Miami if I had to, but I would not live with Abuela long. It would only be a matter of time until Andy could find his way to a job in Miami, or I to North Carolina.

After the big dinner with all of our families, Abuela went to bed early, and Carol, Brian, Andy, and I were plotting to dash out to the Fieldhouse for a round of beers when Abuela called from my bedroom in a muted voice I will never forget. When I saw her, she was clutching her left arm and taking short labored breaths. Andy carried her down the stairs and into the car and Carol and I drove her to the emergency room at the University of Iowa Hospital. She had suffered a heart attack, and doctors said it had not been her first. Her heart was damaged beyond repair, they told me. For the first time in four years, I hated Iowa. I wanted more than anything to take Abuela back to Miami, as if being home could change the diagnosis, but she was too sick to be moved.

For many years, I would rage at myself for not being able to stop Abuela from dying so far from home. Abuela died in a cold hospital in a city she never knew. It is sad to die, but it is sadder to die with only the chilly hand of a tired nurse who says, "*Mawh-mawh*, what's the matter with you this morning?" and the love is lost in the translation, for this kind of regard is strange, foreign. It is not *Mawh-mawh*. It is Mamá, with an accent on the á—as if you mean it with all your heart.

I could not see it then, but Abuela's death far from our home was her last gift to me. She spared me the pain of living in the place where she took her last breath. Her death also became my good-bye to the Midwest. I packed up my things and came home with her coffin. There was nothing else for me to do in Iowa. It was night as we approached the dark cloak of the Everglades. From my lone window seat, I could see millions of city lights twinkling, and as we landed in our Miami, I broke into sobs.

I buried Abuela in a cemetery off Flagler Street where American flags flutter along with Cuban ones in a vast space of manicured grass and shady oaks, a peaceful sea of red, white, and blue where the tombstones are too small for island people used to erecting shrines to their loved ones at home. Her modest grave would have to do until the day I could return her to her rightful rest on the island, alongside her sons and daughters. I vowed that someday I would return Abuela to the place where she belonged, to a forever reunion with her children in our family tomb in Matanzas. But this was something I said to quiet my guilt, and as the years passed, my only tribute to Abuela was to visit her tomb every three months or so. Every time I visited, I tried to talk to her, but I couldn't manage to transcend the silence. All I could do was clean her small bronze tombstone and place fresh white daisies in its silver vase.

PRAYER TO OUR LADY

One match after another fails,
not even a faint flame my hand strikes.
My candle to you is lifeless,
like my faith.
¿Qué nos pasa, Cachita?
We've lost the groove of our ways,
of the blue seas that brought to me your name.
Dead matches, dead souls.
No favors from you today
for this ungrateful
daughter,
mala cubana,
mala católica,
mala hija,
¿Qué nos pasa, Cachita?
I have only words to offer,
to test the waters of your generosity,
of your gifts.
Magical.
Merciful.
Motherly.
Por favor, Cachita,
resuélveme.
Can't you see my wicked will
buckled,
aching,
trembling,
promising.
Oye, mi Cachita,
I kneel before you,

secret altar of my soul,
Ochún's hiding place,
where wayward daughters stash their santos,
ghosts of their Cuban past,
forever present.
Bless this island girl,
Cachita,
feel my heart flutter in your presence,
in your debt,
and fan the flame of forgiveness,
of hope spoken in a larger word:
Esperanza.
For hope belongs to those who cherish it,
as I do you.

WHITE LINEN

11

Miami

After Abuela's death, I moved back into our house as if she were still there, leaving most of it intact, her Sacred Heart of Jesus on the wall of the living room and the statue to Our Lady of Charity, Cuba's patron saint, propped on a small pedestal in her bedroom. I plunged into work with such fury that the years melded into one long stretch. Her death left me shaken, as if every time I took a step, there was not firm ground below me, but a precipice waiting for a misstep. I did not know what to do with my days. I missed her more than I ever could have predicted, only finding consolation in my work at Dade County's Planning Department, where my degree and the connections of old *peluquería* clients helped me gain an entry spot. I buried myself in meetings, research, and fieldwork, and during my free time volunteered at a social service agency helping the lost souls of the 1980 Mariel exodus who did not have family in the United States with whom to claim their little piece of America. In the process of redirecting other lives, I developed an unhealthy fear of becoming a lonely, penniless old lady. In my daydreams, I could see myself carrying my cart of donations around the seedy alleys of downtown Miami and sleeping on borrowed beds.

It was a baseless fear, but like heritage and history, it was a hand-me-down, and in the long run, it served me well.

After her death, I discovered that although Abuela had lived modestly, she had more money than I ever knew. Before the Revolution's triumph, her merchant son had come to Miami in the winters to buy fabrics and jewelry from Jewish snowbirds in Miami Beach. He then resold the goods to the best of Matanzas society from his store in Pueblo Nuevo. Ramiro had used the trips to stash some of his savings at the Central Bank in Miami, and he had invested the funds well. When the decision was made for Abuela and me to join the exiled, he gave Abuela rights to the money. In examining their brief exchange of letters, I learned that Ramiro had instructed her to use the money to begin a new life and to support me. He reminded her that this was his duty, as it was his dying brother's last wish. Ramiro had decided to stay behind, hoping for a miraculous change in the new regime. He had little choice; his wife refused to leave her home and all her family behind. He died waiting. In one letter, when he still had hope, he asked Abuela to keep enough funds in the bank to pay for his family's way out of the country if they were ever to change their minds. All of Ramiro's money, and thousands more, remained in the bank, bequeathed to me. My thrifty Abuela had only used a small portion of Ramiro's money for the down payment on our two-bedroom house, purchased for twenty-one thousand dollars in 1971. The furniture, the French-style living room set she kept wrapped in plastic all of her life, and the matching dining room set with a china cabinet she adored and, like so many exiles, had bought on an installment plan from El Dorado on Calle Ocho. She had managed to make the mortgage payments with her salary, and the small debt remaining was now mine, along with the little house tucked away in a neighborhood of hibiscus fences and shrines to the Virgin in the front yards. It was within walking distance of the bustling quarter of Calle Ocho with its immigrant kitsch and the quaint The Roads with its rows of towering shady oaks and restored old Florida homes.

I inherited Abuela's life, and I could not let go of it. Through the letters from Cuba she kept in a hatbox, tied with a different color ribbon for each author, I learned tidbits about our family: the turmoil in María Isabel's marriage, the death of Abuelo in Havana soon after Ramiro, no mention made of another woman or another wife. Everyone always ended their letters praising her for the sacrifice she had made leaving it all behind for me, and reassuring her that it had been the right decision. I could not help but admire Abuela in death far beyond what I had in life. From the day we descended the airplane's stairwell and were herded into a bus headed to El Refugio, the Giralda-inspired tower in downtown Miami where Cuban refugees were processed as "parolees" and released to relatives—in our case, to a couple who had been family friends in Matanzas—Abuela worked twelve-hour days at the beauty salon. At first she washed the women's hair, answered the telephone, and swept the excess hair off the granite floor. She came early to open the salon and stayed late to close it, eventually becoming the office manager and bookkeeper. In death, I discovered that Abuela was a woman wiser than anyone ever knew. She had left little for me to do, having already purchased her own cemetery plot, arranging with a lawyer for all her possessions to go to me. Although Ramiro's money easily could have paid off the mortgage, I felt the responsibility to keep the funds as treasure that belonged to the family, not just to me. Still, I was far from being a bag lady. I had a home. I made respectable money in my government job, enjoyed benefits, and, following Abuela's example, stashed away earnings, investing them with only two dreams: to explore the world I had studied, and to return to college to further explore what after Abuela's death became a passion—history.

But first there was my own history to occupy. I spent a year unable to clear Abuela's room and closets. I felt her presence each day when I came home and walked through the door past the gardenia bush on the front lawn, or when I had my morning *cafecito* in the backyard, grateful for the aroma the blooming jasmine bush had left overnight. Abuela and our house always smelled of flowers, and I could not let go of their scent. Only after I met Juana did I summon the strength to go through Abuela's clothes. Juana had made the trip from Cuba alone in one of the shrimpers during the Mariel boatlift. Her skin was dry, toasted and wrinkled, her smile toothless, her hair as white as Abuela's had been at the end. She was eighty years old and a longtime widow, although she quickly confessed to having enjoyed the company of many lovers, before and after the title. I loved Juana instantly, but not everyone did. From the day of her arrival, she had bounced from shelter to shelter, from adoptive house to adoptive house in Miami, as social workers could not find the relatives she came looking for. I bought Juana good dentures and gave her most of Abuela's clothes. I was debating with myself over the possibility of bringing her home to live with me when a sister and nephew were found in Wisconsin, and Juana was shipped to reunite with them. When we said good-bye, I railed at the thought of another Cuban exile dying in another cold hospital away from home, but Juana's giddiness as she declined a wheelchair and walked to the gate waving at me in one of Abuela's flowered dresses quelled my distress. If she had ever felt fear, Juana never showed it. She was a true adventurer; her only concern was how to pronounce Wisconsin, which she explained was a worry only because of her new teeth. I had given her a new wardrobe, but Juana gave me a lot more. The only thing I could not bring myself to give Juana was Abuela's favorite perfume. After Juana also left my life, I began wearing Abuela's White Linen, a scent too serious for a woman not quite thirty.

During my years of mourning and cult of work, my relationship with Andy became a long-distance affair, and then, after both of us decided neither one would make the geographic move, it found its way to distant friendship. At first Andy called and wrote often, drawing with words the mountainous paradise I had forsaken by not marrying him and moving to the Carolinas. He had moved back home, and he sent me pictures of the road I had not chosen, as if he were hoping that the glory of nature could restore the woman he had known in Iowa. The photos of him and his brother by a stream in the Blue Ridge Mountains surrounded by trees in glorious shades of mauve, ochre, and burgundy almost melted my heart. That same Christmas, he went on a trip to upstate New York, sending me a Polaroid photo of a snowman he had made. The snowman wore a hat and scarf I recognized, and carried a sign that read "Merry Xmas, Marisol." It made me cry, but it could not make me love Andy, no matter what I wanted to will my heart to do. It is so sad when you cannot fully love a man like Andy Nielsen, a steady man of his word, a man of character. Sometimes in my solitude, or in Chicago, when I visited Carol and Brian and their twin girls who called me "Aunt Mary" and threw themselves into my arms, I craved Andy's company. But I was impatient during his sporadic visits to Miami, relieved to return to my life after he left, and strangely scared when he spoke of marriage and children. Our lovemaking had turned into a predictable routine, and I felt as if I were watching myself without emotion, waiting for another life to unfold. Yesenia, the manicurist with the gifted grandson, explained my own feelings to me one day when she was turning the tips of my nails into a sliver of white moon. Andy was a looker, she said, but in the end, "*un huevo sin sal*," an egg without salt. She recommended sprinkling Russian Violets in my bathwater to send him on his way. I made note of the potion, but in Andy's case, it wasn't the right mix. Time, geography, and a red-haired beauty with green eyes took care of things for me.

12

I did not have Cuba, and my only authentic tie to the island was severed by Abuela's death, but Cuba came to me, exodus after exodus. It came to me in the bodies of an award-winning poet who loved his pizza with onions and pepperoni, a guitarist with a blind eye who canvassed the city's bars playing for food and drink, and a middle-aged engineer with the soul of an impresario. This unlikely ensemble landed in the job-placement arm of the agency where I volunteered, Miami in Action, and I helped the three of them find jobs. The poet went to work as a copy editor at the Spanish-language supplement of the *Miami Standard*; the guitarist began playing at some of the restaurants sprouting up all over town, and went on to teach music; and the engineer started mowing lawns at cut-rate prices and ended up, a decade later, with a million-dollar landscaping business, propelled by the colossal growth in the southern and western fringes of the county. All I did was translate documents from Cuba, help them fill out applications, and make some phone calls to connect them with the right people; but they were grateful, continued to phone beyond what was necessary, and joked that I was their petite *madrina*. When they realized that their godmother was unattached, they took turns trying to romance me with such suave moves that, for a while, their intentions went unnoticed. Their efforts were more comical than serious. They were a Cuban version of the Three Stooges pretending to be smitten by the same woman, and every time they came to visit, their performance was also enjoyed by other women in the office.

One rainy Saturday, they showed up with an invitation to a party that night and a box of *dulces*—yellow cone-shaped *capuchinos* soaked in syrup, flaky French-styled *señoritas* with cream filling, and my favorite sweet of nostalgia, meringue puffs, *merenguitos*, which Abuela made for me as an after-school treat in Matanzas and Miami, roasting sugared egg whites over the flames of her gas stove. The staff and I devoured the treats, but I declined the invitation to the party.

"*Asere*, what do I have to do to win your heart?" the engineer said to me in front of the other two.

I felt my cheeks flush with embarrassment at his public declaration, packaged with that "hey, you" of the hilarious contemporary Havana lingo beginning to congest the conversation in Miami like a bad cold.

"Well, for one, that whole *asere* thing . . . it's not exactly romantic," I replied.

"*Oye, asere*," the poet intervened, "you have no shame, and no idea of how to romance a woman."

He apologized to me on behalf of his friend.

"Well, not all of us can write pretty poetry like you, *come mierda*," the engineer added, defending himself while disparaging his friend.

"*Ay, ya*, you two are wasting your time," the musician chimed in. "Can't you see it's me and my music that she likes? Isn't that so, doll?"

I rolled my eyes.

"Don't you all have anything better to do? Isn't there a lawn begging for your attention somewhere, a new poem to write, a song to practice?"

"Can't you see that it's raining?" the engineer said. "You don't know how behind I get on my rounds when we have this annoying drizzle all day long."

"Well, welcome to Miami. This is Florida. It rains. Listen, I have work to do, rain or shine, and I don't want to be here all day, so thank you for the sweets, and now, shoo, go away."

"That shoo thing you do with those pretty lips and those pretty hands is not very romantic either," the engineer said.

"Good, so we're even!"

"Please try to come tonight," the poet interrupted again. "I am going to read some of my work, and my friend here is going to play and sing with a lovely partner."

The guitarist nodded and smiled.

"Okay, okay. I'll see you at the party tonight."

After that they left, but not before they took turns kissing me on the cheek. The poet commented on how good I always smelled. "You smell of spring, and the promise of a new beginning," he said as he waved good-bye.

But to me, it was not yet time for a new beginning. I smelled of Abuela, of the crisp linen ensembles she wore and the matching elegant scent with which she had perfumed her last years. I had installed myself in the life she left behind, and mine was a borrowed fragrance. Only the city, and the neck-jerking pace of change around me, forced me to rise from the fog of uncertainty each morning. In the city's new characters, I found refuge, humor, and a renewed sense of identity. The poet, the guitarist, and the engineer knew how to raise the sweet meter in the presence of an American woman with a Cuban soul, and I couldn't resist their charm. I enjoyed their attention and their company, yet I was too caught up in my career, too engaged with my ghosts, to consider anything but a casual friendship with them. What I wanted most was to learn all I could about the life I did not get to live in Cuba, and they were eager to share their stories with me. The men indulged me with riveting tales about growing up listening to black market rock-and-roll in a country where playing the Beatles was illegal. They told me about losing their virginity at the state-sponsored *escuela al campo*, where boys and girls were interned in countryside barracks while they worked fields of tobacco and potatoes all day long, from the age of twelve to eighteen. It all sounded terrible, yet when they shared their stories, I could see that the hardships and their clandestine lifestyle had bonded them in a way I had never experienced with my own friends. More so, I became fascinated by their adoration of Havana, and in my mind, the capital became a sensual playground where even the waves splashing against the seawall made music. The poet, the guitarist, and the engineer were friends from the colonial neighborhood of Habana Vieja, and they loved to talk about the nearby corner of Prado and Neptuno, one of the most popular meeting points in the early days of the republic, the staging site for events like Carnival, an intersection immortalized in the *cha-cha-chá* song "La Engañadora" about a voluptuous girl who isn't all that meets the eye. I had often heard the song played on Abuela's favorite radio station, "*la* CMQ *en el exilio*," when she gave our tiled floors a deft shine with her mop on Saturday afternoons, but I did not understand all the cultural nuance behind the piquant lyrics until the men explained them to me. I bought a cassette of *cha-cha-chá* at Ricky's Records and listened to the song with delight as I too cleaned my floors.

The poet, the guitarist, and the engineer had left the island separately, and had reunited in Miami many years later. The poet arrived on the Mariel boatlift, survived two winters in Manhattan, then fled to Miami to start all over again because, as he put it, "the nostalgia for Havana was devouring me, and Miami is the closest thing to my city in this dreadful exile of ours." The guitarist had traveled to Mexico City on a gig, left his hotel room in the middle of the night, crossed the Río Grande with the help of coyotes, and boarded a Greyhound bus to Miami. The engineer, the latest arrival, fled Cuba from a beach town east of Havana on a stolen boat with a large group of relatives. He arrived in Key Biscayne unsure of where he was, much in the same way Ponce de León did in 1513 when, in search of the Fountain of Youth, he came upon the key, named it Santa Marta, and claimed it for the Spanish crown.

We were an unlikely match, this threesome and I, but their humor won me over and they became mentors in my reintroduction into being Cuban, post-Iowa. Whereas my Cuban life with Abuela was defined by her authoritative figure and the discordance of my being uprooted, the culture of my new friends smelled of the heady rum in a Cuba Libre and swayed to the African cadences of poetry and music yet undiscovered by me. My friends introduced me to the soulful Yoruban poems of Nicolás Guillén; to the dissident voice of Heberto Padilla, so eloquent and brave in describing the fake heroes spoiling his garden; to the music of La Nueva Trova, never before played in Cuban Miami due to the musician's official ties with the island's regime. My friends detested the artists' political ties as well, but the music and the poetry they could not part with; they would make that distinction because they knew too well about the masks Cubans wore on the island for survival. They had learned to distinguish between the art and the political game, to read between the lines of a musician's song and a poet's stanza. They too had once been wrong about embracing a totalitarian system, and they told quixotic tales about the transition to becoming free men.

That Saturday night, I went to their party, and it was as if I had entered the set of a foreign movie, or for a moment stepped into the forbidden territory of underground Havana. I had never experienced anything like it in Miami or Iowa.

When I arrived at the address, I came upon a boxy old pink duplex in a run-down stretch of South Beach. I angle-parked on an easement across the street where there were other cars, and when I walked in the door, which was ajar, I could see that the living spaces had been painted black and rearranged with round tables and chairs, set up cabaret-style, a small candle flickering at the center of each table. A young man greeted me and said everyone was being asked to make a five-dollar donation to cover the night's operating costs and to share with the artists performing. I obliged.

"Welcome to *Noches de Playa,*" the host said. "Make yourself at home."

I glanced at the room, searching for my friends, and when I did not see them, I sat at one of the empty tables for two. Not long after, a curtain was drawn to reveal a makeshift black stage with a spotlight on a lone banquette. The poet appeared, his black hair pulled back in his signature ponytail, and took a seat looking very solemn in all-black clothes, a thin book in his hand. He began reading the most gripping poetry I had ever heard, his own, and I later learned that the book had won a big award in Havana. It was the only thing he carried in his pockets when he pretended to be gay so that he would be shipped as "an undesirable" in one of the boats leaving the port of Mariel for Key West. After the poet left the stage to thunderous applause, the guitarist in blue jeans and an olive-skinned woman dressed like a gypsy in a flowing skirt and peasant blouse made an equally dramatic entrance. She had curly black hair which sat on her shoulders like a cape. As he played the guitar, she sang from a repertoire of songs, some vaguely familiar, some new to me—pieces she said were from the era of "*el filin*," in the romantic Havana of the fifties and sixties, when crooners delivered new ballads with refurbished style and feeling. By the time the show ended, all the tables in the duplex were filled, and the crowd called for an encore. " 'Yolanda!' " the engineer clamored from somewhere in the crowd, and several others seconded the request. When I looked back to confirm that it was the engineer's voice I had heard, I saw that he was seated next to a woman who looked like me, only older. The guitarist sang a lovely tune I had never heard, a declaration of love from a haunted heart.

When the show ended, the poet came to my table. I was nursing half a beer, too warm to consume, and I didn't get a chance to say much except that his poetry had touched my heart. Soon we were joined by a tall thin man who wore a beret in summer and introduced himself as the owner of the place. He pulled up two chairs and called over a woman talking to the doorman, a Barbie look-alike with waist-long blond hair who turned out to be the owner's girlfriend and an escapee from Argentina's economic woes. I said little during the conversation. I didn't quite understand the topics of conversation between my poet friend and the man with the beret. All I knew was that they also had known each other in Havana, and that the man with the beret had no job beyond playing the role of an *intelectual,* a highly cultured being.

When *el intelectual* left us alone, the guitarist and his partner, and the engineer and his date, brought extra seats to our table and sat with the poet and me. We toasted to the night, and when it seemed appropriate, I issued an apology.

"Guys, I am sorry if I was rude earlier today," I said. "Thank you for the invitation. This has been a wonderful experience."

"No need to apologize," the engineer said. "We're all friends here—no, not friends, family."

At the end of the night, the poet walked me to my car, stepping ahead of me to gallantly open the car door after I unlocked it. "*Mira*, Marisol," he said, "I know that your life is none of my business, and you can send me to hell if you want to, but why is it that all you do is work? Don't you want something else in your life? Do you ever think about love, about marriage, about starting a family?"

I didn't know what to reply, but I did not want to discuss these subjects with someone who was a stranger to me. I envied the ease with which my new friends meddled in each other's lives and easily fell into the most intimate of conversations, but as much as I welcomed the warmth of the culture, I was far from adopting the instant intimacy for myself. Or so I thought then.

"It's complicated," I told the poet, and I pecked his cheek to signal my intention to leave. "For now, I'm happy with my life and my friendships."

"Will you come again?"

"You bet! I had a great time."

I drove home thinking about love, marriage, family, but not as elements of life that had to be pursued like a career, or like freedom. I thought there was a fated order to life, and perhaps mine had been cast by more serendipitous events than most, and certainly marked by tragedy. To me, love, marriage, family, in that order, were more about tradition than anything else. I did not think of myself as without family any more than I thought myself loveless. To outsiders it may have seemed that way, but to me simply the idea of being Cuban and living in Miami was the same as existing in the embrace of love and family. Cuba, after all, was only ninety miles away from Florida. Even though I could not bring myself to reach for it, the island was always there, like our family of origin, like the promise of forever love. Likewise, I could not ignore another fundamental component of my equation. I felt part of a large, adoptive family, grateful for being able to call myself an American, which was what Abuela had nursed in my heart. I had done a lot of growing up in the country's heartland, become a complex somebody, a citizen who embraced this land as home. Miami belonged to me as much as the idea of Matanzas belonged to my soul. In the afterglow of *Noches de Playa*, I thought of all those existential matters and began to write about them in my journal.

The party became a weekend expedition for me, and after a while, everybody treated me like I too was a friend from Havana. On some nights, after the crowds had trickled back home, the party moved to the seashore under the stars, the Miami moon perched above us like a lantern as the guitarist played. Everyone knew all the song lyrics, and they sang along, except me. I could only join them when they played the songs in my limited repertoire: "Guantanamera," and from my bubblegum days in Matanzas as a *chica yeyé*, "Rosas en el Mar," or "Roses at Sea," a protest song about love and liberty by my Spanish idol, Massiel.

By the time *Noches de Playa* ended and I crossed the MacArthur Causeway to head home, the sun had begun to rise behind me. To my left, a lineup of white cruise ships glistened over the tranquil waters. To my right, a row of Mediterranean mansions curved along the perimeter of tiny islets, and before me stood the fledgling downtown skyline with the Freedom Tower as its centerpiece. It was Miami at its best, my Miami.

By the time my Havana friends finished re-Cubanizing me, the convulsed Miami onto which they had arrived had been transformed. The public battles over bilingualism that plagued the county in the early eighties were fading to the new reality of a region with unbreakable ties—now, desirable economic ties—to the Americas. Every time a flag unfurled or an economy collapsed, Miami became the refuge of choice: Nicaraguans, Haitians, Colombians, Venezuelans, and Argentineans. They were not all penniless, and they brought their money with them, buying stunning apartments in the rising waterfront corridor along Brickell Avenue, settling into the new subdivisions of suburbia. Miami didn't need official declarations of what language was spoken; the region operated in two languages, de facto often in three, and it beat to a Cuban heart. The entire metropolitan area became an effervescent transplant of all that was left behind, virtues and vices included, and Cuban style became the mainstream.

In the grips of growth, the push west brought a stately landscape of new boulevards lined with royal palms, a tribute to the great *palmares* of the island. The music, the art, the literature, and the food of Cuba seeped into Miami's cultural and night life like an energizing elixir. The exiles' collective work ethic, the humor easily conjured even in hard times, the passions stirred by losses, all these carved into Miami a nostalgic soul. But the national vices cast an ugly shadow and discordant notes: corruption, *caudillismo*, intolerance. The unstoppable growth threatened the fragile Everglades as well as the water supply, and I found myself a bit player in the middle of it all, given my job as a junior county planner. "Zero-lot lines" became the code phrase for overbuilding in areas where the infrastructure could not support it. I pushed to protect the ecosystem and the wildlife with the passion for nature born in the lush valleys of my Matanzas and nurtured in the prairies of Iowa, and I fought with the skills acquired through education and experience, but the politicians who ran the region approved flawed plan after flawed plan in the name of prosperity and international status. It was the beginning of a new era, but there was nothing new about the assault upon the land and the corruption that came with it. An ideal setting for land speculators and a variety of corrupt wheeler-dealers not long after its founding in the 1800s as the military outpost Fort Dallas, Miami had its well-honed vices and its corrupt machinery in place when it became the capital of the Cuban exile. The new ruling class of Cuban-born politicians only added another seamless layer to the legacy. In that boilerplate, my days began with one crisis and ended with another, and I was on the proverbial spinning wheel to nowhere. By the end of the 1980s, the weekend *Noches de Playa* had run its course and disbanded. By then, my friends had built a new life and acquired the demands of jobs and family, and it was I who was now yearning for a new start, a new perfume, a new love.

It was time.

On a day when every step seemed to miraculously align to help me change course, my boss called me into his office. He was one of the shortest men in our boxy, beige downtown skyscraper. He had well-groomed, generous graying hair, and I supposed that he had once been handsome, although his Burdines-purchased blue suits could not hide his excessive potbelly or his awkwardly chiseled face, nor could they dress up his odious self-righteous attitude and the demagoguery with which he addressed the staff. I dreaded talks with him, mostly because his eyes darted from my eyes to my breasts, but also because the meetings were seldom about anything other than the pursuit of someone's political or economic agenda. He practiced the art of managing up with enviable dexterity, yet ran his team with a dictatorial hand, as if we were all unruly students instead of a group of collaborating professionals united by the cause of building a great city.

I surmised from the overdose of pleasantries delivered as soon as I walked into his office that my boss was making a great effort to appear friendly. I detested the fakery as much as I did his strong hand. When he had closed the door behind us, he did not waste any time getting to the point. There were opportunities for promotion into a myriad of jobs in government, he said, and I had been identified as "a leader." My volunteer work had been noticed, as had my impeccable attendance record. All I needed was to add some political finesse to my skills, and he could help me with this.

"You have a great future," he said, "but you need to learn to be a team player."

I had heard veiled admonishments before; they came with an invitation to lunch to discuss a project, with "some advice for your sake" after a particularly heated meeting, and not so veiled, under the disguise of stepped-up supervision of my projects. I had survived every test, thrived in the company of coworkers like myself who wanted to do right by the city we loved, but on this day, I saw with clarity that I was robbing myself of a life. The further I took my career, the deeper I was burying my soul's yearning to engage in creative work, to explore the world, to find true love. Abuela's letters from Cuba had fueled in me an archaeologist's craving to dig into and understand the past, and a furious need to write and make sense of it all. I hated to take the coward's way out, but I couldn't forgo the opportunity to tell my boss that I had already made other career plans. I appreciated the coincidence of our conversation, I said, mustering my most cordial smile. I was planning to ask for a leave of absence to travel abroad to study history and art in cities with cultural relevance to Miami. I surprised myself at the eloquence with which I had instantaneously devised a concrete plan for my dreams. When I returned from my studies, I planned to seek work in an institution dedicated to history and the arts, perhaps the Museum of History. My boss seemed thrown off his script by my response, and he was clenching his teeth to keep a frown from fully developing, but to my surprise, by the end of the day I had his approval for a sabbatical. When I walked out of the building that afternoon, the vultures hovering above the downtown skyline, the pigeons pecking at my feet, I felt that familiar euphoric feeling that only comes from the act of emancipation.

I shuttered up my little house filled with memories, plunking down white aluminum awnings that had been used only once before, a decade earlier by Abuela when Hurricane David dabbled close to the coast in 1979, mercilessly teasing South Florida until he changed course. It was now time for me to change mine.

13

Madrid

I landed in Madrid in the middle of a May heat wave.

I was standing in a long taxi line at the airport, fanning myself with my used boarding pass, when I spotted a bus headed to Plaza de Colón, where I had booked a budget hotel until I could find a respectable *pensión* or apartment to rent. I hopped on the two-dollar bus happy to save myself the cab fare, but the bargain and the respite from the heat evaporated when I had to carry my huge suitcase and carry-on bag loaded with my camera and boxes of film up the stairs from the bus depot into the plaza, then down the plaza stairs, and up stairs again to the hotel lobby. When I had but two steps to go to reach the hotel door, a porter appeared to help me. I was sweaty and exhausted and the cool lobby felt as refreshing as ice water, but after I checked in and the porter opened the door to my designated room, I walked into another steamer. It was as hot inside the small space as it was outside.

He blamed City Hall.

El ajuntamiento, the porter said, did not allow the hotel to yet turn on the air-conditioning. The early summer weather had caught everyone off-guard.

"But the lobby is ice-cold," I protested.

"That's different, it's a separate unit," he said.

"So the employees are cool and comfortable and the guests have to suffer through this heat?

"*Lo siento*." He was sorry.

It was no use arguing with the man. I bade him good-bye, tipped him more than he deserved, took off all my clothes, and tried to take a nap. I woke up in a sweat, showered with cold water, and dressed as lightly as I could, given the discovery that Madrid was not the cool European city I had expected, and for which I had packed. I headed downstairs to take my complaints about the lack of air-conditioning to the front desk. The heat wave had been unexpected, the clerk repeated, continuing to give me a different story. The hotel management had not yet hired an electrician to switch from the heater system to air-conditioning.

"What are you waiting for? Hire an electrician," I said. "The heat in the rooms is insufferable."

"*Señorita*, if you don't like our hotel you can move somewhere else."

"I will," I said, walking out the door and into Goya Street to find a more hospitable place to stay and to shop for a cooler wardrobe at El Corte Inglés, the famous Spanish department store I had heard Abuela talk about when she pledged that after my college graduation she would take an overdue vacation and we would go to Madrid together. Abuela's dream of visiting Spain was second only to her dream of a free Cuba, and it was fueled by Yesenia, the manicurist, who went on a trip to Spain organized by one of the disc jockeys on Cuban radio. Yesenia brought Abuela a black mantilla with embroidered flowers and a fan, *un abanico*, bearing a reproduction of Velázquez's famous *meninas*. Abuela started taking them both to San Juan Bosco Church every Sunday, wearing the mantilla over her head during mass, fanning herself during heat spells, all the time daydreaming of visiting *la madre patria*, the motherland. She longed to shop at El Corte Inglés to acquire a selection of mantillas in various colors, and to replace her *abanico*, so quickly battered by the Miami heat.

El Corte Inglés was a longer sprint than the map led me to believe, and when I arrived at the mammoth building, I was starving. I should have stopped in one of the tapas bars along the way, but I knew the store had a restaurant, which my Fodor's guide recommended, and so I ended up in a large cafeteria staffed by a lone older man in a white apron. The only other people there were a couple sipping what looked like Diet Cokes.

I ordered one myself.

"No, we don't have that here," the waiter responded.

"Sure you do, they are drinking it," I said, pointing to the couple.

"Agh," he mumbled, looking annoyed, "that's Coca Light."

"Then that's what I'll have, and the salmon special, and flan for dessert."

He briskly took the menu from me and left without saying a word. I opened a journal with a blue cover of golden moons and stars that I had purchased for the trip and began to write about my disappointing and steamy welcome to Abuela's beloved motherland. The waiter returned a short while later with my order, a smelly salmon smothered in butter and swimming in olive oil accompanied by an insipid yellow rice and a lump of cold *patatas*, Spanish-style potatoes, also dripping with way too much of a good thing. I could not manage more than a bite. I reached for the bread basket to quell my hunger pangs, but the bread was so stale I couldn't bite into it without risking a tooth. The only thing I ate was the flan, not because it was good but because I was starving, and it was the only part of the meal that didn't make me nauseous. As had become my habit during good and bad times, I began to talk to Abuela in my thoughts. "*Viejita,* so far the motherland is not what you imagined."

The waiter came back to ask if I needed anything else, and I requested the check. He looked at my full plate and proceeded to scold me for not liking the food, and for the wastefulness of leaving it untouched.

"Everyone ate this during lunch hour, and no one complained," he insisted.

I paid as fast as I could get the pesetas out of my waist pack, and fled.

I did not fare any better in the women's department, which was overloaded with overpriced American brands and tall-sized clothes. I managed to gather a few items, among them a cotton waist dress in olive green, and headed to the fitting room. I slipped on the dress, but it became stuck at my bust line. I struggled to see if there was a zipper I had neglected to open, but found none. The more I tried to find a way out of the dress, the more trapped I felt, the less I could breathe, and the more impossible it was to move the dress up or down. Some of it was still covering my neck, and I began to feel an overwhelming panic. I could see a saleswoman a few steps from the fitting room, and I called out to her. She looked over and motioned for me to wait. The panic intensified. I shouted that it was an emergency. It did not seem to matter. She did not even look my way this time.

Moments later, she appeared.

"I can't get out of this dress, I can't breathe," I said, almost in tears. "Please help me."

With one fast tug with both hands, she yanked the dress right off me.

"*Mujer!*" she scolded me. "How did you figure you could fit into that dress with those big *tetas* of yours?"

I was too stunned to say a word. I paid for a sleeveless black shirt with white embroidered flowers in a size above what I usually wore, and I left as fast as my legs could carry me. Maybe it had been a mistake to come to Madrid when I could have easily studied anywhere in the United States and avoided all this strange drama. Carol had insisted that Chicago was the place to be, and suggested that if the Windy City wasn't exotic enough for me, I should try living in New York, but I had foolishly set my heart on Europe. The Old World, the classics, they had lured me here, but all I wanted was a hamburger or a Cuban sandwich and my bed in the cocoon of my air-conditioned little house. "The United States is the best country in the world," I wrote in my journal that night, "the most efficient, the cheapest, the most sensible, and oh, God, I never thought I would say this, the one with the better service." Only one thing would save Madrid and recharge my adventurous spirit.

When I walked outside El Corte Inglés that afternoon, I hailed a cab and asked to be taken to El Prado, hoping that visiting the legendary museum would at least make the trip worthwhile. El Prado did more than that. Standing before Goya's haunting canvases, Saturn devouring his children, the *Maja desnuda* and *Maja vestida*, a woman painted in the same luminous pose, one naked, one dressed, I experienced once again the transformative power of art. I could not tear myself away from Goya's paintings, and it would take additional visits to El Prado for me to equally absorb El Greco and Velázquez's masterpieces, as if in the details of every work the mysteries of life unfolded. All of the pieces seem to exist there in eternity, waiting for a pair of willing eyes to discover them as mine had. Madrid redeemed itself through its art treasures, and during my aimless walks along tree-lined boulevards replete with monuments and statues, I could admire how the poets and playwrights of a glorious generation of writers defined the city's culture. But in my day-to-day life, I remained as landlocked in spirit as I was geographically. I could not find a suitable place to spend the summer. I found a budget hotel with air-conditioning not far from my wretched one, but it was too expensive to spend more than a couple of weeks there. I detested most of the typical dishes of Spanish cuisine, as my palate was more accustomed to their Cuban version, and I survived on *serrano* ham and *manchego* cheese sandwiches until I discovered an Italian restaurant in a bargain shoe-shopping district. But on most days, I skipped at least one meal, and got along with nonperishables I bought at the market and brought to my room.

I canvassed the city on foot, quickly losing weight from all the exercise and the amounts of food I was leaving on my plate, until one day I came upon a trendy district away from the tourist throngs where one of the most charming buildings was a lace-maker's school with a big picture window to the street where one could watch both masters and apprentices at work. It was the kind of Spain I came looking for, Old World, gentle, exquisite.

When I saw a rental sign for a studio nearby, I didn't hesitate to inquire. The place was as tiny as a dollhouse, but sunny, and it had an equally small air-conditioning unit, which the woman said I could run until the second week of September at no extra charge. But when she asked questions about me and learned that I was Cuban, she said she had to raise the quoted rent.

"You Cubans take too many showers," she said.

I thought it was a funny thing to note until I realized she wasn't joking. She had rented to Cubans before, she added, and they showered every day, and sometimes twice, day and night.

"It's the Caribbean heat in our loins," I said, so angry that I abruptly thanked her, added that I would think about it, and never returned.

As much as I hated abandoning plans to study in Spain, it was starting to look like I would have to return to Miami no later than by summer's end. But the next Sunday afternoon I went with my camera to photograph a celebration of Sevilla at Plaza Mayor, the big city square, where I met a friendly Spaniard who explained my bad luck to me and suggested a cure for the curse.

The revelry on the square was a celebration of heritage as *madrileñas* young and old donned the traditional ruffled, polka-dot dresses of Spain and promenaded arm in arm. I was captivated by the proud poses of the little girls and their accompanying little brothers, who wore the typical beret, pants, and vest of Old World Spaniards. It was a feast of color and attitude. Delighted, I clicked away until I ran out of film. When I reached into my bag for a new roll of film only to discover that I had mistakenly brought a container with a used roll, I walked to a photo shop I had spotted beyond the plaza's arcade and asked the attendant if he had thirty-five-millimeter film. He did, and when I began putting my new film into the camera, the man began to give me advice on how best to shoot, given Madrid's monotone landscape of grays and the contrast of light with the shadows cast by the surrounding edifices on the squares. I thanked him profusely and told him he was the kindest person I had met on my trip.

"Are they mistreating you here?"

"Unfortunately," I said. "How did you know?"

"Ay, it's those *madrileños*," he said. "People in Madrid are always angry at something."

"You speak as if you were not from here."

"Oh, no, I am not from here! I am from Seville. Nothing to do with these *madrileños*. And you, where are you from?"

"I was born in Cuba, but I grew up in the United States."

"And your parents and grandparents in Cuba, where were they from? They were Spaniards, weren't they?"

"Yes, from Islas Canarias," I said.

"No wonder you are having a hard time in Madrid! You are a twice an islander! They hate islanders here. Poor girl."

It was not a comforting explanation, but he offered a solution.

"Move to Barcelona," he advised. "There are many young people like you in Barcelona, wanderers all, and the Catalans are friendlier. All they care about is that people recognize their independence and their language, but they are more accepting of people from all over, and better still, you will be by the sea. Barcelona is a port city, and I have always heard that islanders cannot live away from the sea."

I returned to the square to take more photos, and reappeared at the shop to leave my film for processing. When José María's tips yielded the best photos I had taken, I also welcomed his advice about leaving Madrid. Two days later, I packed my bags and gratefully boarded a train to Barcelona.

14

Barcelona

José María, the gentlemanly *sevillano*, had provided the telephone number of a relative in Barcelona who would locate an apartment for me to rent. When I arrived at the Sants train station in Barcelona and called the number, a woman gave me the address of a studio apartment in Barceloneta, the city's beachfront neighborhood. The owner would meet me there in a half hour, she said, instructing me to take the subway's red line to the Urquinaona station, then switch to the yellow line until I reached the Barceloneta stop, which was across from the marina. Once in the neighborhood, I should inquire in one of the news kiosks about how to reach Carrer de l'Atlantida, as it was close to the Metro stop. I traced her directions on a map I had bought in Madrid, confirmed the route, and easily found the street, despite the hurdles of construction in the area. I couldn't believe my luck when I stood before the charming turn-of-the-century apartment building overlooking the small Plaça Poeta Boscá. It was only a short walk to the sea.

The renter was a jovial character like José María and as we made our way up two flights of stairs, he addressed some of the neighbors in *catalán*, switching without effort to Spanish to talk to me. When I told him the Catalonian language sounded lovely, and that I hoped to pick up some of it during my stay, his eyes darted from one end of the hall to the other, as if making sure no one was hearing us. "In *catalán*," he said, "we have the loveliest way of saying 'I love you.' " He paused, inserted the key into the locked door, and with a mischievous look on his face whispered, "*Te estimo*."

I appreciate you.

I smiled. "Lovely, indeed."

The apartment was furnished with the basics in a rustic, worn chic look—a brown sofa with throw pillows in various shapes and shades of beige, a nondescript television set, a tall halogen lamp, a small dining table for two, a full-sized bed, and a night table. The only thing on the ivory walls was a set of black and white photographs of bicycles artfully parked at Barcelona landmarks. I appreciated the uncluttered space, the lack of memories, and I personalized the rooms with my books, two bottles of Rioja wine as bookends, a picture of Abuela and me on my graduation day in Iowa, and bouquets of blue hydrangeas I bought during my walks through the famous strip of La Rambla, which was lined with lovely leafy trees and all sorts of vendors. My apartment had a friendly, Bohemian vibe like the neighborhood, where people set their clothes out to dry on a string running across balconies in typical European fashion. Best of all, my walks along the beach at sunrise energized me. It was not my sea, and these were not the fluffy white sands of Varadero or its stand-in, Miami Beach; but the Balearic Sea had its own striking hues of deep blue to admire, and the tightly packed beige sand made for a firmer strut. I could not believe my luck when the rental price was right, and given the dollar's strength to the *peseta*, I could afford to stay for the rest of the year without succumbing to the old nightmares of being destitute. My landlord said I had come to Barcelona at the right time; he expected to double or triple the rent for the '92 Olympics. But if I could live with the construction along the waterfront, the payoff was that I could stay as long as I wanted, and pay him month-to-month or biweekly.

I quickly made friends in the building. Lourdes worked as the cleaning woman during the day, then donned a blue uniform and became a security guard at night. She would bring to the job a portable television set to watch her favorite *telenovelas*, inviting me to sit with her when I returned home exhausted from my explorations of the city, which sometimes I did until her nonstop smoking made it unbearable. Lourdes taught me how to get a good shine out of a window using old bedsheets instead of paper towels. She regaled me with stories about a Catalonian mother's hard life during tough economic times. Lourdes's anecdotes were all dated pre-Franco or post-Franco, as if the Spanish dictator were a benchmark. Nicole was a petite, blond, French twentysomething, also a renter, and the kind of world wanderer I was hoping to be. She spoke three languages with amazing fluency—French, Spanish, English—and was learning Portuguese because she planned to move to Rio de Janeiro with her Chilean boyfriend. Nicole worked in one of the better seafood restaurants near the waterfront, and she assured me that I also could get a cash-only job there without any need for residency papers. I was an English speaker, and they desperately needed help to deal with the throngs of American and British tourists. Nicole introduced me to baby-faced Idris, the building's handyman and a refugee from Sierra Leone. The bicycle-riding Idris taught me how to avoid the tourist traps and find the best deals in town for basic necessities. Soft-spoken and gentle, he had witnessed unspeakable violence as a child in Africa, and he opened my eyes to yet another part of the world.

The only drawback to my new life was that the University of Barcelona campuses were quite a trek away, and so I postponed the idea of formal studies until I got to know the city better and perhaps moved into an apartment closer to campus. Besides, my education had already begun. I was furiously reading the poetry of Federico García Lorca, drawn to sonnets written under the influence of his trips to New York and Cuba. "*Verde que te quiero verde . . .*" Green, how I love you, green, I recited as I flung open my windows to greet Barcelona's summer mornings. I also was reading the novels of Camilo José Cela, who had just won the Nobel Prize, and I was making a serious attempt at deciphering Cervantes' mammoth *Don Quijote*, dictionary in hand.

Barcelona itself, home and canvas to Gaudí, one of the most ingenious architects in the world, held the best lessons in art and architecture. Every neighborhood had its treasures, and the contrast between the Old World and the contemporary made it seem as if the world's free spirits had been turned loose in Barcelona. The city had been home to three extraordinary artists, Picasso, Miró, and Dalí. A young Picasso learned to paint here, and one of the great collections of his art is housed in three renovated medieval mansions. If Madrid turned out to be as disappointing as a bad lover, Barcelona was true love at first sight. I thrived on the lessons contained in walking the city without a schedule, block by block, and exploring its mystical cloak of Gothic and the mix of sophisticated modernist design and attitude. I felt strangely at home here, as if there always had been a plan for me to inhabit this city.

Every day, I walked and walked, not noticing the hours flowing into one another, nor paying attention to the protests of my worn feet. One Sunday, which I had reserved for a walking tour of the city's modernist gems in the upscale neighborhood of L'Eixample, I made two tactical mistakes. I wore pretty leather sandals instead of my comfortable sneakers, and rather than taking the Metro to Passeig de Gràcia, where most of the historic modernist mansions begin to rise like a Disney World for adults, or simply walking the shortest route to the neighborhood from Barceloneta up Via Laetana, I decided to make a side trip to La Rambla to check out the schedules at Gran Teatre del Liceu. It was a breezy day, cool for late June. Dressed in a white linen shirt and lightweight beige pants, I felt invigorated by the sudden burst of nature's air-conditioning, which made me think of the chilly malls in Miami. I did not notice how far I was walking. At the end of La Rambla, I crossed the mammoth Plaça de Catalunya to find Passeig de Gràcia, and by then I could feel the tender soles of my feet starting to burn. A couple of blocks later, I could see welts in the making, and worse than the blistering pain, I was in monumental need of a restroom. But everything in sight, from the designer boutiques nestled in turn-of-the-century buildings to the restaurants on every block, was closed. The throngs of tourists were nowhere to be found, and the residents seemed to have abandoned the city to its ghosts while they went to church. It was not only a day of worship and rest, but the siesta hour in Spain, when most establishments shut down to reopen late in the afternoon. I cursed my excesses. Both my feet and my bladder had given me plenty of warnings that I did not heed.

My only option was to bear the pain and walk ahead, perhaps to the public restrooms at the Metro station, or to a spot where I could see a small crowd in the distance, and the map indicated that would be Gaudí's famous Casa Batlló with its curved roof and blue and green ceramic cladding, designed to resemble a dragon, with windows and balconies shaped like the skulls and bones of its victims.

As I approached Batlló, I realized that I had reached the strip known as Manzana de la Discordia, literally "Apple of Discord." Quite the mythical name, but more likely a play on words, since *manzana* is also the word for block in Spanish. This stretch of Passeig de Gràcia was so named because of the competition between the three modernist rival architects who designed historic houses in a wild mismatch of styles. It was then that I saw it at the end of the street, like a beacon—a restaurant, its door wide open and with the typical row of hams hanging from its bar. As I approached it, I saw the sign that said the bathroom was only for customers, but I resolved to put on my best smile and beg. Little did I suspect that I was about to begin my life's most intense love affair, my own little Greek drama at the aptly named Block of Discord.

A man in white jeans and a black T-shirt was the first person I saw when I walked into the empty restaurant. He was standing in the middle of the room, looking into the eyes of a young woman in a matching black and white waitress uniform. He was cradling her face in his hands as if he were about to give her the sweetest kiss. Something happened to me at that moment as I stood there, my body aching, and I would never be sure exactly what it was. But I wanted to be the woman whose face was in those hands. I was captivated by their thickness, their manly shape, by the endearing pose, as if those hands were holding the most precious of sculptures. I could not will my eyes away from the man's hands, generous and impeccably manicured. I stood there for too long, and he did not kiss her, but talked to her with gentleness, as if she were a child. When they became aware of my presence, he let her go and turned to me.

"Can I help you?" he asked.

"I—I am so sorry to interrupt," I said, stuttering and nervous, "but may I use your restroom? I know the sign says it's only for patrons, but I can purchase food and drink, anything, if you just let me—"

"Please, go ahead, *no hay problema,*" the man said, pointing to the end of the room. "Through that hall, make a right, and it will be on your left."

I detected in his speech the Havana accent I was so accustomed to hearing in Miami, but I had no time for introductions or pleasantries. I thanked him and walked to the back as fast as I could. I don't know how long I was in there, but I soaked my feet, one after the other, in the sink. The cool water soothed my blisters, and after I patted them dry, they were still throbbing. I would take a taxi home. When I came out of the bathroom, the man was sitting at the bar and the young woman was behind the counter pouring him a beer.

"Thank you so much," I said to them. "Yours is the only restaurant open in this entire area."

"We're not open for meals," the man said, "just preparing for the afternoon shift. We open at four, come back then if you want to eat."

I nodded, and was about to leave when the words spilled from my lips: "Are you Cuban?"

"Yes," the man said, "and you?"

"Yes, *matancera,*" I said, anticipating what was always the second question when you met a fellow Cuban.

"*Habanero,*" he said, extending his hand. "I'm Gabriel and this is my sister Mariela."

His sister, his sister, she is only his sister, my foolish heart screamed in silence.

"I'm Marisol," I said extending my hand. "How nice it is to run into fellow Cubans."

"Have you been away long?" Gabriel asked.

"I live in Miami," I said.

"I live in Havana," he said.

"Oh, oh, the enemy," I said with a laugh.

"I could never be the enemy of such a lovely *matancera,*" Gabriel said, and I blushed. He stood up, pulled out the stool to his right, and invited me to join them. "Come, sit down, have a *cavita* with us, Marisol, and tell us all about Miami."

WRITER'S MOON

A PRAYER

Orange-soaked,
spectacle of a Miami sunset,
she gives birth to words.
Spinner of wisdom,
sun of the night,
mother my spirit,
light the road home.
Walk with me,
moon,
dress me in your shadow
to wander and search.
Shape my contours,
fill my dreams
with the essence of you,
and of my city.

HABANITA

15

My *city* . . . Miami was my city, and in the distance, I felt a strange need to defend her, to make this man from the other side feel what I felt for her.

"Miami has extraordinary moons," I said to Gabriel, accepting the seat and the glass of cold draft beer he offered. Mariela served us from behind the bar, where the cured hams hung over our heads, before she disappeared like a phantom without saying a word. "You have not seen the moon until you have experienced the many moons over Miami. Orange, purple, silver, white, blue."

Gabriel was devouring me with his intense olive-green eyes, which were too small for his face but inquisitive and distinguished, and it seemed as if he and his eyes were trying to read me, to figure out the answers in order to pass a test. The more he looked at me this way, the more I persisted in my aimless monologue.

"Thanks for the invitation and the hospitality," I said, switching subjects. "I can use the rest. I overdid the walking and my feet are burning and blistered. I walked all the way here from Barceloneta . . ."

Gabriel looked down with concern, as if he were going to inspect my sandaled feet, and I noticed that he had slightly graying temples, as if time were drawing tentative lines, dimming the luster of his dark hair. He had the weathered features of people from the islands, the premature lines around the eyes and mouth, the thick sunbleached hair; but in clothes and manners he displayed the polish of a diplomat. He smelled of cool waters, as if he had just stepped out of a shower. I guessed that he was older than me, although not by much. His white designer jeans and leather moccasins seemed too expensive for an ordinary thirtysomething from the island. His biceps bulged slightly beneath the sleeves of his black T-shirt, made of a fine silk. His arms were as manly in shape as his hands. Something about Gabriel did not add up, given what I knew about Cubans on the island simply by living in Miami, but the cloak of mystery made me wonder all the more what it would feel like to have those arms wrapped around me.

"If I were a sculptor," Gabriel said, still looking at the floor, but now with delight, "I would want to immortalize those feet. They are perfect, delicate, so small."

"Perfection is not very interesting," I said. "Artists look for the complete opposite of perfection."

"And what is that?"

"Authenticity."

"Well said. Are you an artist?"

"No, I am only a student of art and of history, but I would have loved to have been born an artist. And you, what do you do?"

"I make movies," Gabriel said. "I'm a producer."

"Then *you* are the artist."

"Unfortunately, I spend more of my time being a bureaucrat and a negotiator than making the movies I want to make," Gabriel said, and that was something I could relate to. "My job is to find the money to make films, to find partners to finance our projects. The fun part is to make the movie, but that, like all good things in life, happens too fast, and the other stuff, the stuff you don't want to do, takes forever."

"You do this work independently or for a studio?" I asked, deciding to feign stupidity. It would have been tough to live in Miami, with one wave of refugees after another landing on our shores, and not know that there was only one employer in Cuba: the state.

"I wish," Gabriel said, without excessive melodrama, his voice taking on a melancholy timbre. "I work for the Cuban Film Institute and the Ministry of Culture, and we make movies in partnership with entities in Europe, especially Spain.

"Don't look at me that way," he quickly added. "I assure you I am not the enemy."

I was about to assure him I wasn't thinking that, although I was, when Mariela glided into focus with two small white plates and a tray of tapas, a bowl filled with olives, tiny pickles, and onions, chorizo slices on top of crusty slices of bread, and anchovies arranged in a circle.

"*Gracias, hermana,*" Gabriel said to her.

Mariela nodded and disappeared again. Gabriel told me that Mariela had married a Spaniard who visited Cuba two years ago. He was part owner of the restaurant, and although Mariela loved him, she was homesick for the island, her friends, the family left behind.

"*Lo de uno,*" he said.

One's own. I understood.

We ate, made small talk about our lives, and when customers began to trickle in for tapas and drinks and the noise in the restaurant began to rise with the bustle of workers and the demands of the hungry, Gabriel asked if he could give me a ride home. He didn't have a car, he said, but he could take me on the bicycle he had borrowed from Mariela's husband. He could at least leave me at the Metro stop, which wasn't that far, and it was better than walking on my blistered feet.

"How can you give me a ride on a bicycle? Where would I ride? We're not kids, you know."

"*Princesa,* I can tell you are from the other side of the pond, the privileged side." He smiled. "I can travel the whole world on a bicycle if I have to, because, well, I have to travel all over Havana on a bicycle. Wait for me around the corner, and I will show you what this *habanero* can do."

Gabriel came around the corner of Passeig de Gracia and Carrer del Consell de Cent in a five-speed, teal-colored bike with too many scrapes to inspire confidence. He looked at me as if he were studying a movie subject, then patting the bar in front of him, said, "Hop on here. I thought you could ride more comfortably on the handlebars, but not with that cushion." I blushed. I started to have second thoughts about the ride and it showed when I went to jump on the bar and missed. It was the Abuela in my head screaming at me, *Marisol, what the hell are you doing with this* comunista, *about to ride on a bicycle all over Barcelona?*

"Wait a minute," Gabriel said. "Let's do this differently."

Gabriel lowered the kickstand and with those strong arms of his, scooped me up on the bike in front of him. By now I was tomato-red and trembling. Sports had never been my strong suit. I hung on to the handlebars. "Relax," Gabriel said, getting back on the seat and gently moving my hands to take command of the bike. "The trick is staying in balance. Let me steer the bike, and you hang on to my arms, lean into me if you feel unsteady. But don't make any sudden movements, or we'll both go down. Relax, just relax and enjoy the ride."

I had no choice but to trust him, and I so did. The minute I felt the breeze, I leaned into Gabriel, hanging onto his arms as languidly as I could manage, and the fear began to dissipate. The ride down Via Laietana, past the splendid Palau de la Música Catalana, built in 1908, past the wedding-cake-like structure of the bank Caixa Catalunya, was smooth and refreshing, and there was less traffic than usual. Before we reached the busy intersection with Passeig de Colom and the entrance to Barceloneta, Gabriel steered the bike onto a side street.

He stopped at a lovely medieval wall accented by a sweeping arch encrusted with drooping moss. Gabriel dropped the kickstand and helped me get off the bike, inviting me to sit on a short ledge that wrapped around the perimeter of the wall. We were on the edge of the Barri Gòtic, the city's Gothic Quarter.

"Let's sit here and catch our breath," he said. "This is one of my favorite spots in Barcelona. One can sit here and imagine what life was like when this wall was erected. Can't you see the hay and flour traders, the blacksmiths, the royal court with their fancy clothes making their way through the mayhem of the markets?"

I could imagine it, but the place was now deserted, except for a couple walking a dog, and an adolescent riding on a bike too small for him. I began to wonder if I should be here. It was already late afternoon. All of a sudden Gabriel's face also showed concern, and he said in a way that I knew he was not kidding, "Are you for real? Are you really from Miami? You speak too much like a Cuban from the island to be from Miami. We are alone here, it's just you and me, and you can tell me the truth. If they sent you to spy on me . . ."

I couldn't believe what I was hearing. When I came into the restaurant and he heard my Cuban accent, Gabriel told me, he was sure that I was a spy sent by his bosses to figure out if he was about to become part of a lengthy list of defectors from the artistic ranks.

"Are *you* for real?" I said. "Of course I'm from Miami. Why would I lie about that?"

"Because they always send a *niñera* after me when I travel alone."

"A *niñera*? A babysitter?"

"Yeah, so that I don't stray."

"Ridiculous, my God."

I spent the next half hour trying to convince Gabriel that I was not a spy, telling him enough about my life in Miami for him to believe that I had nothing to do with the Cuban government. When he did believe me, I turned the tables on him, arguing that it was now his turn to convince me that he was for real. He professed to have a job that was hardly believable. He dressed better than anyone I had ever met from the island. Could *he* be the Commie spy, or worse, simply a fraud? Spies were said to be a dime a dozen in Miami, so why not in Barcelona?

Gabriel laughed.

"It's amazing what they have turned us all into, isn't it? A bunch of paranoid people who can't believe they could just meet by the grace of good fortune," he said. "Can we go someplace where we can talk in peace?"

"I believe there are no spies in my apartment," I said, "and I really need to go home and soak and bandage my feet."

Gabriel carried the bike up the stairs without effort, and parked it at the entrance to my apartment. It was Lourdes's day off and the building seemed desolate. There were no smells of frying fish wafting into the halls, and except for towels, no laundry was set out to dry on the balconies. I didn't run into anyone on the way up, and I was grateful for that. Gabriel was an enigma and I wanted to decipher him without witnesses. It was reciprocal. I could see from the kitchen that Gabriel was studying every inch of my apartment as I poured two glasses of cold water to refresh us and surveyed the refrigerator to see what I could offer him to eat before I went to clean and bandage my feet. He asked to use the bathroom, and on the way there through my bedroom, he paused at the picture I kept on the nightstand, Abuela and me at my graduation in Iowa, our last photograph. When Gabriel came out of the bathroom, he came back with my hand towel, wet and warm. I met him with the glass of water, and as if we had known each other all our lives, he took a seat at the edge of my bed, put the glass on the nightstand, asked me to sit next to him, and he began to pat the bottom of my feet with the wet towel. The warmth felt soothing. He asked me to lean back on a pillow and relax. With one hand he held the towel on my feet and with the other he reached for the glass, and drank the water in one gulp. We continued to talk, I nervously in my suggestive position on the bed, Gabriel walking back and forth to the bathroom to re-wet the towel and nurse my feet. When he finished, he suggested that, instead of bandages, my feet needed some air. He saw the fan at the foot of my bed, pointed it at my feet, and turned it on. Then he walked to the other side of the bed, propped up the pillow, and lay back on the bed, his hunky arms folded under his head.

"I want to know all about your life," he said, "from the beginning."

And so I began to tell him about my life, or what I knew of it, although not from the beginning, and if Gabriel registered that, he did not say so. I could not remember most of my childhood. It was as if life had begun in 1969 when man landed on the moon and Abuela and I landed in Miami, and that's the story I told Gabriel. He, in contrast, told his story with a cinematographic memory and the engrossing voice of a radio personality. I listened to him, enchanted.

His parents had a fairy-tale romance. His mother, Sonia, had been a typical Havana society girl of the 1950s, the thin-waisted type with the upside down umbrella skirt, a bob haircut, and membership in the Havana Yacht Club. His father, Alberto, was a law student at the University of Havana, and they met on the steps of the law school when Sonia went there to meet her father for lunch. He was a law professor, and Alberto, an activist as well as a scholar, was one of his most promising students. It wasn't long before Sonia and Alberto were headed to the altar with the blessings of their families, but two weeks before the wedding, Alberto disappeared. The gossips whispered that Alberto had left Sonia for a woman in a nearby town he visited too often. The politically inclined attributed his disappearance to the political violence sweeping Havana. Sonia knew better. Her man had joined the rebels in the Sierra Maestra range, and her job was to pretend to be the jilted girlfriend to those who favored the Batista dictatorship; the bereaved girlfriend to the supporters of the fight against the dictatorship; and a little of both to those who were on the fence about the political strife. Only Sonia, Alberto, and their designated contact in the underground knew that Alberto had left for the mountains. Alberto believed it was a lifesaving measure. Goons loyal to the dictatorship had been zeroing in on him in his increasing role as a leader of the clandestine movement. It was not difficult for Sonia to act the part of the forlorn girlfriend, as she truly was pained to spend her days without Alberto, and she told herself that this was her sacrifice on behalf of the fatherland. By the summer of 1958, her father could no longer stand Sonia's morose mood, and he sent her to vacation with relatives in Varadero, hoping that the days on the beach with her cousins would lift her spirits. Before she left, her father made the mistake of telling Sonia that he was a finalist for a fellowship to study and teach at a New York university that fall, and he spoke of how timely it would be for the family to be able to spend some time in the United States until a more peaceful atmosphere reigned in Havana. Sonia feigned excitement, asked for money to shop at El Encanto for a few items she would need for the trip to Varadero, and instead rushed to the university to find her contact and only link to Alberto. Sonia barely had time to write Alberto a note, but Alberto received it days later with details of her whereabouts at El Rincón Francés in Varadero, and news about her father's plans to take the family out of the country. Alberto did not hesitate. He sent two of his best men to fetch Sonia from among the throngs of Cubans frolicking, *veraneando*, in beachside cottages and pristine beaches. Alberto sent word that he would put her up in a safe house in the countryside in Oriente, where her father would never find her, and where Alberto could visit her. They would marry in a church sympathetic to the cause; it would be a simple ceremony but sincere and blessed. Although Alberto had become a *guerrillero*, he was still a gentleman and a man of conventions and faith. Besides, Sonia would be more useful to the rebel movement closer to the Sierra Maestra than she was in Havana. On her fourth night in Varadero, Sonia disappeared overnight, leaving her family a short, cryptic note. "*Todo por la patria*," it said, "My love, Sonia." All for the Fatherland. Seven months later, when the rebels took their victorious ride across the island from the Sierra Maestra to Havana in the early days of January 1959, Gabriel's mother and father were in the caravan, and Sonia's belly was protruding from her oversized olive-green jacket.

Gabriel was born in Havana the night of the rebels' triumphant celebration, two months premature, as if he were in a hurry to join the fray. If he had remained in his mother's womb to term, we might have shared a birthday. Gabriel and I discovered that we had led almost parallel lives, his in Havana, and mine first in Matanzas and then in Miami. We had both been the top students of our grade school, he a proud Communist Pioneer, me the daughter of *gusanos*, pariahs with little choice but to seek exile. When I was studying in Iowa, he was studying in the Soviet Union. When I was building a career in city government, he was rising through the ranks of the Ministry of Culture, aided by his title "Son of Heroes of the Revolution," and by the official dictate that out of his generation would rise "*el nuevo hombre*," the new man created by the Revolution his parents had helped into being. While I had shunned marriage, preferring to wait for the elusive perfect lover, Gabriel had married his childhood sweetheart and had left a trail of lovers everywhere he had been. Before he had traveled to Spain seeking partnerships for his movies, he had divorced. He preferred not to talk about that relationship, simply saying that his ex-wife was "*más loca que una regadera,*" crazier than a water hose, and that, thankfully, there had been no children.

At this point in his tale, we moved from my bed to the kitchen, where I heated leftover paella from El Rey de las Gambas while we commiserated on how we had both become disenchanted with our lives on the road to thirty. We had no answers, only questions and unfulfilled dreams. Only one thing separated our lives, yet it made all the difference: I had the freedom to pursue my dreams; Gabriel felt chained to his.

His mother had worked all her life in the Ministry of Education close to the woman who was the wife of Cuba's second-in-command, and in lieu of a first lady, the woman had assumed that role as well. His father never went back to law school, and instead chose a military career, rising to the rank of commander in the early days of the war in Angola. During one of his short trips back from war, Alberto had died of a heart attack in a military barracks in Havana. Or so his mother was told, and when Sonia began to repeat this too often—"*Eso, por lo menos, fue lo que se me dijo a mí*"—she inadvertently planted the seed of doubt in her son. Up to that moment, Gabriel had been raised on revolutionary rhetoric and dogma, and accepted them without question. He believed that all his efforts, and the meaning of his life and his work, were centered on the principle of preserving the hard-fought Revolution. But something about his mother's words began to change the way he observed everyone around him, and he developed an inquisitive streak that his instincts told him to keep to himself. Yet the new feelings and observations fueled his career in film, as if with a camera he could capture truth, or the lack of it. And he did. He began to question everything, including his own history, and he saw, with all the brightness of color, the fiefdom that *el comandante en jefe* had created for himself at the expense of a nation, at the expense of Gabriel's family, at the expense of Gabriel's soul.

Before the night was over, Gabriel confessed: He had come to Barcelona to plant the seeds of a possible escape from the island. He had no relatives abroad other than his younger sister. Mariela and her marriage to the Spaniard were his ticket to survival, but only once he had figured his best way out. He could work in the restaurant with them for a while, and he had been doing just that during his stay. He already had a bank account in Barcelona, and he was putting a little money away. Yet taking food orders, stocking the inventory, cleaning up at night's end, was not the life he wanted, even if it was only temporary. He wanted to find a place in Spain's film and television industry, and he was scoping out the possibilities as he pretended to everyone else that he was here in an official capacity. It was true that he was talking shop on behalf of the Cuban Film Institute with moviemakers in Spain, and he reported on his activities every week to the cultural attaché at the Cuban Embassy in Madrid, but his intentions were to stay in Spain as long as possible. He knew he was being watched by Cuban authorities closely in Madrid, and before he left, he had made it a point to report that he was visiting his sister, who had not broken with the regime but was simply an emigrant by marriage. When Gabriel told me all of this, my heart leaped at the possibility that he might not return to the island. Only later, when I sat alone in my apartment ruminating over the day's events, would I realize the brunt of what I was feeling, and the impossible affair into which I was diving.

Right away I told Gabriel that if there was anything I could do to help him gain his freedom, I would. He thanked me, but made it clear that he also had complicated feelings of alliance to the island

and its fate, to his mother and her fate. He was not yet ready to commit to the move. Besides, he added, perhaps what once seemed improbable may happen now: The Soviet Empire was crumbling, and Cuba was one of its satellites.

"Change," Gabriel said, "feels so near. How can I leave it all now?"

Throughout the conversation, Gabriel and I had moved from the dining table, where we shared the seafood paella, warm bread, and a chilled bottle of sparkling wine brought by Nicole one night from her restaurant, to the beige couch, and when he talked of the possibility of democracy blossoming on the island, I felt the urge to embrace him. We both wanted the same thing for Cuba. Politically, we were not so different after all. But I remained at my end of the couch caressing my empty glass of wine.

Gabriel stood up to refill my glass, but there was not one drop left in the bottle. He offered to buy more, and we walked out into the Barcelona night, but not before Gabriel lovingly bandaged my feet. We began to search for one of the little storefront markets dotting the city late into the night, and we ventured into the narrow alleys of the Gothic Quarter. We could not find a store open, and I was telling Gabriel that I did not want to walk farther when we came upon the sounds of live jazz coming from a dark little club. "I love jazz," Gabriel said. "Want to check it out?"

It was close to midnight, but the nightlife in Barcelona was only beginning. Gabriel and I walked into a cave filled with smoke, rhythms, and the smell of the collective consumption of too much alcohol.

"What do you want to drink?" he asked.

"I think the night calls for a Cuba Libre," I said.

He smiled.

"A *mentirita,*" he said to the bartender, who did not understand.

A little lie.

I had thought this was only a Miami joke.

"Nah, we say it in Havana all the time," Gabriel said with a laugh. "Behind the horse's back, of course."

Gabriel Santamarina did not talk like the enemy, did not think like the enemy, and as I would shortly discover, did not feel like the enemy.

By the time we walked out of Harlem Jazz, it was past four in the morning and Gabriel and I had downed three rum and Cokes apiece. Gabriel had related the history of jazz in Havana between sets, planting another layer of love for the musicality of the city in my heart. As we walked back to Barceloneta, the cool breeze coming from the sea sent a chill through me, and soon I felt Gabriel's protective arms wrapped around me. I felt dizzy, as if I were inside a dream out of focus. We walked like that, he embracing me and almost holding me up, for a few blocks. I had forgotten all about my sore feet, and once again I could feel them throbbing. When I complained, Gabriel stopped, picked me up, and carried me for several blocks all the way to my apartment, stopping only for the traffic light at Passeig de Colom. When he put me down, he was soaked in sweat. We were at the bottom of the stairs, and I would have said good-bye there but his bike was upstairs. We had brought it inside the apartment before we walked out into the night, and Gabriel had to come up to retrieve it. As he went to pick me up again to carry me up the stairs, I felt sorry for the man, assuring him I could make it up all by myself. My feet could stand it. It was then that he brought his hand to my chin, pulled my face close to his, and planted a gentle kiss on my lips, an unforgettable first kiss. His lips were as sultry and inviting as his arms, as his hands, as his conversation. The intimacy of it startled me, and

I did not know how to respond. I let it be simply a kiss. I felt vulnerable, suddenly undressed, and when I rescued my senses from the moment, I dashed up the stairs as fast as I could, like a frightened child. Gabriel followed. I could hear his feet methodically reaching one step after another, and with each one, my heart beat a little faster.

16

If I had done what I wanted to do, I would have left the door ajar for Gabriel and dashed into my minuscule shower, and certainly his assured steps would have followed me there. If I had done what I wanted to do, I would have invited him to cleanse the night smells from my body with the French soap that exudes a bouquet of gardenias. I would have returned the attentions, and ours would have been a dance of falling water and rousing aromas in the expansive space of desire. My minuscule shower would turn into something like the old Cuban dance of yesteryear that Abuela once recalled with a sigh. "There is nothing like dancing on one *ladrillito*, cheek to cheek," she said. Nothing like dancing close together in the space of one lovely Cuban tile and its perfect geometry. I could only imagine Abuela and Abuelo in those happy days. But Abuela had warned us about Cuban men, and in Gabriel's case, I took her warning seriously. Gabriel exhibited all the suave moves of a contemporary dandy, the self-possessed swagger, the penchant for silk fabrics and leather, the choreographed gestures of sensual politeness, and he had succeeded in making me feel that I could not live another day without him. I prayed for a sign from the beyond, and restraint came to me in a thought: I had not yet found a proper fragrance to inspire a new love affair. I was in between perfumes, long past the sensibleness of White Linen and not yet enamored of another scent.

I did leave the door ajar, and Gabriel found me in the bathroom, but instead of bathing in the nude, I was propped up on the vanity, in the most unromantic of positions, soaking my sweaty, achy feet in cold water.

"I guess I should say good night," Gabriel said.

"Or good morning," I said. "Thank you for a great day. That bike ride was unforgettable."

"The conversation too," he said.

"And the music."

"And you."

"Good-bye, Gabriel."

He pecked me on the cheek and walked out the door. My heart sank. I swung my feet out of the sink, almost toppled over, and made a mental note to buy for my next soak a good *palangana*, the staple washbowl of Cuban households and of cheap pedicures at Cuban beauty salons. I patted my feet dry as quickly as I could and rushed to lock the door after Gabriel. When I ran past the bedroom wall, I stumbled right into him.

He had not left.

"Can I see you again tomorrow?"

"S-sure," I stuttered. "Great."

"I have to help Mariela open the restaurant and work until a little past noon, but I can come afterward and maybe we can hang out at the beach," he said.

"You have to work in the morning? It's almost morning. When are you going to sleep?"

"I could sleep right here with you, but then you know I wouldn't sleep, and I wouldn't go to work."

"Ha! Really? The thought had not crossed my mind."

"That's why I am leaving right now," Gabriel said, shamelessly looking me up and down, and walking backward to the door. "You are a nice girl from Miami and I am the enemy."

"*Adiós*, Gabriel."

I closed the door as soon as he was out, and he protested a little too loudly for the dawn hours.

"What? No good night kiss?" he said from the hall.

He was going to wake up my neighbors.

"Shhhhh," I whispered without opening.

"Don't they kiss good night in Miami?"

I opened the door with a blunt swing. He was standing there with his hand extended to the wall, as if he had known that I would yield. He was so sure of himself. I glided over to his body, ran my hands from his chest to his neck, and offered my lips. He began to kiss me softly, his hands cupping my face as I had seen him embrace Mariela that afternoon. I thrilled at the rush along my spine. Then Gabriel moved his hands to my hips, and he pressed me against all of him, and I felt everything I needed to feel. If I wanted this man, I had to send him home, and so I did with the promise of a tomorrow.

I went to bed restless, my mind filled with all sorts of questions, my heart throbbing with warnings, but I slept soundly given the high doses of liquor and my physical exhaustion. I woke up four hours later with a headache, and I could have gone back to sleep, but I forced myself to get up and make strong *café con leche*. The elixir kicked in and so did the energy of anticipation. I had two missions for the day—shop for a new perfume, see Gabriel again.

I had perused the perfume department at El Corte Inglés in Madrid and in Barcelona, but all I could find was the past: the American designer scents, the traditional French perfume de rigueur of socialites from Coral Gables, and Spanish fragrances like Maja and Maderas de Oriente that conjured the culture of flamenco and *mantillas*. Their spicy aromas seemed outdated to me. Spanish perfumes were sold all over Cuban Miami, in the grocery stores and pharmacies, and their familiar scent of citrus and clove reminded me of early exile, when the decorative black and red box of Maja powder, the wrapped sets of soaps, or the bottles of perfume were small luxuries, gifts to give or receive for Christmas or a birthday, and to be used and worn only for evening events and special occasions. And so I had abandoned my search for a perfume in Spain. A new man on the horizon, however, a special man, unlocked my senses. I felt virginal, devoid of prejudices, full of expectations, and ready to choose a new scent.

It was not to be. I canvassed the old neighborhoods of La Ribera and El Born, and somewhere along the narrow old streets on the way to Museu Picasso, I found a storefront with a window display of stacked perfume bottles. I smelled as many perfumes as the storekeeper was willing to let me experience, but resolute as I was, I could not identify a scent that felt at home on my skin. The storekeeper soon lost his initial patience, and said I was a difficult woman to please. There were only so many fragrances he was going to let me test. He was right, I was a difficult woman to please, and I went home empty-handed. It was already noon, and I did not want to miss Gabriel's promised visit.

I fell asleep waiting for Gabriel and reading the laborious beginning of *El Quijote*'s second chapter. "*¡Oh, Princesa Dulcinea, señora de este cautivo!*" It seemed a good place to succumb to sleep, with Don Quixote a prisoner of love.

Gabriel arrived midafternoon, greeted me with a kiss on the cheek, and apologized for being late. He brought from the restaurant a boxed plate of tapas, an assortment of sweet and spicy sausages and cheese, bread, and a bottle of red wine from the Rioja region. I had slept through lunch and was starving. I set the table and Gabriel brought in his mini-feast from the kitchen. He opened the bottle of wine, offered me the first taste, poured two full glasses after I nodded my approval, and raised his glass in a toast.

"To our new friendship and another great day," he said.

"*Salud*," I said, somewhat disappointed at the label he was already placing on us. It was too early for me to consider Gabriel a friend, a title I reserved for a small circle of significant people I loved. It also was too early for him to declare our relationship a friendship, and not a love affair, which was straight where I was headed, and where I thought, after last night, that he was reciprocally headed.

Perhaps I was reading too much into the toast, but Gabriel seemed to have lost his steam in the course of the last few hours. He devoured the food with relish, drinking the wine as if it were water. He had assimilated well the Spanish art of consuming red wine at every meal except breakfast. I could not. I still lived on bottled water and the infamous Coca Light.

"I've been thinking of you all morning," he said between bites of *manchego* cheese.

"Oh, really, what about?"

"I thought you might like to see what I have in my backpack."

"What is it?"

"You have to see it."

"I can't wait. I love surprises."

And now I too ate with relish.

When we finished, I got up and took the dishes to the sink, ran warm water and squirted liquid soap over them, and let them sit there soaking. I returned to pick up the rest, but Gabriel had already cleared the table, thrown the used boxes back into the plastic bag, tied the ends into a knot, and put the garbage by the door. Could this man be any more perfect? If only he would kiss me again, I thought as I wiped the table clean and went back to the kitchen to wash the dishes. There wasn't much to wash, and it didn't take me long to tidy up.

"Leave that and come here," Gabriel called out from the living room.

When I turned the corner and saw my coffee table, I could not believe my eyes. It overflowed with vintage photographs in black and white and sepia. It didn't take but a glance to realize that they were from Havana. One of the first I saw was the view of the famous seawall, El Malecón, and the fortress of El Morro in the distance. The seafront boulevard was lined with two- and three-story colonial mansions side by side, bearing stately balconies and columns. The street was dotted with old cars, dating the photo to the 1950s. Another photograph captured a triumphant moment in a car race along another stretch of the same boulevard. There was a joyous parade featuring marching bands, decorated floats with *rumberas* riding on top, and convertibles bursting with couples. In the background of another photo, I could see children dressed in fine linens leaning from their balconies to watch the street party unfold. There were many old family photos as well, portraits of elegant men and women, and some of those dated back to the early days of the republic. In one of the photos from the late 1950s, his smiling parents and grandparents were gathered around a table at the famous Tropicana Nightclub. "It was their last outing before my father headed to the mountains," Gabriel said. There was a great-grandfather in a distinguished military uniform. "He was a *mambí*, a freedom fighter, and he fought in the War of Independence, then he became a general in the Republican Army," Gabriel explained. I could not tear myself away from the photographs. They were captivating, as if the characters in a book were coming alive before me. Most remarkable were the fashions. No matter what epoch, no matter whether they were photographs of family or of a large gathering at an outdoor event, the men were dressed in sports jackets and pleated pants, the women in an array of smart dresses and Louis XV heels.

Next, he showed me pictures of Ernest Hemingway celebrating his Nobel Prize with *la crème* of Havana society on October 28, 1954, the women in pearls, the men in jackets; and another of Hemingway celebrating New Year's Eve, 1951, in the company of Gary Cooper at El Floridita bar. Nine months later, Hemingway published *The Old Man and the Sea*, Gabriel told me. He knew a lot about Hemingway's life, and had come to own these photographs while he was working on a documentary about Hemingway's life in Cuba. The production work on the documentary had been one of the turning points of his life. As he delved into the life of the most famous American in Cuba, he understood all that had been lost, all that was betrayed.

"I thought you would enjoy seeing what Cuba was like," Gabriel said. "Havana was the Paris of the Caribbean."

It was the first time I had heard the poetic comparison, and I could see and feel Havana in all of her old glory, enchanting in her architecture, and adorned with the elegance of characters that spanned generations. Gabriel's personal collection showed a sophisticated city with the soul of a debonair woman in her prime. I was falling deeply in love, and I wasn't sure if it was with the *habanero* bringing La Habana to me, or with the romantic idea of a great city, now fading, dilapidated, and lost to history.

"Havana, the Paris of the Caribbean," I said, the tears swelling in my eyes. "That is lovely."

"Someday—" Gabriel started to say.

"Someday," I hijacked his sentence, "I will dance in the streets of Havana."

I let my tears run free, tears so quiet they were silent prayers. Gabriel slid his hands through my hair, brown and flowing to my shoulders, and he brought me to his chest. He let me cry in his arms for a long time, and then he kissed my tears, my hair, my face, my lips, my neck. We made love on the sofa without a moment of hesitation, his photographs on the table like an altar, our bodies submerged in a deep ocean of unconsciousness. When I woke up from the trance and the depletion that had lulled us to sleep, my head was resting on Gabriel's chest, and his arms were wrapped around me. This was where I wanted to be for the rest of my life. I had found my island. Gabriel was my lovely, lovely island, unspoiled by fate, unblemished by history.

"Are you thinking what I am thinking?" Gabriel whispered in my ear.

I only wished.

He did not wait for an answer.

"I think I am falling madly, wildly in love with you," he said.

"And I with you," I said before I kissed him on the lips.

He kissed me back, so hard and passionately and for so long that it hurt, then he let me go, helped me untangle myself from his body, and we both stood up. He caught me off-guard when he slid his arms under my knees and scooped me up.

"I am not done with you yet, *mi novia matancera,*" Gabriel said as he carried me to bed. "Like Cortázar said, '*No haremos el amor, él nos hará.*' "

We will not make love, love will make us.

After that day, Gabriel never slept away from my apartment. We spent weeks living in a Barcelonian utopia of avant-garde art show openings in the blossoming contemporary art scene, of soirees with local musicians beginning to experiment with fusing flamenco and international rhythms. One event generated an invitation to another, and soon we were swept into a nonstop cycle of late-night get-togethers at *tablaos* or at people's homes. Some were attended by movie and television directors and producers, and every now and then a famous personality would pop in. Gabriel and I were treated as a couple, and I had every reason to suppose that we were on our way to building a life together.

In 1989, Barcelona was a great place to be. Bon Jovi and Pavarotti played to sold-out crowds, and the city exuded the energy of an athlete training, on the way to achieving great things, breaking a new record. It was as if the entire metropolis had undertaken the job of creating grand spaces in preparation for the 1992 Olympic Games. Tall cranes dotted the waterfront and the leafy hilltops of Montjuic, Barcelona's "Magic Mountain," where designer pavilions, vast exhibition warehouses, and an Olympic stadium and concert halls were being built. Catalonians referred to their state of construction as if they were pregnant with child, and it was impossible not to embrace their enthusiasm. "*Estamos en obra,*" they called it.

Gabriel and I adopted their phrase.

"*Estamos en obra*," we would say to each other about our fledgling relationship. We were under construction.

Sometimes it seemed as if the whole world shared our karma. In the Soviet Union, the newly installed leader spoke of change, and he christened the idea of democracy with two words—glasnost and perestroika—that flew around the world like ambassadors of hope. The Berlin wall came crashing down, chiseled away chunk by chunk. The Czech parliament ended Communist domination. The Romanians too rose against dictatorship. Our *tertulias* with the Spaniards were filled with conjectures about Cuba being the next satellite to be released from the nightmare of subjugation. Gabriel and I could only watch, love, and hope.

Ours was a wildly passionate affair, yet from the start it was not an ebullient love. It was a love entangled in the shadows of history, and silently cast adrift by the uncertainty of the future. From the beginning it came with pain and sorrow, even if to me it felt like a complete love. I wanted Gabriel to leave the island, to live the adventure of freedom with me. He was always on the fence. At times, it seemed as if Gabriel knew that there was no way back from this point, no return. If the fall of communism was like a game of dominoes, Cuba had been left holding the losing double-nine tile. Despite that dark view, there were times Gabriel could not envision anything but returning to the island and sustaining his commitment to help foster change from the inside. His flip-flops were like knife wounds to my soul, and I was covered with them. I began to feel depleted, chained to tragedy, hopelessly entangled in his demons. I wanted to run, but the physical connection to Gabriel was unbreakable. A desperate look, passionate words, and all was forgotten for another leap into the precipice of his body and his history. In his bewitching embrace, one day would fold into the next, and I would find another reason to stay. Gabriel seemed oblivious to the pain he was causing me, but I understood that his pain was greater, that there was more at stake for him than for me. I took note of his pattern of operating in a flux of off-and-on behaviors, but accepted it as circumstantial. I forced myself to be patient. I learned to drown my grief and satisfy my sexual desires. In bed, there were no quarrels, no geographic dislocations, no distance between our points of pleasure. In bed, we were home.

One afternoon, Gabriel arrived at the apartment from the restaurant in a hopeful mood. He had found an art dealer in Madrid who wanted to purchase his collection of photographs. I did not understand the cheer at first. Those photos were so precious that I had been afraid to touch them too much, and now Gabriel was selling them. But the news was followed by questions about life in the United States, and in my mind, Gabriel was designing our future, and I welcomed his desire to build a financial base as a good sign. I did not see that I was jumping many steps ahead. I did not ever imagine that the vulnerable man who quoted Cortázar, who shed tears at the thought of giving up on his Havana, would turn into a self-possessed narcissist who squandered his freedom, changed his coat with great ease at the slightest change in seasons, and ultimately betrayed our love. All I could see from the hopeful days of Barcelona was an open road, and Gabriel and I walking it, hand in hand.

I did not see what was coming.

When the sale of his photo collection went through, Gabriel came home with a single red rose. He kissed me with a passion I had come to crave, and we made love. Afterward, in the most awkward pause of my existence, Gabriel told me he had to return to Havana.

He had been contacted by the cultural attaché in Madrid; he was wanted back in Havana, and he would return. He had made up his mind. He did not want to discuss it further.

I became so angry I lost control of my words, and I delivered every feeling I had swallowed in one word.

"*Vete,*" I said. "Leave."

Leave already.

He tried to reason with me, to beg me to hear him out, but it was a monologue. I got up, walked to the door tying a red silk bathrobe around my naked body, and I held the door open. He quickly dressed. After Gabriel left, I began writing in my journal, trying to make sense of what was happening to me. It did not help ease the ache in my heart. How could he do that after all we had lived, after all we had become?

17

A persistent knock startled me awake. Sleepy still and wearing my flowery pink summer pajamas, I dragged myself to the front door and asked, "*¿Quién?*" Gabriel answered, and I couldn't open the door fast enough.

"What's wrong?"

"Nothing, everything is right, for now. I have a surprise."

He was holding papers in his right hand, and with his left he grabbed my waist and pulled me into him.

"I can't take you to Havana with me, but I can take you to Paris for the weekend," Gabriel said. "Look, two tickets for the overnight train. We leave tonight, and we'll be there early tomorrow morning."

I had never dared to dream of seeing Paris on a whim, nor as a consolation prize for losing to a country a man I craved more than I was willing to admit. Paris was supposed to be the most romantic city in the world, a lover's paradise. People went there on honeymoons, dream vacations; they fell to their knees, produced a diamond ring they had zealously guarded all trip long in their pocket, and proposed marriage under the Eiffel Tower. I did not want Paris forever linked to a man I was about to lose. As much as I wanted to surrender to Gabriel's proposal, to live in the moment, as he begged, I could only muster a look of concern, not the enthusiasm he had expected. I was still angry, hurt, disappointed at his decision to return.

"I thought this would make you happy," he reproached me, letting go of me and placing the train tickets on the dining table.

"Going to Paris with you would be a dream, but this does not change the fact that you're going back to Cuba, does it?"

"It doesn't change reality," Gabriel said. "We've already been through all that, but let's forget about it for a weekend. I want to show you Paris, the real Paris."

"And then?"

"And then, like Bogie said, we'll always have Paris."

A sharp pain pierced my heart after he said that, but I drowned it by offering Gabriel a long, provocative kiss, and to further choke my tears, I dragged him to my bedroom. As he stood there shaking his head with a grin on his face, I took off my pajamas and slid into my disheveled bed, pushing to the floor the poetry books that had been my overnight companions. In our short time together, I had learned that sex was the best way to drown out the noise of Gabriel's complicated life. When his tongue found its way to the most persuadable of my geographies, I whispered in my last moment of consciousness, "Yes, I'll go to Paris with you."

The Barcelona-França train station was only a few blocks from my apartment, and the minute we checked in and took a seat on a bench at Track Six, I began to fret. I was restless. I could not wait for the train to arrive, and I kept walking from the bench to a small news kiosk nearby to flip aimlessly through the magazines, looking over my shoulder as if I expected someone to snatch this moment away from me. Gabriel remained seated, calm and smiling, but I could tell he was keeping an eye on me, and when our glances met, he winked and threw me kisses from afar. What he did not see, or ever acknowledge if he did figure it out, was that after he left my apartment, I walked to the train station and upgraded the cheap tickets he had bought to first class so that we could travel in a private sleeper car. Finally, the long train, royal blue and white, pulled into the terminal, and as soon as it firmly stopped, we began to search for our compartment: Number 65.

The space was tiny, and there was just enough room for our lone carry-on bag, but it was ours alone. A porter in a navy vest and cap arrived at our door, checked our tickets, showed us the hidden sink in the compartment, towels and toiletries, asked if we would be ordering dinner à la carte, and gave us a rundown of the itinerary. We told him we were exhausted, would skip dinner, and simply wanted to read and sleep. He said he would return at ten-thirty to turn down our seats and pull out the beds, and he wished us a good trip. We thanked him, closed the door, and made sure to lock ourselves in. We took our seats, and when our eyes met again, I knew we were thinking the same thing, doing the same math, sizing up our bodies and the horizontal space.

"Evil woman," Gabriel said.

"One for the road?"

"*Ou deux*," Gabriel said, showing off his French.

"It's a small space, how could we possibly manage it?"

"That only means we'll have to use our imagination."

"I like that . . ."

And then the shrieks of two children outside our door interrupted our mind games.

"*¡Nos vamos a París! ¡Nos vamos a París! ¡Qué suerte!*"

Lucky for them, but for us sex was going to be a challenge with two children next door. If we could hear these children, they could certainly hear us.

"*¡Qué suerte!* What luck!" I mimicked the kids.

"Shhh, behave," Gabriel whispered in my ear. "I have a plan. Wait until the train gains some speed. But you'll have to be very quiet."

"I don't know if I can do that."

"Trying is half the fun."

"I'll drink to that," I said, raising an imaginary glass.

During the first twenty minutes, the train seemed to be traveling in slow motion, but as soon as we left behind the graffiti-filled walls of the city, it began to speed up. It was nine-thirty, but there was still plenty of light outside. I was sitting by the window, lost in the bland landscape of wild weeds and distant hills, when Gabriel stood in front of me. Slowly, he began to unzip his blue jeans, and before his pants fell all the way down to his ankles, I had the best of him staring right at me. I went to close the drapes, but he pulled my hand away.

"I like the light," Gabriel said, and then, caressing my hair, "Dinner, mademoiselle?"

"Hmm . . . sure smells good."

"A splash of Jean Naté for the road," he said.

"Jean Naté! What a girl you are! Delicious."

Many pleasurable minutes later, Gabriel took my place on the window seat, and I took his, standing there so filled with anticipation that I could not breathe. He took his time pulling down the zipper before he escorted my jeans and bikini underwear all the way down, past my ankles, and flung them into the empty seat. He slid to the edge of the chair, inching as close to me as he could. He inhaled, and before touching me with his lips muttered, "Just how I like it, *au naturel*."

"For now," I sighed. "I'm going to buy a new perfume in Paris."

The porter arrived fifteen minutes earlier than he had promised, as Gabriel and I were grudgingly dressing, exhausted from our reckless play and the day's emotions. He asked us to step outside, and for a moment I thought we were in trouble. But all he did was close our drapes, fold up our seats, and pull out two beds from the wall. When Gabriel saw the beds, one above the other, we looked at each other with longing, and again thought the same thing: Terrible. We would have to sleep in separate beds. It was a good thing. I needed the rest, and I easily fell asleep with the rocking of the train in darkness. The night seemed short, or at least the time for sleep. Before sunrise, Gabriel had hopped from his top bunk to mine, and figured out how to fold his back into the wall.

"If you can be very quiet so that we don't wake up those children next door," he said, his hands traveling down my belly, "I can be very good to you."

I was about as quiet as a woman madly in lust can be, and Gabriel was bursting with pride at his newfound power over me. I surrendered, but not before I made Gabriel promise that no matter how badly I wanted to get my first glimpse of Paris when we arrived, we would not leave the train until everyone in our car had left first, lest they turn us over to the train police for lewd behavior. Our porter had other plans. A little after seven, he knocked on our door, announcing that it was time to wake up. Breakfast was being served in the restaurant car.

"Thank you," Gabriel hollered.

"I don't want to go outside," I protested. "I'm too embarrassed. What if people heard us?"

"Don't be silly, no one knows who we are," Gabriel said. "I'm starving, let's go eat."

It was a beautiful, postcard-perfect morning and the sunlight cast a golden glow on the restaurant car. We lingered over refills of café au lait and not enough croissants as we passed through the charming Parisian suburb of Bretigny with its terra-cotta-tiled roofs, beige facades, and white-lace-curtained windows. My fear of recognition had been unfounded; our fellow travelers only paid attention to each other, or to the uniformed waiter, overdressed for the morning shift in a tuxedo bow. No one seemed to be particularly aware of our existence, and I liked that. On the train to Paris, Gabriel and I existed in a cocoon, as if the rest of the world was in a holding pattern. It would never again be like that.

After breakfast, we went back to our car, hoping to cuddle in our bunk and sleep some more, but the porter kept coming by our compartment, knocking on our door three more times before we arrived in Paris.

"Madame, monsieur, last call for breakfast."

"Madame, monsieur, could I see your tickets please?"

"Madame, monsieur, five minutes to Paris!"

When we got off the train at the Austerlitz station, I wanted to sprint like a child at the entrance gate to Disney World to get my first glimpse of the city, but I had to hold on to Gabriel and catch myself as I took my first steps. It felt like Paris was moving sideways. I had disembarked, but my head felt as if it were still back in the train.

"Motion sickness," Gabriel said. "It will go away in a little while."

But Paris did not stop moving for a good part of the day. From the train station, we found our way to the Latin Quarter on the subway, and I had to stay at a café, sipping a sturdy espresso and writing in my journal, while Gabriel and his rudimentary French found us a hotel nearby. The narrow cobblestone streets were transformed from nearly empty when we arrived in the morning to bustling with merchants and tourists by midday and into the dawn hours. Our hotel room was almost as small as the train's compartment, but it packed Old World charm in its over-the-top burgundy and olive drapery with gold tassels and its reproductions of masterpieces in gilded frames hung in strategic places. When we realized our double bed consisted of twin beds pushed together, I joked that by our trip's end I would be able to write a manual on how to make the most of your sex life in small spaces. Gabriel interpreted my words as an invitation.

"Ready to baptize our room?" he said, scooping me into his arms.

"Get away from me, you crazy Cuban, or we are going to spend the day in this room."

He kissed me. "That sounds like an invitation to me."

He kissed me again and again.

"Gabriel, please, I want to see Paris."

"*Me vuelves loco*," he said, diving into my body with such relish that I too became swept up in his passion. It was an odd moment to think of it, but I remembered my Catalonian landlord and his gentle "*te estimo*." There was nothing gentle or easy about loving an *habanero*. It was an all-or-nothing dive into the gulf of desire. Loving Gabriel was like striding into a dark *callejón* in Havana from which there was no return. In Gabriel's arms, I lost all of my senses. He loved in the language of my soul, and I could not resist the temptation to dissolve every inch of me into all that he was. By the time we left the room, it was afternoon.

I was enchanted by our neighborhood's view of the Gothic towers of Notre-Dame, tickled and frightened at the same time by its gargoyles. The Seine enchanted me in the way only rivers can. Like the Miami River at dusk, purple and orange, like the iced-over river in Iowa on a beautiful winter morning when it is framed by a particularly bright blue sky. I could have been happy simply sitting at the Café de Flore for the rest of my life, but Gabriel insisted that there was no more proper introduction to Paris than a stroll along the Champs-Élysées. He had been in Paris twice in his official role with the Cuban Film Institute, and seemed to know the city better than I ever imagined. We went underground at Place Saint-Michel and took the Métro to Place de la Concorde. When I emerged from the ground, I recognized in the distance the unmistakable stamp of Paris, the Eiffel Tower, enveloped in a soft haze, the clouds above it illuminated by the setting sun. It was my first view of the famous structure, and I stood there transfixed. I took out my camera and captured the image, as if by framing in the viewfinder the distant tower in its glory I could make Paris forever mine. I could take it with me and make it mine, only mine. I had no reason to suspect it in that instant, but no matter how many times I photographed the tower after that, it was this photo that would serve me well in the tumult of the years ahead. When faced with the contradictions of love and history, it would be my salvation.

"This is the place where Marie Antoinette lost her head," Gabriel interrupted my contemplation.

"In the guillotine," he added.

"Oh, yes, the French Revolution, I studied it in Iowa. You know what I think? If you must lose your head, this looks like a magnificent place to do so. I wouldn't mind if this was the last place on earth I saw."

"If you put it that way . . . can I help you lose your head, my queen?"

"You already have, *cariño*," I said, and I pecked his cheek.

Gabriel took my hand, folded it into his arm, and we greeted the evening traversing the most famous boulevard in the world. It was there that I found the most precious bottle of perfume I have ever seen, a two-toned bottle in black and gold, a relief of Egyptian motifs running all around it, and the word "*Habanita*" superimposed in red letters. Even before I smelled the perfume, I knew I had found the scent I wanted to wear. I was predisposed to like Habanita, and for the next decade it became the only scent that perfumed my days. It smelled of patchouli, vanilla, jasmine, and roses, and I had to be careful to apply it only in small doses. It was an overwhelming scent, the kind you never forget. It almost made me dizzy, but I loved the sensation of it bathing my skin. The package, the perfume, and the man were irresistible.

We were in Paris, but Gabriel and I seldom spoke of French history again. We were in Paris, but we talked about Havana, as if with our presence and my new perfume, the Cuban capital had invaded Paris. Had invaded the cafés, the squares, the fountains, the stately Père Lachaise Cemetery, where Gabriel and I communed with the illustrious dead, Morrison and Chopin, Wilde and Molière, Signoret and Montand, strolling the leafy walkways hand in hand.

As we explored the City of Light, in my heart I was waiting for the miracle of waking up in Havana with Gabriel, as if our hotel were the Ambos Mundos, where Hemingway spent his drunken nights, as if Café de Flore were La Bodeguita del Medio, with its walls filled with the scribbled musings of half a century of patrons, as if the Lido and its dancing beauties were the Tropicana and its spectacular *mulatas* parading in minuscule ruffled bikinis and sequins. It was reasonable for me to dream. When we stood at a news kiosk on the Rue de Rivoli and surveyed the headlines, I could only be hopeful. The newspapers were full of stories detailing how the Iron Curtain was coming down for good, layer by layer. I was charged, at least for brief moments, with the hope that the seawall between Gabriel and me, between Havana and Miami, also would crumble.

In Paris, Gabriel completed the task of cementing his Havana in my heart, and I walked alongside him with a conflicted mix of awe, gratitude, and regret. I soothed the dark corners by taking Gabriel's photograph, changing my film from color to black and white so I could preserve the essence of him forever in my memory.

But Paris did not change our destiny. Our last hours in Paris and the trip back to Barcelona were cloaked in sadness. Gabriel remained firm about returning to Havana the next day. In the darkness of our train compartment, I fell asleep to tears. Gabriel spent the night cradling my body in his arms, and in the middle of the night, when I reached for his face, I felt the wetness of his.

"I cannot leave her as if she were an old rag, no longer useful to me," Gabriel said of Havana, and I so loved him for the feeling, the sincerity with which he spoke the words. I knew then that there would never be another man for me. When we arrived in Barcelona, we said our good-byes at the train station. Neither of us wanted to prolong the separation.

18

Not long after Gabriel left Barcelona, I too packed my bags. I did not leave as light as I had arrived. I had to buy an extra suitcase to carry all the art, ceramics, books, and mementos I had acquired in Barcelona and Paris, in essence my new life, and by Christmas I was back in Miami. I felt closer to Gabriel there. If Europe had been reveling in the dawn of a new era, Miami was even more ebullient. I came home to a city reeling with the hope that a democratic shift was afoot on the island, a people engaged in premature predictions of the last days of tyranny. Some had gone as far as preparing a set of luggage, ready to make the trip to the island on the first plane back. It was impossible not to dream, and for me the preparations for the future began with renovations to my house. It had taken me almost a decade to build the courage to transform Abuela's house into my own. In six months, I turned the house into my oasis, which included a sunny kitchen with white cabinets, yellow walls, and a view of the backyard. I stayed in my bedroom, but I traded in the pink and green rose pattern Abuela had assigned to my linens for a soothing Oriental royal blue and white design. I turned Abuela's room, the larger of the two, into an office with a daybed for overnight guests. It took a while to land the right job, but I returned to work when an opportunity for a bilingual archivist came up at the Museum of History.

A year flew with little news of Gabriel, as if my letters did not reach him. Our only contact was his sister in Barcelona, and whenever I called the phone number in Havana that Mariela gave me, a neighbor's house, the old woman who answered said Gabriel was not in the city. Mariela was not much help. All she would tell me was that Gabriel was traveling across the island filming a new documentary. Mariela sounded bothered by my calls, and so did the neighbor, and the echo of my voice on the phone line between Miami and Havana and Miami and Barcelona became an abyss through which the idea of Gabriel, and with him my sanity, had disappeared. Brokenhearted and perplexed, I gave up trying to reach him, and once again I immersed myself in my work, this time piecing together the threads of Miami's history and writing poetry about love and loss. Gabriel's decision to return to Cuba, and the aftermath of his silence, painted a coat of doubt I could never again wipe clean from my heart. My nights were saturated with nightmares in which I played out all sorts of scenarios of betrayal. Sad as I was, or perhaps because of that sadness, I did not give up on my dream of studying history, and I refocused my interest in art history. I didn't return to Europe, but instead enrolled at The University of Miami, and once again my nights and weekends were filled with the task of learning, a respite for my aching soul. I traded in my nothingness for the world of Picasso, Juan Gris, Dalí, and their artistic production in early twentieth-century Paris. I was home one Saturday writing a paper on Picasso's *Les Desmoiselles d'Avignon*, documenting how the painting was the launching point of Cubism, when a man who identified himself as an American saxophonist called my house. His name was David and he was returning from a trip to Cuba. He had an important message to deliver to me from someone on the island, but he did not want to talk on the phone. Could he see me? Given the cloak-and-dagger of our brief conversation, I could only hope the message was from Gabriel.

The saxophonist was staying in an old, renovated Art Deco hotel along an oceanfront strip of South Beach that was undergoing a renaissance, and we agreed to meet in the area. Restoration and new construction were dramatically turning what had been a retirement haven for snowbirds and a source of cheap housing for penniless refugees into a nascent playground for the international jet set. The scene of trendy locals and Europeans flocking to our paradise was not far from where *Noches de Playa* had brought Havana and the night to my shore, and the memory sent me to my beloved bottle of Habanita before I left the house. I sprayed a tad behind my ears and near my heart, hoping that the tonic would bring me good news from Cuba and my beloved *habanero*.

David and I were to meet at one of the outdoor tables of the News Café, my new favorite haunt for a bagel with cream cheese, strong coffee, out-of-town newspapers and magazines, and people-watching. He was already seated when I arrived, and was easy to spot, the only man with an instrument case by his side. He was tall and burly, with brown skin that had been bronzed by the Caribbean sun to a deeper shade. He had bloodshot eyes and a jolly smile that made me feel at ease right away.

"You are as pretty as Gabriel described. *Linda*, Gabriel said to me, unforgettable."

I smiled, but my heart also ached at the mention of his name.

"I haven't heard from Gabriel in more than a year," I said.

"I know. He told me to tell you he was sorry about that, but it was necessary. He got into a lot of trouble when he returned to Cuba. They knew all about the two of you. He had a lot of explaining to do, and he told them it was just a fling. He couldn't take your calls, and he had to pretend that he didn't want them."

"Who is they?"

"The government people who watch the artists when they travel, the security agents in the Ministry of Culture."

I was having a hard time buying the story, and the saxophonist could tell.

"They told him you are the daughter of an enemy of the Revolution."

I had never heard this before, not put this way, and the tagline on my father's history caught me off-guard.

"My father died a long time ago," I said. "I know very little about him and the circumstances of his death, but I doubt he was anyone of any significance to the Revolution. He was a dandy, for sure, but he and his older brother were shopkeepers in Matanzas, hardly the enemy. This is all very bizarre, but you said you had a message for me."

The saxophonist looked straight at me.

"Do you still love him?"

I could feel my eyes water, and despite my best efforts to contain them, the tears began to roll down my cheeks.

I did not have to answer the question.

"Gabriel wants to defect, he has an opportunity coming up, and he needs your help," David said. "He has a plan, it's risky and it might not work, all sorts of things can go wrong, but he told me that he would do whatever it takes to be with you, to have a life with you."

I so wanted to believe that to be true, but Gabriel had made clear to me his commitment to playing a role in the island's future, to remaining on the inside, where he could help foster change. I admired his resolve, even loved him all the more for it. Why had he changed his mind?

"He now believes that nothing is ever going to change in Cuba," David explained. "There is not going to be any glasnost or perestroika or military coup, or anything other than more of the same. More dissidents sent to prison, more economic misery without the Soviet subsidies. He has made up his mind. All he wants to know is if you will help him defect, or at least, if you will be there for him if he manages to break free."

Without waiting for my answer, David laid out a transatlantic plan for Gabriel's defection, and it felt as if my life had suddenly become a Hollywood thriller, and Gabriel and I were the protagonists. The saxophonist said he needed a decision by the end of the day. He would be playing that night at Mojazz, up the road on Normandy Isle, and he invited me to the show. He was meeting another American musician there, a bassist who was traveling to the island next week. He would send Gabriel my answer with him. But I could not, David warned, discuss the plan with anyone else. Gabriel's life was at stake, and it was impossible to know who was friend and who was foe. Not even his sister in Barcelona could know. All the bassist was supposed to tell Gabriel, if I agreed to help, was that there was a great movie to be made in Miami and that the financing was in place. That had been the agreed-upon code.

I did not make David wait for my answer.

"I will do whatever it takes to help Gabriel gain his freedom," I swore to David, and mine was not a false certainty. I was madly in love with Gabriel, and if there was more lust than love involved, now was not the time to dwell on such details. I could smell the promise of Gabriel on my skin. I had my Habanita to remind me what it was like to rest my head in the best place in the world, the cocoon of Gabriel's arms. That night I went to see David perform before a quintessential only-in-Miami crowd, among them a former Black Panther turned champion of the Cuban exile cause after spending years in a Cuban prison among political prisoners. Gabriel and his movies would fit right in.

After David and I said our good-byes, I could not sleep for several nights, tossing around the plan in my head, running through all the what-ifs, imagining my life with Gabriel in Miami.

In only a month, I would see Gabriel again. The meeting point: Madrid's Barajas Airport. The date: September 9, 1991. Gabriel would be traveling to Spain, then supposedly on to France and Italy, with a delegation seeking to seal a deal on several projects with three of the largest cinematic production companies in Europe. Given the domino effect of the Soviet fallout and the crumbling of the Berlin Wall, Cuba had become a hot destination. Journalists, photographers, and filmmakers from all over the world wanted to come to the island to chronicle what were supposed to be the last days of the regime. The delegation from the Cuban Film Institute and the Ministry of Culture was to return from Europe with a full report on the economic and political advantages of opening the door to foreign filmmakers, with controls, of course.

Gabriel's instructions to me were to go to the luggage carousel where passengers from Iberia's Havana-Madrid flight were supposed to pick up their bags. If all went well, my American Airlines flight from Miami would be arriving a little earlier than Gabriel's from Havana. I was to remain in the baggage area, pretending to have lost my luggage so that, in the tumult of arriving passengers, I could approach the Havana-Madrid carousel as if I were looking for my bags.

I could not speak to Gabriel. Only our eyes would meet, and when he gave me the signal—he would rub his neck as if it were sore from the nine hours of flight—I was to head for the bathroom, which we both knew, from previous trips, was close to the carousel but tucked away enough so that the doors were not visible. Gabriel would pretend to be going to the men's bathroom, but would instead dash into the women's side to meet me. My job was to reserve a stall for him to hide and wait. In case it was crowded, I was to keep women from making a fuss if they realized there was a man there and became alarmed. How I would do that was not explained to me, and I assumed I would have to improvise, use my imagination. I wondered what would be worse, Cuban agents in pursuit, or a handful of angry women fearful at the sight of a man in their bathroom.

Once stashed away in a stall, Gabriel would transform himself. I was to bring in my carry-on bag a woman's wig and I was to wear one myself on the trip or dye my hair and change my look. Gabriel was sure the Cuban secret police had photographed us together in Barcelona or Paris and could recognize me, so I needed to take precautions, given the need for my presence in the carousel area to make contact. I also needed to bring in my carry-on some women's clothing that would fit Gabriel. He would change, disguise himself as a woman, and when the baggage area was clear of the Cuban agents who were sure to be looking for him by then, we would make a mad dash for a cab, or head to another area of the airport where we could safely contact authorities and Gabriel could ask for political asylum.

Nothing went as planned, except for my change of hair color and my pixie haircut. Once more in my life, I went blond, but this time part blond, with professionally brushed highlights. Judging by the solicitousness of the suited Brazilian businessman sitting next to me on the plane, my hyphenated hair was becoming, and I wasn't sure if that helped or hurt our plan. Adding to the stress, my overnight flight from Miami was delayed, first an hour, then two. I wanted to scream from the helplessness of watching our plan become more improbable with the passing of time. Unless the winds were in our favor and the pilot made up the lost time in the air, our plan of meeting in baggage claim at about the same time would fall flat. I would miss Gabriel's arrival. Gabriel would have to pick up his luggage and go on with his delegation, and then all I would have as a contact was Mariela in Barcelona, and she wasn't supposed to know a thing. I couldn't sleep. I couldn't read. My bid to become a heroine had not started well. I did not have a leading lady's nerves of steel. If my hands trembled at the thought of having to explain the contents of my carry-on bag in customs, what could I possibly expect when Gabriel and I were actually on the run? I fretted in my seat until the Brazilian businessman offered to buy me a drink. I lied to explain my excessive fidgeting, said I was a nervous flyer. I declined the scotch on the rocks he ordered himself, but accepted a tiny bottle of cabernet sauvignon, regretting the plastic cup. We indulged in small talk about wines from South America versus Europe, about our experiences with difficult *madrileños*, then fortunately the Brazilian put the airline's burgundy blanket over his head and said good night. He did not wake up until it was time for breakfast and Madrid was only an hour away.

I was so on edge, and now also drowsy from lack of sleep, that as soon as the flight attendant handed the coffee to me, I brought it to my mouth too quickly, and I burned my bottom lip and the tip of my tongue to a furious pitch of pain. "We're almost there," the Brazilian said, and I appreciated his effort to soothe me. We chatted the rest of the way about his business ventures importing jewelry made from wood and stones from the Amazon until the captain announced our approach, adding that thanks to favorable winds, indeed he had made up most of the time lost on the ground. I thanked Cachita, my beloved *virgencita*, in silence; what to the captain were winds, to me was divine intervention, Cuban-style.

I went through the immigration and custom checkpoints without incident, and was again relieved to sense that our plane had been first to land, as the lines before me were short and behind me and my fellow passengers quickly grew out of sight. And so I hurried to baggage claim, my heart ticking faster than the seconds, the minutes until I would see again my Gabriel. Perhaps it was naïveté fueled by the euphoria of landing and the positive turn of events, perhaps it was that a free person cannot fathom otherwise, but the moment I spotted Gabriel in the midst of a maddening crowd gathered around Carousel Number 23, I was no longer as afraid of the badass secret agents as I was about all the other circumstances that could have foiled our plans. If Gabriel had boarded that plane in Havana and landed in Madrid, there was no way I was going to let anyone pry him away from me. I walked to the carousel slowly without taking my eyes off Gabriel. He was dressed all in black and he looked like he was waiting for his luggage like everyone else. I had to quash the desire to run to him, embrace him, and never again let go. He looked up and saw me, and instantly he began to rub his neck. For a minute I was paralyzed, unsure of what to do, but when I panned the crowd to both sides of Gabriel, I saw two men, one with a thick mustache, the other bald. They were badly dressed in navy polyester, and had that unmistakable dated look of hired thugs trying to blend in, to appear presentable. I bolted for the bathroom, and when I made it inside and saw the line in front of the women's stalls, I nearly fainted. The women's bathroom was packed, as usual. What was I supposed to do now?

The answer came swiftly. A strong hand grabbed my arm, pulled me too hard, and before I knew it, I was inside a men's stall with Gabriel holding on to me, his body trembling to the rhythm of mine. We did not speak, we could not speak. We simply stood in the small space, the stench of urine and feces thickening the air around us, and held on to each other for a long time until a loud knock brought us back to reality.

"Is everything okay in there?" a thunderous voice asked.

The man had a Spanish accent and we were relieved.

"My wife is sick," Gabriel said, "and I am assisting her."

"Let me help you," the man said. "I am a police officer."

Gabriel looked at me, and I could sense the question in his eyes. Was he for real? I followed my intuition and nodded.

Slowly, Gabriel opened the door.

To our relief, the man was dressed as a police officer. I was so pale and shaking that I could tell he believed that I was sick. But as soon as he began to tell us that he could take us to the first-aid station, the two Cuban men who had been standing around Gabriel burst into the bathroom, agitated, red faced, and sweaty.

The minute they saw Gabriel, they reached for him, but I screamed, stood in front of Gabriel, and shouted, "We want political asylum, don't let these criminals take him!" A man who was washing his hands ran to my side and also stood between Gabriel and the others.

The police officer grabbed his radio and asked for backup.

It was only then that I heard Gabriel utter in what was almost a whisper, "I want political asylum." I felt a load of tension leave my body. In seconds the men's bathroom was filled with police, and I saw the two Cubans back up, heading for the door.

"*Te salvas tú, pero nos jodes a nosotros, maricón,*" one of the men yelled at Gabriel. Gabriel was saving himself, the man said, but he was getting them in a lot of trouble.

"Make up whatever story makes you look good," Gabriel shouted back. "You're good at that."

"Don't forget that your mother is still in Cuba," the other man said. "You're going to regret this."

I saw the look of terror again in Gabriel's face, and when the men were out of sight, Gabriel embraced me and we both broke into sobs. Every man who had gathered around us, police and civilian, began to clap furiously. We were safe. Gabriel was finally free, and for the first time as a free man, Gabriel hugged and kissed me. He kissed my eyelids, my tears, my forehead, my nose, and my lips. I have never since known a moment of greater happiness.

19

"Words cannot describe freedom. It is too grand for words," Gabriel said to me the moment we were alone, past the danger, and done with the paperwork that begging for the opportunity of a new life entails. I knew what he meant, and the shared experience only inspired me to love Gabriel more. But this time I could not stay with him in Spain for long. I was building a career I loved back in Miami, and the only thing left to do now was for Gabriel to remain under the radar of Cuban officials roaming the city while he waited for his petition for political asylum in the United States to be granted. He had to go underground and I had to return to work. Before I left, I offered Gabriel marriage as a way to expedite the paperwork or as an option if his claim was denied. We were in love. We planned a life together, didn't we? What difference did it make when or where we married? Gabriel became tearful. He seemed moved by my offer, but insisted on "doing things right" at this stage of his life. "You deserve better," he said. "I don't want to shortchange you." I felt strange, relieved, and at the same time disappointed, but I did not say so. After the toasts to new beginnings, I went home.

Once more I waited for Gabriel, preparing my little house for another inhabitant, talking in my mind to Abuela and her things with endearment. I gave away more, stored more of the memories, and made room in closets and drawers for Gabriel. Three months later, Gabriel called me collect from Madrid with the good news. He was arriving in three days. Once more we lived the thrill of a reunion, toasting with a bottle of champagne and an exquisite French-style meal of almond-crusted sea bass, delicate green beans, and chocolate mousse I picked up from the best chef in Coral Gables.

"*Soy tuyo, todo tuyo,*" Gabriel said, cupping my face with his beautiful hands. He was all mine, he promised. We were living a dream, and that night I visualized the future in full color.

My rhapsody went like this:

Gabriel and I were married at San Juan Bosco, a church without pretensions, where service to the most humble immigrants, the elderly, and the neediest of children was still the ultimate charge of saints, those on the pedestals and those who roamed the halls carrying out the most selfless calling of service. Ours was a simple ceremony attended by the women from Abuela's beauty salon; my closest friends from work; the poet, who read lovely verses he had written for the occasion; and the guitarist, who accompanied the singer, now his girlfriend, for the Ave María. The engineer was there too. He sat in the pews, an arm draped around his wife, who cradled a well-behaved toddler dressed in frilly pink on her lap. Carol and Brian flew in from Chicago with the twins, my flower girls, the only members of the court. I did not have a maid of honor, as Gabriel did not have a best man; all of his friends were back in Cuba, or by now exiled across the world. I dressed the twins in miniature versions of my dress, a simple V-

necked gown with no veil. Our hairdos, coiffed into buns with drooping curls by Abuela's heirs at the beauty salon, were spotted with baby's breath. I held long-stemmed lilies on my way to the altar, where at the end of the ceremony I left the flowers before a statue of Our Lady of Charity. I invited Andy to the wedding, and at first he said he and his wife Cindy would come, but days later he excused himself, saying a business trip to New York City had come up and that, anyway, Cindy was too far along in her pregnancy to travel.

It was a happy day. Abuela would have approved, and sent me a sign of her blessing from heaven.

But this was the reality:

The day after his arrival, I was showing Gabriel my Miami, and nothing less than euphoria filled my heart. I was driving along the stately stretch of Collins Avenue that people call Millionaire's Row. It was a glorious afternoon. The waters of the intercoastal shimmered as if diamonds floated on top. Gabriel and I were flushed with the victory of his escape and the ecstasy of our night of love, driving through the most scenic artery of Miami Beach with nothing but the future ahead of us. I pointed to the high-rises along the beachfront and found myself telling Gabriel that I had often daydreamed of selling Abuela's house and moving to the beach. There would be pros and cons, I said. The sea and sun at our window would be my definition of paradise, but a house with a backyard is a better place to raise a family. It was then that Gabriel said to me, with chilling coldness, his eyes fixed on the road ahead, "Don't ever think that I am going to marry you, and have children with you, and have *that* kind of a life."

The woman who changes her perfume would have stopped the car, let him out, and gone shopping for another fragrance, but the woman who wore Habanita was a fool. *Forgive him, he has been through a lot. Forgive him, he did not mean it that way, he is confused. Forgive him, he is a good person. Give him time.* At that moment, I swallowed my feelings and became an award-winning actress. I had long ago learned that I could perform any role, and do it well. Without missing a beat, I answered, "Why would I want *that*?" My heart was screaming, rebelling, suffering, wanting to ask a simple, "And why not?" But my mouth, in the same cold tone that Gabriel had chosen to address me, began to spin tales about how Miami Beach had become an entertainment hot spot after a stand-up comedian named Jackie Gleason began to broadcast his weekly television show from Miami Beach. I promised an outing to Miami's version of Havana's Tropicana, the Club Tropigala at the Fontainebleau Hotel, recited Art Deco history, and ended the driving tour with a stop at the News Café on Ocean Drive, where his saxophone player friend had delivered the news of his wish to defect. Throughout the monologue, I perfected the schoolteacher pitch of a tour guide for better effect, and Gabriel seemed riveted. He asked a lot of questions about Miami and its history, and I answered them. I ended the tour with a stroll along the boardwalk at Government Cut as the sun was setting in the distance behind the city's skyline, an orange ball in purple skies.

"This is a fascinating city and you are a fascinating woman," Gabriel said. "You are the most interesting woman I have ever met."

We kissed, and he pressed me against his body like that first time in Barcelona, but I was broken. If there was ever a time in my life in which I betrayed myself, that day was the launching-pad moment. There would be many others in the years to come, and with each one, the light inside me would dim a little more. I turned myself off so that Gabriel could shine a little, or at least feel like he did. I so wanted him to love me.

I sidelined my own pursuits to help Gabriel realize his dreams. Gabriel wanted to continue to make films, but that, I had warned him back in Barcelona when we first met, was a lot like writing poetry. It wasn't a living. The Medicis of Miami were not interested in supporting artists. Gabriel refused to sideline his vocation during his job search, and I admired him for it. But I did not want the failures to sour him. I knew it was a long road from Miami to Hollywood. For a while, Gabriel was content with the job I helped him get in the county office that negotiated and facilitated filmmaking ventures in Miami. It helped that Gabriel was bilingual, having studied English in, of all places, the Soviet Union. All his rustic English needed was practice, and the job gave him access to international filmmakers as interested in filming in Miami as they were in Cuba. It was not a bad place at all for Gabriel to begin, yet on most days he was in a foul mood, frustrated with what he said was a suffocating office job. He brought up the subject of returning to Spain almost weekly, and at some point it began to feel as if he were threatening to leave me. I didn't want to leave Miami, where the arts scene was bursting with new work smuggled out of the island and new artists coming from Cuba, but I would have done anything to build a life with Gabriel. I kept my heart open to the idea of settling with him in Spain, but after a while Gabriel spoke of it no more.

Six months into the job, Gabriel announced one weekend, as if it were the most normal development, that he was planning to move to an apartment in the Little Gables, where a lot of newly arrived Cuban artists were renting studio apartments and mother-in-law cottages behind quaint homes.

I was stunned.

Weren't we a couple? Why were we taking a step back?

"You've been very kind, but I don't want to be a burden to anyone," Gabriel said. "I have to stand up on my own."

"You are not a burden to me, Gabriel, I love you."

"I love you too, but I need my own quiet space to work."

Gabriel further explained that he wanted to bring his mother Sonia from Cuba soon, and that he did not want to impose her on me. He had to rent something to determine if it would be appropriate for her. I understood the commitment to family, and once again I was left admiring his devotion to the right causes and thinking that perhaps my discomfort was selfish.

"We will always spend our weekends together," Gabriel promised, and so I helped him move into his studio apartment on Mendoza. We scrubbed and painted together, ending the job in a horizontal celebration of our skills on the kitchen's wood-laminate floors. Before I left for home, Gabriel gave me a key to the apartment, and I felt stupid for having doubted his intentions. I hoped I was not turning into one of those neurotically jealous women I so detested. Gabriel and I were both bohemian souls, people with artistic sensibilities, and our relationship could not be boxed into traditional roles. We were soul mates, mirrors of each other, inextricably bound by the greatest love.

I began to like our arrangement. At first it seemed to keep us in a state of romantic courtship. The first time Gabriel came back to my house after he moved, I was in the kitchen making dinner, and when I heard his key as he tried to open my door, I joked to myself, "Here comes the Cuban version of 'Honey, I'm home.' "

I was glad, in a strange way, to have my house back to myself. Gabriel always kept a change of clothes in my closet and in a drawer, and I did the same at his apartment. It was all very chic, very hip, very modern, I told myself. I always had a writing project to spread out over vast amounts of space, and the aloneness became a source of inspiration to me. Yet as time went by, our arrangement became awkward, tiresome, as predictable as a twenty-year marriage. Sonia never came from Cuba. She flew to visit her daughter in Barcelona, and Gabriel met her there. I was not invited to the family reunion, but again, I understood. They did not want to bring strangers into a delicate situation. Although she was retired, Sonia was still revolutionary royalty in Cuba, and she did not want to leave Cuba for good in her old age.

Still, I accommodated Gabriel's dance, and sought refuge from the demons through my poetry and my journals. Somewhere along the path, I began to feel genuine only in my writing. Somewhere along the path, I began to know a man who was deeply in love with himself and his desires, a man for whom, more and more, I was only a decorative accent. I wanted to leave him, but I could not. At first I felt an obligation to see Gabriel through the beginning of his life in exile. I felt guilty for having fanned his desire for freedom, and I wanted to make sure he would be successful in his new life. Then, as one year folded into another, I loved him more than I loved myself. The thought of leaving Gabriel brought me unspeakable pain. I loved the man and I loved his city and his island; and for me, these loves became so intertwined that I no longer could feel the difference. I lived in a haze of nostalgia for all things Cuban, and of a scent so strong it became inseparable from my own. No matter how angry, no matter how disappointed I ever was, the sex between us and the connection I felt to the island through Gabriel were like Super Glue.

A foolish woman, a blind woman, a woman who doesn't know she deserves better, can spend a lifetime waiting for a miracle. I spent more than ten. I loved a self-absorbed man who had painted his life with romantic brushstrokes, but it was all a mirage, a tall tale as fake as Las Vegas.

Freedom did not make Gabriel a better man, and I would forever grieve the horror of this as I watched him turn into the most trivial person I knew, a man without depth, without a soul. Gabriel became obsessed with his looks, with preserving his youth, and he began to tell me what I needed to do to improve my appearance. Lose a little weight, wear stilettos, sport makeup from sunrise to sunset. "Put a little lipstick on," he would say. "Not that one, the red one." He spent the weekends shopping, fanatical about the latest fashion trends, and always in the pursuit of the elusive Hollywood. I had to watch with him every movie made, not for the pleasure of cinema, but as if it were homework. I seldom again encountered the complex, committed, struggling man I fell in love with in Barcelona, the one with whom I engaged in the best conversations of my life, the man with whom I walked the streets of Paris in awe, the man who made me love Havana as if it were my own. He no longer wanted to hear about Havana or Cuba or even about Miami.

"Fuck Havana, fuck Miami," he would say. "Fuck them all."

I did not know how to help him along this road. I did not know how to be with him anymore. I spent the years waiting for the return of the man I had met, the man I loved, the man he never was again. With every day I waited, with every week, with every month, with every year, the cheer in my soul faded until I no longer recognized my portrait. I spent the years thinking that if I was patient, if I continued to support Gabriel's dreams, nurse him through his growing bitterness, if I drowned my own desires to live chained to the routine of our packaged lives, Gabriel would then find his way back to me, find that thing he could not name but that was always beyond reach, and I would be there whenever the miracle occurred. I would be there, me, his refuge, his *eterna novia matancera,* his true love. It was a lonely, lonely wait, without poetry, without perfume. My bottle of Habanita had long expired when the end came, fast and without warning, the way thunder strikes in Florida.

20

February 8, 2002
A Friday in winter

Sometimes, there is virtue in silence. When I ended mine, I could not conjure any goodness. The words spilled from my lips devoid of poetry. I could no more muster compassion for Gabriel than I could for myself.

Gabriel phoned from work. He wanted to know what we would do that night. It was a rhetorical question. We always did what he wanted to do on Friday night, and Saturday night, and every other night of my life. I don't know why I didn't submit to more of the routine of our lives that day. Perhaps it was the double dose of exhaustion from lugging around the weight of the relationship and the pressures at work, but when I heard his voice, I felt exhausted from the noise in my life. Politics colored everything in Miami, and its tentacles had reached the museum like a metastasizing cancer. Every exhibit, every project, and every participant was put through a test of the community's sensibilities, and the subject of art and artists from Cuba was the latest hot-button topic. Unlike previous waves of exiles, some of the intellectual defectors of the 1990s did not want to take to the airwaves and discuss their disenchantment with the regime openly. The newly arrived called themselves emigrants, didn't care for political discourse, and sometimes went back to Cuba as soon as they could to visit relatives. They did not seek a complete break, and this was not readily understood in a Cuban Miami reeling from the wounds of a revolution betrayed, of summary executions and life sentences dictated for the sole crime of dissenting. I stood in the midst of the divide, and understood both sides, but it was sad to see artists being strong-armed into declaring themselves public enemies of a regime to sell a painting, to play the piano, to find employment. Wasn't freedom from all that what they had come looking for? In time, some of the distance between generations of exiles would shrink, but in the midst of change and transition, Miami's leadership miserably failed again. Instead of fostering open discussions, the knee-jerk reaction of those in charge was to exercise censorship behind closed doors at the slightest divergence from the established views of the long exiled. It was always a mistake to attempt to stifle free debate in a free country, and every episode of censorship was followed by sessions strategizing on how to control the public relations damage. To me, it seemed as if every controversy played to a predictable script written in Havana and performed in Miami.

Gabriel's call arrived in the midst of that cauldron and the aftermath of my latest scrimmage at the museum. The last thing I wanted to do that night was what Gabriel and I did every Friday night: Go see another bad movie so that Gabriel could feel more miserable about not being involved in making them; then, later, make love to "*limpiar el sable*," clean the sword, as he started calling our sessions in an attempt at humor that only served to deepen my resentments against what he and I had become. My life, it seemed, had also become a script written in Havana, and that realization infused me with a rage I had never known before. I loved Gabriel with every inch of me, but I no longer wanted to lose myself in his arms only to return, when the moment of ecstasy was but another speck in history, to a reality I could no longer negate. I was drowning in revelations and large truths. There was no tenderness left in his way of relating to me, there were no vulnerable tears in his eyes, there was no love in his heart. It was time for me to surrender. I did not know how, and I grappled to find adequate words.

"Gabriel, the time has come to define our lives," I said.

"What do you mean?"

"I want more than a part-time lover."

"Is that all I am to you?"

"That's what it feels like."

"Well, what is it that you want me to do?"

"We have to fix things between us, or we need to end it all. I'm tired of the burden of carrying on a relationship that never seems to jell. I'm tired of having a husband who isn't a husband. I'm tired of mediocrity, of spending our days in useless and meaningless pursuits. I am horribly unhappy. I want peace in my life. I want a family I can count on. Maybe I want children, or not, but I don't want to be with a man telling me he doesn't want to have a family with me."

"Why complicate our lives like that, Marisol? I don't understand why you are saying all these things now."

"Because our relationship, as it is, has long run its course. It needs profundity, it needs fresh waters to navigate, it needs a new scent, it needs to become something."

"What you want is for us to marry?"

"I could care less about the piece of paper. What I want is something else, and you know exactly what I am talking about."

"Let me think about it."

"Time is up, Gabriel. Come home and let's solve this once and for all."

"Let me think about it. I want to keep my options open."

"Gabriel, enough. We either work this out tonight, or we don't and we're finished. Time is up."

I knew Gabriel would not come, but I hoped he would. A lifetime of exile turns people into perennial fools expecting miracles and reversals of fortune. I spent the night waiting for Gabriel in the darkness, meditating by candlelight to no avail, and I promised myself it would be my last night pining for a man who was lost in a world all his own. At midnight, I walked to my dresser, took the bottle of Habanita from its place of honor, and hurled it against the tiled floor of my bedroom. The bottle didn't break. Only the faintest of aromas oozed from it when I held it in my hands, intact. There was no tonic left, only the empty carcass of a beautiful bottle that wouldn't break, to remind me forever of my powerlessness.

The aftermath of a painful breakup was an uncharted landscape for me, and I did not know what to do with the wounds dripping fresh blood, the feelings choking me, the regrets flooding the banks of my life. I could not see beyond the storm of grief, could not feel anything but the sting of pain, ancient and new, and my pain and I wandered the city like ghosts.

The Sea Within

You were the voice of the sea
caressing my dreams
when they were fresh,
clear,
like mornings in eastern cities.
We played hopscotch,
my dreams and I,
bouncing on a sidewalk awash in beginnings,
and your voice, then but a whisper,
tempting,
conspiratorial,
skipping steps,
to propel us to certain victory.

You were the voice of the sea
chaining my body
to waves of pleasure and spume.
I knew you,
breathed you,
and breathed for you,
and in your blue soul
I deposited my prayers,
tender with the chastity of new love.

A hundred moons,
and you are the voice of torment,
of vacant nights,
thoughts thrashing,
powerful giants,
like the mountains of the Southern cone,
cold,

stoic,

fatal.

Your damning voice drowns my heart

and I beg the shadows of winter for mercy.

Remember the game?

The dream?

The pleasure?

And you, oh sea, so silent.

MIRACLE

21

Some loves are simply a page, an instant of connection, a haiku.

Blas had the saddest eyes I had ever seen, but they were beautiful: hazel, oval, and framed by the kind of long, lush eyelashes that could make a woman envious. He also had the saddest smile, wide and curved like an elongated half-moon, and easily conjured by a kind word. His thin auburn hair, streaked by a lifetime of sea and sun, cascaded down to his concise waist. As soon as he woke up, Blas pulled up his locks in a ponytail, and revealed a body sculpted like Michelangelo's David. Once, when he got up naked from bed to open the shades and let the morning into his studio apartment, I studied all of him from behind, still drowsy but delighted to have the vantage point of my place on his bed.

"What a view," I said, and, startled by my voice, Blas turned around.

He said he agreed that the apartment's location, steps from the bustle of beautiful people and edgy characters on South

Beach's Lincoln Road, was unbeatable, but when he realized that he had misunderstood my words, that it was his body I was admiring, he seemed embarrassed by the lust in my eyes. He walked away, pulled on a pair of khaki shorts, and glided a few paces to the kitchenette to make us a thick, dark, sweet *café cubano* topped by the amber foam he learned to make in a Hialeah cafeteria, his first job after he sailed to freedom on a homemade raft made of inner tubes, a plank of wood, and a bedsheet for a sail. In exile, Blas quickly mastered the technique of making *café cubano*, and the old Cuban barista who taught him, a matronly woman with chocolate-cherry-colored hair, used to rave about how her student had surpassed her. I could understand why, given the intense concentration with which Blas poured four teaspoons of sugar in a tin cup, caught the first few drops of the brew dripping from the machine, and beat the mix to its amber richness with a lot of heart.

When I met Blas at a restaurant on Lincoln Road where I was eating a grilled chicken Caesar salad and he was busing tables, he practiced yoga and meditation, and in his presence, my convulsed soul felt a strange sense of peace. I told him this the second weekend we spent together when Blas was driving me home Sunday night in his old topless Jeep, my left hand locked in his right as we crossed over the Julia Tuttle Causeway to catch I-95 south.

"All I need right now, Blas, is the peace I feel sitting here by your side," I said.

"I'm glad," Blas said, squeezing my hand tighter without taking his eyes off the road. "I need it too."

I did not detect then all of the demons Blas was desperately trying to keep at bay. Blas was almost ten years younger than me, and in Havana he was known as a *friki*, a take on the word freak and designating the youthful members of an underground made up of artists and musicians who clamored for freedom. The *frikis* wore their hair long, listened to heavy metal rock, and composed music and works of art that packed the punch of social protest. Some of the *frikis* went as far as injecting themselves with the AIDS virus to protest the totalitarian regime, which had imported Soviet communism but crushed the democratic shifts toward glasnost and perestroika. In his youth, Blas had been a promising art student, but at eighteen he was sent to prison, denounced by his own mother, who was so frightened by his looks and his talk that she thought jail time "would set him straight." He spent three years among common criminals.

"You haven't seen anything until you see a man with his throat sliced open by a homemade knife, contorting like a slaughtered chicken, squirting blood until he stops and dies," Blas told me one night during one of our long conversations at the beach, sitting on the sand and contemplating the stars. When I prodded Blas to tell me more about his time in prison, he dissolved in silence, his stare lost to the horizon. I dared not interrupt his thoughts. I had learned to let him be when the lost haze came over his gentle face. I always wondered where he went when he faded, and once, only once, I worked up the courage to ask him.

"I visit my mother," Blas answered. "I fly from wherever I am, spreading my wings over the Straits of Florida, and I land in the *azotea*, on the rooftop of our apartment in Centro Habana, and I sit at the kitchen table while her watery coffee is dripping from the *tetera* into a tin cup, and I have a conversation with her."

"What does she tell you?" I asked.

"She tells me that she has become an expert at making her monthly ration of *café* last longer," he answered.

"And what do you say to her?"

"I tell her that it's good to know that."

I hugged him, and he returned my caress, and silence reigned between us again for a long time. I knew that Blas was in conversation with his ghosts, and I began to conjure mine as the breeze from the Atlantic cooled our souls.

Blas knew about my demons and my ghosts. He knew about Gabriel and his betrayal. I told him parts of the story the day we met under the red awnings of the Van Dyke the Saturday I went to eat lunch there alone and brought with me a copy of Virgilio Piñera's collection of poetry, *La isla en peso, The Weight of the Island*, hoping that the text would fill the empty hours of leisure Gabriel had left in my life. Blas saw me first. He watched me read, and after my salad arrived and I put down the book repeating in my head Piñera's glorious phrase "*la maldita circumstancia del agua por todas partes*," the damned circumstance of water everywhere, Blas approached my table. He was a waiter at the restaurant, and mostly worked the jazz bar upstairs, but that afternoon he had picked up a coworker's shift. Piñera was one of his favorite writers, he said. In the six years that he had been in Miami, he had never seen anyone reading the highbrow Piñera, much less in this funky place better known as a haunt for up-and-coming Hollywood starlets and Latin American *telenovela* stars. Nobody came here to read a dead Cuban poet from the 1950s who until his death in 1979 lived marginalized for being a gay man, and for refusing to pay tribute to the regime in his literature.

"That's what makes Miami so great," I said. "You never know

what you're going to get, where you are going to find a soul mate, or at least a literary soul mate."

Blas smiled that unforgettable smile, sincere and generous.

"Do you live around here?" he asked.

"No, I wish. I live in the city."

"I have an apartment near here," Blas said. "If you want to live in Miami Beach, you should look at my building. There are always studios and apartments coming up for rent."

I did not want to discuss the safety net of my home with a stranger, the little house Abuela had so lovingly left me and that I could never leave, so I told him that beach rents were too high for me. As I spoke, he borrowed a pen from a passing waitress, grabbed a napkin from the table, and scribbled his cellular number.

"You'd be surprised," he said. "My apartment is very small, an efficiency, but I only pay four hundred and fifty dollars a month. You can see it anytime you like, or just call me when you want to talk about literature. I used to walk by Virgilio's house all the time when I was a boy in Havana."

It was easy for Blas and me to become friends. It also was predictable that a quiet passion would swell between us. I began to enjoy my weekend trips to the beach, and I no longer thought about Gabriel when I strolled along Lincoln Road. Sometimes I ran into Blas when I visited the bookstore near the Van Dyke, or the hippie shop with all the paraphernalia to align the chakras, or the gelato parlor for coconut ice cream. We began to take long walks together in the late afternoon, starting with the fifteen-block stretch of Ocean Drive with the renovated Art Deco hotels in a rainbow of pastels, returning via Washington Avenue, where another rebirth was under way and rundown storefronts were being turned into upscale restaurants. The walks soothed my rage at the passing days without a word from Gabriel, cleared my thinking about the future, and restored hope that my life was best lived without him. Blas was like an angel, who despite his broken wing was gently holding my hand through the flight of night.

I liked being by the water and my communing with the sea became an almost daily routine, as it had been in Barcelona. When I started to consider investing in a beach property, Blas insisted that I check out his apartment building, and one Saturday afternoon I called, proposing to visit. But he had been asked to work, and instead invited me to the jazz club at the restaurant. "Better yet, why don't you come to the show tonight? There's a great Cuban saxophonist here who used to play with Irakere when it was the greatest jazz band in the world."

I loved my hyperbolic Cubans. Everything about Cuba was grand, and I believed it. I only had a lingering question for myself: *Habaneros* exist in a perpetual state of infatuation with their city, *enamorados* to the bone of the grande dame, but how could I love her so deeply when I had never cast my eyes upon her? There was no reasonable explanation for my longing, only layers of fantasy.

When I arrived at the club, Blas was still working, and I took a seat at the bar as the night began melting away under the spell of Latin jazz. The ballads made me melancholy, and I could not help thinking of Gabriel and the many nights of jazz I enjoyed with him in Barcelona and in Miami. Blas seemed to read my heart, and every time I searched the room I would find him in some corner, looking at me. He winked and smiled, and I would return from the flashback to the past. Finally free after his double shift, Blas shared the last half of the last set with me, and we downed one *mojito* after another in celebration. The band was cooking: the pianist, the bassist, and the saxophonist were all Cuban, a mix of musicians grown in the island and in exile, and the drummer was a German with a lot of soul. After the show, we shared another round of *mojitos* with the musicians, and Blas and I were high on our chemistry and the scene.

He invited me to see his apartment.

"It's really late now," I said.

"You can't drive home," he said. "You've had too much to drink."

"I know. I was going to stop for coffee."

"Come home with me, you can stay the night."

"I don't even know your last name," I said.

"I'll tell you my last name—"

"No," I interrupted him. "I don't want to know, not now. You can tell me tomorrow."

Blas smiled and kissed me, and we walked the short blocks to his apartment holding hands and necking like teenagers alone for the first time. At the traffic light on Alton Road, night stragglers beeped their approval from their passing cars. We waved and laughed. When Blas opened the door to his apartment, I felt as if I were walking into my version of heaven. It was an artist's studio. The walls were filled with paintings, some framed, some taped to the wall. The living area was stacked with rows of cardboard, wood planks, glass, white canvases, and empty frames. Any surface was a canvas for Blas to unleash his spirit into a work of art. The only place to sit or rest was on a mattress on the floor. That night I slept surrounded by faces of a woman whose head grew palm leaves like tendrils, by a contorted figure drinking blood, his heart exposed behind bars, and by a ghost sitting at a bar.

When I woke up and began to stir, Blas opened his eyes with effort, handed me the book on his nightstand, a Spanish edition of *Oriental Tales* by Marguerite Yourcenar, and instructed, "Read this, and let me sleep. When you finish, wake me." I read several stories, and I liked them all. At the end of the one about the beautiful and terrible Kali, the goddess who roamed the Indian plains with "eyes as deep as death," I came to a dialogue Blas had underlined:

"We are all incomplete," the wise man said. "We are all pieces, fragments, shadows, matterless ghosts."

I took out the tiny notebook I carried everywhere in my purse and I wrote what the wise man said. Then I dropped back down onto the empty space in Blas's bed and began observing all of Blas's artworks from the floor. There was something odd about them, and when I realized what it was, my eyes darted from one to another to confirm my discovery. Blas had not signed any of his paintings. When I later asked him about it, he said, "What for? I know they are mine." In a world of oversized egos, Blas was one of a kind. He was good for me in the same way that medicine heals a grave illness, and I like to think that I was good for him too, that our time together was worth something to him. But I also knew that it was finite. Our friendship could be infinite, our memories tender, but Blas was not the man for me, nor I the woman for him, and I knew this after our first night together.

When Blas finally woke up, he walked to the small refrigerator in a corner of the tiny kitchenette, took out a cold Corona, and chugged the beer as if it were water, in one long gulp. Some endings are written at the beginning, and so it was with Blas and me. When we returned to Lincoln Road that Sunday for a late lunch at the café of Books & Books, I left Blas perusing art books and went to shop for a new perfume. I saw the pretty pink bottle right away. I did not have to smell the fragrance to know it was what I needed: Miracle. I would learn to like it; it would grow on me and protect me. Like Blas, it was only a perfume of transition, a scent of refuge from all the others.

22

Sometimes miracles come in sets of two. After spending another weekend with Blas, I came home on a Sunday night to a letter in my mailbox. It had a West Miami return address, and the sender was an A. Castellanos. The last name rang familiar, but I couldn't place it right away. I walked inside the house, turned off the alarm, dropped my purse and overnight bag on the couch, and sat down to open the envelope. The letter was written in college-lined paper, penned in blue ink.

Dear Marisol,

I hope you remember me. I am Alejo, your childhood friend from Matanzas. Before I left Cuba, your relatives gave me this address and said it was the only one they ever had for your grandmother Rosario, and for you. I hope this letter somehow reaches you. I have been looking for you since I arrived. I have visited this address several times, but I have not been able to find you. I even called a radio show that helps people find lost relatives, and I gave them your name, but no one has called me. People tell me that the postal service forwards mail, and that even if this is not your right address anymore, you might get my letter in your new home. I hope it works.

Do you remember me, Marisol? I remember you clearly. I remember the time our parents took us to Varadero for a vacation. You were always so well behaved, but I was the devil. I climbed on the balcony railing of our hotel room on the first day, and I got into big trouble. My parents almost drove me back to Matanzas, only they didn't want to leave you all alone with the adults and your grandmother had gone to Havana to visit your uncle Ramiro in his new house. Do you remember how much fun we had playing jacks on the floor of your hotel room? You were the champion of jacks in all of Matanzas. I couldn't beat you either. But I could swim better than you, and you almost drowned trying to follow me. Remember how mad your father got? How he screamed at your mother for not watching you closely, and how your mother then screamed at you when he left with my father to get more beer? You could do no wrong in your father's eyes, but your mother, she was really hard on you. Good thing she never found out about Robertico. Do you remember how you fell in love with my friend Robertico and how I helped the two of you kiss?

I remember everything, Marisol, and I can't wait to see you, to see the wonderful woman that I am sure you have become.

All of my love,
Alejo

I remembered.

I remembered following Alejo into deeper water and feeling the pull of something that felt as if a hole had opened in the sand. I remembered the ocean swallowing me, my father pulling me out on my last breath. I remembered the women screaming, the aftermath, the recrimination. But most of all, I remembered the virgin-bride-white sands of Varadero, and it filled me with joy. I remembered sinking my hands and feet into the silkiest, softest mounds in the world, the sands of my best childhood memories. I also remembered what I had tried for so long to forget, the last I saw of Alejo, my best friend, the day I left Cuba, his sad face and his little hand waving me good-bye.

When I finished reading Alejo's letter, I shed many more tears for my lost past, and I thanked Abuela's *virgencita* for the recovered memories, and for bringing Alejo to me. That night, I went to sleep conjuring the memory of my beach, my sand, my sun, and sleep descended like a mother's embrace. In the sweet cradle of memory, I was blissful.

The next day I called the phone number Alejo sent me in his letter, and I could not reach him until he came home from work at the clinic that afternoon, but he drove immediately to my house, and I never let go of him again. Alejo's tales surpassed those of anyone I had ever met. In his desperation to flee the island, he married a newly divorced Canadian tourist he met in Varadero at the nightclub where he was singing, only to find out that she was part of an Italian Mafia family. When she returned home to process Alejo's exit papers and delivered the news to her family that she had married a Cuban crooner, her brothers descended on Alejo's show in Varadero just like in the movies, threatening to kill him if he did not divorce her, which he gladly did. He did not even like women, anyway. "We are all adults here," Alejo said to me the first time he told me this story. "You know what I mean." But he did not give up on finding a way out of the island. Alejo prayed to every deity and saint he knew. He consulted every credible *santero* and *babalao* in Matanzas about the state of his future. He wanted the priests of *santería* to help him convince the entire Yoruban pantheon of *orishas* to clear the road, to deliver a sign that he should leave. He had to wait another year, and it was not a peaceful one. Sometimes he prayed on his knees, made offerings of fruit and flowers, begged for a way out to appear. When the *orishas* failed to deliver, he punished them with banishment from his altar. He was ready to give up when Alejo hit the jackpot: He won the U.S. visa lottery. He promised the goddess Ochún and her Catholic counterpart, our beloved patron saint La Virgen del Cobre, an altar all to herself in his new home.

"No raft for me," Alejo joked, "I was sent first class by the saints."

With Alejo in my life, I too felt as if I had won a lottery. I acquired family, a brother, a warm and humorous man I could love as much as I had my grandmother. He was the bridge on which I could make a long-overdue crossing to the yesterday I had needed to forget in the bitter distance of my forever exile. My sliver of Cuba, that narrow space which I called home, had finally come to me. But I was afraid to remember. I could not bear it if the sands of Varadero were not as soft, not as white as I remembered them, not as soft, not as white as I treasured them. I could not bear it if the royal palms did not rise tall above the Yumurí. I could not bear it if the rains didn't run fast like a river along the sidewalks of my house in Matanzas to empty in the bay, and if those were not my paper boats racing downstream with them. I could not bear it if that little girl on the beach, in the countryside, on the porch playing jacks, the girl I saw in my dreams, were not me.

Alejo assured me that everything was the way I was remembering it. But if it ever was not that way, if our sands were to ever be swallowed by the ocean, if my paper boats did not float out to the sea, if the royal palms ever lost their majesty, he would be there with me to lament it, to grieve it, to set it free. Alejo helped me embark on the road back to memory, weaving the golden yarn of my early life, one spool at a time. He knew that only then would I be able to make peace with my ghosts.

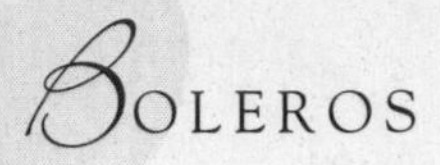

BOLEROS

Boleros,
sweet songs of love,
anthems
in my mother's adolescent voice.
I hear her sing,
I hear her sway,
back and forth,
back and forth,
in the big sillón *with the cane weave*
and the undulating lines of the seas.

Singing, swaying,
she sheds quiet tears
while I pretend to sleep
embraced by the shadows
of the white tulle of childhood.

I listen.
She weeps.
He's gone.

Boleros
songs of my Cuban soul,
dictionary of life,
maestros del amor.
Mami,
sing me a ballad,
the one about "Nosotros,
que nos queremos tanto . . ."
And tell me
the story of the girl with the weak heart

who died in the embrace
of such a love.

Sing to me, Mami.
Boleros are a Cuban girl's nursery rhymes.
But why do they make you cry?

RUSSIAN VIOLETS

23

Matanzas, Cuba
1959–1965

Mar y sol. Sea and sun. *Mar y sol. Marisol,* as if the sea and the sun were one, as if they had come together to give me a name. Abuela had told me that my father gave me this name, a good name for an island girl, but Mami thought it vulgar and plain. Mami preferred Carolina, the name that the stunning Grace Kelly, the perfect Grace Kelly, gave to her own daughter. Mami thought it was the right name for her first-born. Mami loved the golden princess of Monaco with a childlike adoration. Mami's friends knew of her infatuation, and called her Grace, or *la princesa americana,* the golden American princess. This was no exaggeration. Mami's locks sparkled with the same golden touch, only Mami's curls were richer, thicker, because hers were touched by the Cuban sun. In my dreams, Mami was a Cuban princess, the only kind of princess I ever knew or wanted to know. To go with her regal looks, she had full, round hips that swung to the rhythms of *el guaguancó,* as if Los Muñequitos de Matanzas and their drums had invented their soulful music just for her. Her hips always betrayed Mami, and it was a legacy that she would pass on to me.

Papi did not want a regal name for his island girl.

"Why the hell do we have to give the sun of my life the name of a stupid European princess, the name of a repented American?"

"She did not renounce her American citizenship, Ricardo. She kept it, and she has dual citizenship."

"Graciela, why should I care about what somebody else names their daughter?"

"*¡Ay, Ricardo, por favor, contrólate!*"

Control was not among Papi's talents.

"In this house," he ended every quarrel, "we do as I say. You know who wears the pants."

Their arguments were that silly. Mami burst into tears, long and sloppy tears that messed up the perfect black lines around her green eyes. Papi did what he always did. He strutted out the front door with the self-assured swagger of the dandy *el guapo* that he was. Mami stayed in the house shouting back at nothing and no one that Papi was a bossy idiot who got his way with everything, like giving me the name he wanted.

I like my name. It fits. I was born on an island embraced by sea and sun, *mar y sol,* and that's what I've always been and always will be, an island girl.

Marisol.

When my mother had me, when the doctor pulled me from her ripped womb, she looked into my squinty eyes and asked my Abuela Rosario, "Is she as pretty as me? Will she love me? Will she be mine to keep? Will she be the perfect little girl I can show off to my friends at the Yacht Club? Will her father, your son, love me forever now that I have given him this precious gift? Will he stay home, away from the bar girls who leave their sweaty perfume on his shirts, their lust on his breath?"

"I will love you forever," Papi said upon laying eyes on me, his first and only daughter. It was not clear to whom he was speaking when he said this, but Mami held it close to her heart that, surely, he was speaking to her and about her. But Papi did not, he could not leave the bar girls who served his Johnnie Walker straight, on the rocks, and their loving upon demand.

Abuela told me that I came home on a rainy day bundled in hand-embroidered white linen and lace, my supple wisps of hair perfumed with Russian Violets. Short, thick bursts of rain came and went that day, the way rain falls in the tropics, as if the heavens were trying their best to rinse the collective sins of our hearts, our restless hearts. When Mami walked me through the mahogany doors of our home perched above the bay in Matanzas, the rain was coming down in thin streams and the sun was shining with a blinding hue of transparent yellow.

"*Se está casando la hija del diablo*," Abuela said. The devil's daughter is getting married.

Abuela took me from Mami's arms and rocked me in the old rocking chair. It went creak, creak, creak, as if it were singing a nursery rhyme. Sun and rain, it was like a curse the day I came home, a bundle wrapped in the finest white linen the aunts could buy in Havana's El Encanto, the store called The Enchanted, which it was.

When I was old enough to want things, on a day when rain and sun once again headed for the altar, and Abuela once again noted the occasion, as if by saying it over and over— *la hija del diablo se está casando*, the devil's daughter is getting married—she would shoo away Satanic spirits, I asked her if we could go to this wedding.

"*¡Jesús! ¡Niña! ¡Ave María Santísima!*" Abuela cried, making the sign of the cross repeatedly from her forehead to her heart, to her left breast, to her right, and finally kissing her thumb and index finger. "Never, never say that again! Ask Papá Dios for forgiveness right now."

I didn't know how to want forgiveness. I didn't need it then. I didn't want to waste my wishes asking for it. Instead, I stood before the tallest window, the one looking out to the wilted rose garden, and I asked Papá Dios to make my mother stop crying. This was a better wish. I could see Mami's tears from my bed every night through the thin veil of my pearl-white mosquito net. Mami sat on the cane-backed rocking chair all night but she didn't rock, and her rocking chair didn't go creak, creak, creak in the darkness of the living room. Fading in and out of my dreams, I could see Mami's tears rolling down her cheeks. I imagined the tears rolling down her pointed breasts, over her stomach, bloated with the child she would not have, rolling down her thick thighs to her bony calves, over her bare feet and onto the terrazzo floor. They flowed and flowed and did not stop. In my dreams, the tears filled the room. They rose to Mami's knees, to her waist, thickened by my empty place, up to the breasts I had suckled, up to her mouth, sad but painted a torrid red, and above to her smooth thin nose. I imagined the tears almost drowning her, but I could never imagine the ending. I would be asleep by then.

Papá Dios must have been very busy that day. He did not hear me. He did not grant my wish. Mami cried for many more days, many more nights that Papi did not come home. Mami left me at Abuela's house and disappeared. When she finally came back for me, as suddenly as she left, she was like a wandering spirit in our house. She did not look at me, she did not speak to me, and when I looked at her, I saw that her eyes were very pink and almost swollen shut. She did not speak to me as she dressed me in a new black dress she brought out of a big box, an ugly dress for a girl of six. We walked to Abuela's house and there was Papi, who had fallen asleep inside an even bigger box than the ugly-dress box. All kinds of people came to see Papi. He too was dressed up in his best churchgoing suit, a *drill cien* of creamy linen, too dressed up to just lie there in this box-bed. Mami sat by him all day and all night and wept, kissing his clasped hands, whispering things to Papi no one could hear. But Papi wouldn't wake up. Her whispers flew with the island's capricious winds, as did her tears. People came all day and night to Abuela's house, all the way from the skinny end of our island to the thick part that juts out like the rear end of a triangle far, far away to the east. All of them wore black like Mami, like me, like Abuela, like everyone I saw that day. The men wore elegant tailored suits and matching hats, the ladies wore black dresses, and all the statues of the saints in Abuela's house were draped in black veils too, as if it were Good Friday.

The people who came to visit my sleeping Papi were kind to me; they stroked my droopy brown curls and said I was beautiful like my mother. Papi's best friend was especially kind to me. With an unbearable slowness, he ran his thick olive fingers along my face, down my neck, and down the front of my dress. "You and your mother don't have to worry about anything," he said. "You have me."

I was not worried. Not then. I only worried, and only for a brief moment, when two men I didn't know closed the box where Papi fell asleep and Mami and Abuela let out a scream that came from somewhere deep inside them, but not their mouths. Then the men put the box in an ugly black car and drove away. Mami and Abuela went after Papi in another black car, and the other people followed them too in theirs. They left me at Abuela's house with the wife of the man who ran his olive fingers along my face, down my neck, and down the front of my dress. This woman had black eyes, small and squinty, but kind, and when she pressed me against her chest, she sobbed in short spurts. I did not want to cry. I knew Papi always came back.

For the longest time, I believed Mami and Abuela had not been able to catch up to the car with my sleeping Papi in the box. I was still not worried. I knew he would come back. He always came back. But I never saw Papi again, and for a long time I thought about how he must have lost his way after his car passed the big curve by the church of La Milagrosa, The One Who Performs Miracles, and then disappeared onto the road to the beach. I imagined him losing his way among the tall royal palms of the Valle Yumurí. Everyone in school said the valley was haunted. How could Papi not know *el Yumurí* was the hiding place of the ghost of Hatuey, the noble Indian burned alive by the brutal Spanish conquistadores? For many nights, I fell asleep thinking about this and imagining Papi running in his good suit through the thicket of *ceiba* trees and royal palms, and Hatuey, confusing him for a Spaniard, raising his ax in pursuit of my Papi.

In the mornings, for many, many mornings, I asked Abuela when Papi was coming back. Not *if* he was coming back, but when he was coming back. Abuela looked around the room for my mother, but she didn't see her.

"*Se fue al cielo*," she said to me. He went to heaven, that's all.

"I want to see him," I said.

"You can't. He's with Papá Dios."

By then, Mami and I were spending every day in Abuela's house. My mother walked through the kitchen door in her white lacy night-gown, and Abuela asked me to be quiet, but that day I wanted desperately to know when Papi was coming back from heaven. Abuela snapped: "*Las niñas hablan cuando las gallinas mean*." Little girls speak when hens pee. And we all know hens never pee. So I never asked again.

Mami wanted more than anything for Papi to come home, even if he smelled of the perfume called Bar Girls, even if he told me he loved me more times than he told her, so Mami went to see a woman who said she could bring Papi back. For this outing, Mami dressed me in a pink piqué dress embroidered with tulips. After Abuela left for the corner bodega to get the morning's ration of bread, Mami grabbed me by the hand and took me to a bus stop on General Betancourt, which was the big street where cars passed all day long. I was happy just sitting there watching the girls walk by, swinging their hips this way and that, when Mami grabbed me again even harder and shoved me onto Bus Number 32. I thought surely we were going to find Papi because the bus kept going and going. When it passed the church of La Milagrosa everyone made the sign of the cross, from the forehead to the heart, to the left breast, to the right, and finally a kiss to the thumb and index finger. *Amén*. I was so busy watching everybody that I forgot to make my sign of the cross. Mami pinched my arm and I did not know why she pinched me, and I said, "*¡Ay!*" I almost really said, "*Ay, coño*," that's what I wanted to say, but I didn't because I knew better than to earn myself a slap in the face. When I did not make the sign of the cross on time, before the church disappeared in the distance, Mami pinched me again and said, "Such disrespect, Marisol, will win you a place in hell."

"And what is hell like?" I said. "Will Papi be there?"

Mami slapped me in the face even though I did not say *coño*.

I did not say any more and the bus kept going and going until there were no more houses or churches or beaches. Only green hills and long, slow curves. The bus went *s-s-s-h-h-h-h-h-h* and stopped in a place where the road turned to red-brick earth. I looked out the window and all I could see were rows and rows of lemon groves, fruitless lemon groves.

"We're in Limonar," Mami said to no one in particular. I thought she was speaking to me, but she really wasn't. As she said this, Mami had a distant look on her face, as if her pretty green eyes could see something the rest of us didn't. We were the only ones to get off the bus in Lemon Grove and when the bus left, I could see in front of me a street corner with a white house made of wood, a black streetlamp, and another short road off to the side. We took the longer road, and as we walked and walked, the red dirt began sticking to my black patent leather shoes, and the town of Limonar began to appear block by block, frame by frame. A bull was pulling a *carreta* packed with sugarcane stalks down the street. A bunch of golden roosters and white hens parted to make way for the beast carrying its load. All along this dusty promenade of Limonar, ladies in colorful housedresses sat on their front porches fanning away the heat and flies with white rags and cardboard. They rocked in tall wooden chairs back and forth, back and forth, to the tune of their talk.

"There goes the widow from Matanzas," I heard the one in the blue-flowered dress say. "I knew she would come. Look at the little girl, such sad eyes."

Mami paid them no mind. I did not think they were speaking about us.

I lost a father to the ways of the island. That day in Limonar, the town called Lemon Grove, I lost a mother to the ghost of a man she loved more than me. All I remember from that day is waking up in a hospital room that was all white, where strangers in blue uniforms hovered over me. A mask was covering my nose, and I could breathe well. I didn't see my mother again for many years.

"I'm done, I can't go any further," I told Alejo when I could remember nothing more.

Sweat was dripping down my spine. We were sitting in my living room, and I got up to turn the air-conditioning on full blast. My cheeks were flushed, and I wanted to think it was due to the bottle of Rioja that Alejo and I had consumed, even though I knew it was the effort, the exhaustion of returning to the past.

"Can you see her now?" Alejo asked me.

"No, I cannot see her face. I have pictures of when they were young, of their courtship, and one of their wedding in the cathedral. They are in a box in storage. Abuela brought them from Cuba when she went to visit, but I don't like to look at them."

"Have you ever met a woman from Matanzas named Lucía?" Alejo asked.

"No, Abuela didn't keep in touch with many people. Sometimes, when I was in Iowa, she would write me that so-and-so came to visit, that so-and-so came from Cuba, but they were like phantoms to me. Now I wish I had paid more attention, but back then all I could think about was getting out of her house so I could breathe."

"I will try to find Lucía," Alejo said. "She knew your mother well."

"I only want to know one thing, Alejo. I want to know how my father died."

"That I can tell you because it is one of those stories that travels throughout Matanzas like the legend of Hatuey," Alejo said, to my surprise. "I don't know how much is true, how much is myth. You never really know with families."

The year was 1965. My father had been left in charge of the family store by Ramiro, who had moved to Havana with his new wife and her family. Ramiro had met Victoria when her family stopped at Las Cuevas de Bellamar, the famous caves in Matanzas, on their way to a vacation in Varadero, and there was no stopping Ramiro from divorcing his first wife. Unlike what my grandmother did to Abuelo, his wife did not banish him from Matanzas, but Ramiro chose to exile himself to Havana. It was only natural that he would leave his younger brother Ricardo in charge of the store he had built through countless years of effort. My father took on the job of running the store with gusto, and he expanded it to include a counter with barstools from behind which he could serve his customers drinks and conversation. My mother hated the family business from the beginning of her courtship with my father, and the feeling only grew with the years, as the store became the operating center for everything he wanted to do behind her back.

"She was so in love with your father, and she was a very jealous woman," Alejo said.

"I know all of this," I said. "What I don't know is why he died, or how."

He went on to tell me how the soldiers in olive-green fatigues came into the store carrying their rifles, with orders to confiscate the business on behalf of the government. They were doing this all over the island, and to them it had become almost a routine operation. The owner was asked if he wanted to remain on the job as an employee of the state. If he didn't, he had to hand over the keys, and the business was shut down until someone else could run it for the government. If he decided to stay, the owner became one more employee in his own business.

When the two *milicianos* arrived, it was after lunch, and my father was at the counter drinking with a couple of friends and their girlfriends from "the easy life," who wore flowered sundresses and too much makeup. As soon as the military men announced their intentions to confiscate the store, my father's friends said their good-byes and left. No one knows what happened exactly after that. The last they heard was Ricardo talking amicably with the *milicianos*, offering them a drink. Then, after a while, several shots rang out. When his friends rushed back to the store, Ricardo was bleeding from his chest, dying on the floor behind the counter. One of the *milicianos* was dead, and they could see a bullet hole had pierced the center of his forehead. The other was sprawled on the floor screaming and clutching his shattered knee. My father had shot them both. His aim was right on target the first time, but his trembling hand missed the second mark, and the soldier shot him before he went down. No one knows if it was regret that cost my father his life, but everyone agrees that he was a dead man anyway. He would have been executed, as were so many others who defied the government.

"Ramiro, I couldn't let them take your store," were the last words his friends heard my agonized father say.

Alejo's story did not ease the pain of my family's absences, but it explained my exile, Abuela's sacrifice, and her inability to open the door to too much truth. The dead man's family had threatened revenge. The episode had put my family in the bull's-eye of the Revolution and its frenzied supporters. Now I understood why Gabriel had been told that I was the daughter of an enemy of the Revolution.

Now I knew why Abuela had been so fearful of a return. Now I understood Ramiro's generosity with his money. All that was left was the mystery of my detachment from my mother. If only I could see the face of the woman who gave me life, perhaps I could put the past to rest.

"For that, we must find Lucía. She must be an old woman by now, but she was your mother's friend," Alejo said. "But I think you've had enough remembering for now."

Alejo and I seldom spoke of the past again, except to relish it in small moments of connection, when we came to know how similar we were, even though we had become adults so far away from each other. Alejo was the first person to read my poetry, and he fanned the flame of penning my passions. Despite all his sad songs he was a festive spirit, and we began to host get-togethers at my house for our ever-growing group of friends. Those nights always ended with someone on a guitar and Alejo singing. Then came the day when Alejo met and brought Gustavo into the circle. It wasn't long before we transferred the party permanently to Dos Gardenias, where José Antonio entered my life.

24

The Riverfront Hotel,
December 31, 2004
7 p.m.

When I rise from the bed at the Riverfront Hotel, I am in a fog. My head aches, and so do my limbs. My jaw and my chest feel tight. I struggle with my senses to confirm that I am alive. I do not know how long I have cried, nor for how long I have slept in the aftermath of my breakup with José Antonio. I draw back the curtains and confirm that the sun has set. It is night in Room 1701, and in my city as well, which is all lit up like Paris, I am alone. José Antonio did not return. I have to say it to believe it: I am alone. The only signs of life in the room are my breathing and the persistent flash of my silent cellular phone. I don't have to look to know that it is Alejo. After all, it's New Year's Eve and we're scheduled to open the show at Dos Gardenias to a sold-out crowd.

"Where the hell are you?" he screams into my ear when I pick up after one ring.

"I'm still at the Riverfront. I broke up with José Antonio, and I don't know, I lost track of time. I fell asleep crying and forgot to turn the cell phone back on."

"I've been to your house. I've called you fourteen times. I was worried."

"I'm sorry."

"Marisol, you have thirty minutes to get to the club. The tables are filling. It's going to be a full house. "

"I don't know if I can perform tonight, Alejo."

"What? Listen to me, woman, Rosario San Martín didn't raise a *pendeja*. You get out of that lousy hotel room, go home, take a shower, wear that hot black dress we agreed on, and the droopy earrings, and you get over here, and you use all that mess that the *doctorcito* and that *cabrón* of Gabriel have inspired, and you put it into the show."

"I don't know if I can . . ."

"You can and you will. You know what they say in show business, honey, the show must go on. Now hurry up, you blessed woman."

Without letting me say another word, Alejo hangs up, and I know that I must do what he says. I know that I can perform, and I know that I will. If there is anything I have learned about grief, it is that I have no vocation for self-pity. When I leave Room 1701, I slam the door as hard as José Antonio did, and it feels good. I ride down the elevator by myself, and I avoid the mirrors. No use in remembering the woman I am leaving behind. On my drive home, I look for the moon and cannot find it. That only tells me that it is perched above the water, luminous, as it always is in my Miami.

I try not to think as I jump in the shower. I just need to get through the night, plunk all I have into the words, make my performance as good as if it were my last. I surprise myself with that thought. Why would it be my last? But it helps me get through the shower, and the water restores my physical vigor. It is easier to get dressed. I'm not the kind of woman who obsesses over her wardrobe, not now that Gabriel and his judgments are out of my life, not since Alejo helped me settle on the wardrobe for our New Year's Eve show. I slip into the black dress, a slim fit that ends above the knee and has a subtle plunging neck. I think the rhinestone earrings and bracelet are too gaudy. If I'm going classic, I prefer subtle jewelry. If I'm casual, I prefer my hippie hoops. But I'm dressing for the job, and like Alejo struts around saying, "This is show business." What a hoot, I am now in show business.

The cell phone rings.

"Where the hell are you?"

"I'm walking out the door, I swear it."

Alejo hangs up.

It takes me a few minutes to drive to Dos Gardenias and park in the back behind Alejo's car. It is then that I realize I am not wearing any perfume, but it's too late to do anything about it. People come to hear me, not smell me, I tell myself. The second I walk in, I feel the energy of the music blaring from every corner of the dark club, and I wish I didn't have to perform. I just want to dance, lose myself in the rhythms of my music. People are already jamming the dance floor, shimmying to recordings of what I call the Cuban Top 40 Here, There, & Everywhere: Celia Cruz, Willy Chirino, Polo Montañez, Los Van Van—the dead and the living in a mélange of song. It used to be such a scandal to play Los Van Van in Miami, but few make a fuss anymore. Like Alejo says, everyone knows that Los Van Van are as *jodidos* as everyone else is in Cuba. I love Celia the best. The Queen of Salsa launched her career with "La Sonora Matancera," and in Dos Gardenias, Gustavo plays the old clips from yesteryear, followed by the glitzy video of her last big hit, "La Negra Tiene Tumbao," the one with the stately *mulata* strutting down the street, naked and awash in gold paint. The clips and videos play on the oversized screen in front of the dance floor, as if the dead were invited to the party. And they are. Joy fills the house.

I am soaking in the scene when an arm grabs me by the waist from behind, and I know it is my shadow.

"*¡Al fin!*"

"Let's go over the lineup, *muñeca*."

I manage a half smile.

"So you sent the old man to hell," Alejo says.

"I don't know what came over me, but being somebody's mistress is not my idea of a life. The rendezvous might be exciting for a moment, but you end up staining a lot of pillows with the runny mascara."

"And now you know," Alejo says. "Turn the page."

"All done."

"Then I guess I can give you the news. He canceled his reservation."

"José Antonio had a reservation?"

"He had booked the big table in the center, didn't you know?"

"Nope, he didn't tell me a thing."

"Maybe he was planning to surprise you, and you surprised him."

"I really didn't know what I was doing, Alejo, it wasn't premeditated."

"Whatever it was, it was good for you."

"It came out of nowhere, but it felt right."

"It was the light of your guardian angel."

"That it was."

Showtime.

It's a full house, indeed. Gustavo has no trouble filling José Antonio's table from the waiting list and walk-ins grateful to find a spot on New Year's Eve. Alejo comes out first, says a few words, introduces me, and I coax my best smile from my lips as I come onstage. We take our seats on the barstools, as a three-man band plays the first notes of Alejo's first song. It's a gala night and silver and white streamers hang from the ceiling. Tonight there's also a tall table behind us with two glasses of champagne to incorporate into the show, and I am grateful. I need the drink.

At first I only see his shoes, black leather, so shiny they blind you like sunlight on a mirror. Gabriel is sitting at the bar alone. He is wearing a tuxedo, his necktie undone, as if he had fled from a gala like a movie star being chased by paparazzi. He is staring at me. I pretend that I don't see him. I look past him, only to find Blas moonlighting behind the bar, helping the two regular bartenders. Blas smiles when our eyes meet, and I smile back, wink. I have a soft spot in my heart for him. Gabriel smiles, thinking I have smiled at him. I want to run, but instead I take a sip of my champagne. Alejo is singing "Dos Gardenias," the vintage bolero penned by the great Isolina Carrillo, and which gave Gustavo's club its name.

I am supposed to be longingly looking at Alejo while he sings, pretending it is me he is loving with the song, but I need another sip of champagne. Alejo croons: "*Dos gardenias para ti,*" "Two gardenias for you," I translate the lyrics in a fruitless effort to calm my nerves. I sip champagne, and I sip champagne, and I do not look at Gabriel, nor at Blas, nor at Alejo. I search the crowd with my eyes, and find a tall redhead leering at my neckline from a table. He will do. I focus my fake lust on him.

It's my turn now. I don't need to conjure the persona of femme fatale. I am her, Cuban-style.

On the bed of history
I slept,
intoxicated by your love,

the smell of you imprinted in my hair,
my lips hurting from your kisses.
I trembled,
I felt
as if your blood ran through my veins.

It was the wrong poem for the song, and Alejo gives me a hypocritical smile that tells me he wants to kill me. I know it is the wrong poem, but I cannot deliver the other, "When You Come Home," with Gabriel sitting there, looking at me with desire in his eyes. Alejo tells the crowd the old story about Cuba and Mexico and their golden era of boleros, and he says that on this night of endings and new beginnings, he wants to sing one of his favorites, "Mucho Corazón," or "A Lot of Heart," by the lovely *mejicana* Emma Elena Valdelamar. Bolstered by the lyrics of a woman who confesses that she did not need a reason to love, only a lot of heart, I deliver the poem I wrote for Gabriel when I still had hope.

When you come home,
I want to unfreeze my heart,
awaken my pale skin to your touch,
hear you say "me vuelves loco" *when we make love.*
When you come home,
I want to forget the absences,
the anguish caused by other names,
the years wasted,
the journeys untraveled.

When you come home,
I want to live with you,

marry you,
die with you,
have our ashes spread
over the waters of Government Cut on a windy autumn night.

Today, I wanted to tell you that when you come home,
I will be here.
But you did not hear me,
and my words fell into the hollow abyss of your memory,
and my fatigue.

When I end my poem, Alejo begins to sing "Júrame," or "Swear to Me," and I see Blas serving Gabriel another drink. Their interaction seems to be taking longer than necessary. They are talking, and I am getting more nervous. I drink more champagne. Alejo jokes with the crowd, midsong, that I am celebrating early, and asks Blas to walk over and refill my glass. People clap and egg me on. I raise my glass in a toast. They raise theirs. Alejo has managed to avert another disaster. Give him a microphone and a stage and he can turn anything around. We finish the show on another high, with Alejo urging the crowd to get up and dance to "Lágrimas Negras," as he grabs me and dances a few steps with me. Only Cubans could write a song so dark and so upbeat at the same time. "Okay, *gente*, time to party! A Happy New Year to you!"

The crowd breaks into applause, and Alejo and I hold hands and bow, thank them. We leave the stage waving, and I blow a kiss into the air. I am relieved. I am sure of it now. This will be my last performance. New Year, New Life. I don't know why yet, but it feels like good-bye. When we are alone in the back, Alejo and I hug. We always hug, but this one feels tighter, as if we needed to reassure ourselves of the connection more than ever.

"You had me a little worried there with the champagne," he says.

"It was either that or run. Did you see that? Gabriel and Blas, both of them looking at me, talking. All that was left was for José Antonio to walk in!"

"I knew they were both here, but I didn't want to tell you before the show."

I punch him in the arm.

"Traitor."

"No, savior."

"Now what?"

"You decide. What do you want to do? Where do you want to be at midnight?"

"Not here," I say. "I know it sounds preposterous, but the only thing I want to do tonight is talk to my grandmother. She's the only ghost with whom I want to commune," I say. "Maybe I should go home."

"Don't turn around now," Alejo says to me, and grabs my arm. "Just follow me, and don't look back."

I don't need to turn around. As we exit the club, from the corner of my eye I see the blinding shine of black leather shoes behind us.

Alejo whisks me into the back office, locks the door. I grab my purse instinctively, and we take a side exit to the parking lot. "The key?" he asks. He walks me to my car, opens the door for me, then walks around, sits behind the wheel, and drives off. When we turn the corner, I see Gabriel wandering the parking lot.

"Where are we going?

"We are going to see Lucía," he says. "You are ready now."

Alejo tells me he found Lucía three months ago. He was going to tell me when I began my relationship with José Antonio. Lucía wants to see me, he says. He parks at a peach-colored duplex in a Little Havana street with a yellow sign that warns "No Outlet." I am trembling when he opens my door, helps me out of the car, and walks me to the door. He rings the doorbell, and as soon as he does, an old woman in a peasant skirt and embroidered blouse opens the door. Alejo greets her, kissing her on the cheek.

"Lucía, this is Marisol. She is ready to see you."

The woman embraces me as if she had known me all of her life, which she says she has. When my mother was pregnant, Lucía tells me, she rubbed an egg around my mother's belly to ward off the evil eye from the life growing in her womb, to protect me.

"*Hija mía*, I have been waiting for you for so many years."

Alejo interrupts to tell us that he needs to return to the club, but he will return for me when we are done. He drives off in my car. It is past eleven, and I realize that unless this visit is short, I am going to greet thc New Year here. Lucía seems happy to have company. It is as if she had been expecting me. She wants to know about my life. Alejo told her some things when he recently visited, she says, but she wants to hear it all from me. I give her the highlights, and she tells me with a certainty I cannot help but envy, "That man, the one with the shiny shoes, will always be your shadow. But that is all he is, a shadow. We all have our shadows. Do not fear him. Just let him go."

Next, she speaks of Blas.

"The young one with the gifted but trembling hand, he has another path. Some people are only meant to be in our lives for a little while. His time in yours has past."

"And what is my path?" I ask.

"Come, sit with me at the table, and we will find out."

Lucía gives me a yellow pad, and she instructs me to be prepared to take notes when she tells me to. She grabs a deck of Tarot cards and begins to shuffle them, cut them into three bundles. I am feeling queasy, but I try to focus on her reassuring words once she has spread the cards on the table. They do not speak to me, but they do to Lucía.

"Your path is across the seas, your future is in a trip, your happiness will come from your pen, from papers. I see paper and photographs and flowers in your future."

Lucía says that I must make an offering to Yemayá, my protector, and she will guide me on this journey.

"You are the daughter of Yemayá," Lucía says.

And me, all this time, all these years that my heart's been in captivity, I've been praying to Ochún, my *virgencita* de la Caridad, lighting candles to her on my knees, asking her to bring me back the wayward man who taught me to love, who made me believe in love long after I had discounted the possibility of its existence. But it is Yemayá, the motherly deity, and its Catholic equivalent, la Virgen de Regla, who has been watching over me.

"I have been praying to the wrong saint all these years?"

"Ay, *mi hija*, they work together. You are the daughter of both Ochún and Yemayá. They both protect you and your house. You are the daughter of a land of crossing rivers and abundant sea. Ochún is the deity of love, the flirt. Yemayá is the mother figure. You are both, you need both."

I do not understand the mysteries, but in the strangest way, it all makes sense to me. Next, Lucía says that I need a cleansing.

"You have a deep hurt, a deep wound, and you need to pray for healing," she says.

She asks me to write down on the yellow pad a ritual that I will perform at daybreak for nine consecutive days. I must line up in my bedroom nine small glasses filled with water in sets of three. Every morning, I am to pick up one of the glasses, pour the water over my shoulders, and make the same invocation: "As water cleanses all, so it will wash away my pain, in the name of the Holy Spirit."

She also tells me to put seven sunflowers on a tray, take it outside at daybreak, and facing the sun, I must pray, "As you rise in the mornings, so will I rise from my pain. As you shine on the world, so will I shine in my work, in wisdom, in love. And as you fall each day, so will my enemies."

The end of the prayer frightens me a little. I don't have enemies, I think. But Lucía has left the room and she returns with a bowl. She hands it to me and says, "One more thing."

I take the bowl, but I become so spooked by what I see inside—it looks like blood—that I drop it on her white tiled floor. The bowl shatters and blood splatters everywhere. I begin to scream. I don't want to, but I begin to scream.

25

"She tried to kill me.

"She almost killed me."

I am screaming to Lucía, yet it is not me, it is another who is speaking the words. It all comes back clearly, the memory of that day in Limonar with my mother. A part of me wants to put it back where it was, but something has been uprooted inside of me. I can feel the tears spilling faster than I can wipe them from my face, and I feel an overwhelming need to clean up the mess I've made on Lucía's clean floor. I want to clean and run. I rip the papers from the yellow pad, drop to my knees, and start to cover the red liquid. I clean the mess and I wipe my tears with the back of my hand, and I don't realize that I am staining my face red. For a moment, I think I am in a nightmare. But I am awake, I am crying, and I am remembering, and I know I need to remember. I can no longer shove the memories away, as I have for so many years. I am not dreaming, and all of it comes to me with the force of an instant, in an unplanned, horrible instant. I remember. I remember it all. I remember her. I remember the ghost of him that never was. I remember how I paid the price for his absence.

The day we went to the Lemon Grove, Mami visited an *espiritista*, a medium who claimed to rouse the dead from the grave and bring them before the living. At first Mami left me outside, sitting on the porch, and she went into the dark house, such a strange house for a street that smelled of sweet jasmine. I sat on the rocking chair in the porch and tried to imitate the proper ladies of Limonar. I crossed my legs, tried to grip the rocking chair with both hands, but it was not comfortable. I folded my hands into each other, pushed my body forward, and rocked. I liked the way my hands looked folded, so elegant, and I imagined my fingernails painted torrid red like Mami's before Papi left us. Mami's nails were always manicured in the most beautiful shade of sexy scarlet. She accented the polish with *lunitas*, a half-moon design at the very top of the nail, and she finished the ends with a curvy, glossy white edge. Her lipstick always matched her nails. I thought she was the most beautiful woman on earth.

I was thinking all this when I heard the voices coming from inside the house.

"Ricardo, present yourself. Your wife is here," the *espiritista* said.

"Ricardo! Ricardo! I am here. Come to me, my love," I heard my mother beg. "Come to me."

"I can feel him. I can feel him," the old woman mumbled.

Then I heard Mami's voice again, rising, anguished, as if she herself were in the grave. "Are you here? Are you here, Ricardo? Speak to me. Speak to me, Ricardo."

Mami's pitch rose above the *espiritista*'s. She wanted to talk to the dead. But her beloved was not listening. Her voice was angry now, like when they fought about his overnight trips.

"Ricardo, I command you to listen to me."

The medium tried to soothe her.

"Graciela, the dead must feel peace to communicate with us. Be still."

There was silence for a while.

"He must feel your love," the medium said calmly. "He loves you more than anything in the world and he wants you to be well."

There was silence for a while, but suddenly I heard a chair fall to the floor. I jumped as if I had heard thunder. I wanted to get up and see, but I couldn't manage to move my shoulders. Only my hands felt free. I clutched one of the rectangular arms of the rocking chair, and it felt clammy, as if it were a living thing.

I could hear my mother's cries.

"*!Te odio, te odio!* You hear me, I hate you, you son-of-a-bitch. I hate you."

I heard another chair crash inside, and Mami burst through the door. She came out to the porch, her curls undone and looking like she had lost something very precious. She scooped me up from the rocking chair and pushed me back through the door. The room was very dark. I only remember the orange shutters, the old round mahogany table and the cane-backed chairs around it. There were three chairs upright, and two strewn on the floor. A crumpled picture of Papi, like the one Abuela kept on the wall above a vase filled with fresh white roses, lay on the table near the medium.

The *espiritista* wore a white gown and a red hibiscus over her right ear. She looked pale, thin. She sat to the left of Mami, slowly chewing on the stub of a homemade cigar. When Mami brought me into the room, the medium looked me up and down. She was an old woman with many wrinkles. They flowed from every bit of her left uncovered by the white dress, which was made of frail cotton, sleeveless, and came down below her knees.

I looked at the old woman for a long time, and she stared back at me.

"She's a beautiful child," she said.

She seemed to be speaking to someone else, not my mother, but she was looking at me.

Then she shook her head and told my mother, "No, Graciela, do not do this to the child, do not offer the child. That is not necessary."

My mother looked dazed.

"*Sí*," she said. "*Sí*, he loves her, he loves her more. It is she he loves and not me."

Mami took me by the shoulders and turned me around to a darker corner of the room.

"*Mírala, mírala*, Ricardo, here she is," Mami screamed at the air, at nothing, nothing at all, shaking my thin shoulders like the madwoman she had become. "Look at her, look at her. Is that what you wanted, your precious little girl?

"Come back to me, Ricardo, come back!" she yelled to no one.

With each scream, I could hear a rawness overtaking her throat, as her hands gripped my shoulders harder and harder.

I looked back, wanting to escape her grip, but then I saw her tears.

"*Vuelve, vuelve*," she moaned until she no longer had words.

Vuelve.

Then came the silence. The sudden silence was worse. My head hurt. I closed my eyes, and at first I felt relief. A warm breeze embraced my waist, and I felt hands cradling my neck. At first it felt comforting. The last thing I felt was the overwhelming tightness. I don't remember her hands taking me so close to death. I don't remember them closing in on my throat, tighter and tighter, squeezing, squeezing until the townspeople—*las chismosas* in their rocking chairs, *los trabajadores* toiling in red earth, the *abuelas* and the *tías* nursing the young—all of them rushing into the house with the sweet smell of jasmine outside, and the rancor of death inside.

All of them rushed in just in time to pry me loose from the hands of the woman who gave me life.

When I woke up, I was in a hospital, and from there I was taken to Abuela's house, and I did not see my mother again until I turned ten and she came to my birthday party, my last birthday in Cuba. She no longer looked like the mother I'd had, and she did not seem to recognize me. As for Papi, he never returned. I was not allowed to ask about him, but sometimes I couldn't help myself. I was a curious girl despite the chains around me. In the beginning, after Papi died and Mami was carted away to the psychiatric hospital Mazorra, I nagged Abuela day and night. "*Where is Papi? Where is Papi?*" I would say over and over again until I drove her from the house in tears. *¿Dónde?* His memory, however, faded like lost hope, little by little, day by day, night by night, but deep in my heart I waited for him to come home. I never asked Abuela anymore, and for many years, for a lifetime, I could not remember what happened that day in the Lemon Grove of red dirt streets and fruitless trees. I did not want to remember. It could not be love, the madness of it all. It could not be love to leave a daughter for a ghost. All of my yearnings came to this: What I wanted so badly was to have a mother, a mother so strong she could love me more than she loved her man.

Lucía tells me that now that I know, now that I remember, I can go in peace, live my life, realize my dreams. She has only one last thing to tell me, she says. The *espiritista* who robbed my mother of her last shred of sanity was Lucía's mother.

"Forgive us," Lucía says. "No one knew how truly affected your mother was by your father's death. All we wanted to do was help her."

I know Lucía is sincere. I know she has waited a long time to unburden her family, as long as I have waited to learn the truth. She tells me not to worry about the mess on her floor. The red potion has served its purpose.

"Go live your life, my child, and be happy," Lucía tells me at the door, before she kisses my cheek. "You were born to be a free spirit, to roam this earth like a butterfly."

Alejo drives me home in my car, and Gustavo follows him in his car. I tell them I am exhausted and kiss them both good night. I am home, and for a long while I sit on Abuela's old rocking chair, another transplant from Cuba purchased on Calle Ocho as soon as she could afford it. She loved to sit in front of the black and white TV on her chair and watch her *telenovelas*. *Corazón salvaje*, *Wild Heart*, was her all-time favorite soap opera, and mine too. I sit in Abuela's rocking chair and I have a long-overdue conversation with her about the past and the future. "I need to leave, *viejita*. I want to leave. We were happy here, and I am so grateful for everything you were to me, but the world is so big and beautiful, Abuela. I want to see it all." For the first time in my life I am sure that she approves.

It is past midnight, and I want to glance at the New Year's moon, wish her a happy one. I always want to see the moon. I walk out the back door, and what I see is the Angel's Trumpet in full bloom. I remember when Abuela warned me that it is a very beautiful but poisonous flower, and that I must not touch it, pick up its flowers, and bring them close to me. The Angel's Trumpet hangs from its mother bush upside down. It looks like a bell with its girlish pink petals facing downward as if they wanted to swallow, to suck in all of Earth. When the Angel's Trumpet is in full bloom, as I see it now, it is breathtakingly celestial, and if you look hard enough, close enough, and with some imagination, you can almost see the angels circling the tree, reaching for their instruments. I learned to love it from afar.

And now that I know all that I know, I want to sleep in the embrace of the fine white veil of my childhood, perfumed by the scent of Russian Violets, in the company of ghosts who no longer haunt me. I settle into bed and pray. *Sleep, come to me, whisk me to the Other World.* I pray and I pray, and white shadows call out to me, "*mar y sol, mar y sol,*" and familiar hands reach out to smooth the covers over me. I see Mami without tears rocking on her wicker chair. Papi smiles and says he loves me. Abuela runs her fingers through my hair and whispers to the wind, "*Pídele perdón a Papá Dios. Pídele perdón a Papá Dios.*"

And I do. I ask Papá Dios for forgiveness, and he parts the veil. I see my mother's face. She looks like me.

When I wake up, it is past noon on New Year's Day 2005. I am joyful and at peace, ready to embark on a new life. I find my largest suitcase, and I pack for a long trip, for all four seasons: my favorite clothes, my black leather winter jacket, my boots, my favorite sneakers and sandals, the black dress I wore last night, my photo of Abuela and the old ones in the storage box of my parents, my poetry journals. Once more, I shutter up my little house in the bosom of Cuban Miami. Behind the house, in the potted bromeliad, I leave Alejo my key. On the living room coffee table, next to the Cuban art books, I leave Alejo two letters, one to send to the museum director, and another addressed to him. I take a taxi to the airport, and buy a ticket on the seven o'clock flight to Paris.

ESSENCE

26

Paris, France
2005

For the first few weekends without me, Alejo sang his boleros alone, and in the process, revamped his repertoire. He now opens the show with "Alma con alma," or "Soul to Soul," and performs with the three-man band every weekend, ending with a new, upbeat arrangement to "Lágrimas Negras" to which people get up and dance. I can clearly imagine my people dancing with joy to their black tears. During his first Friday night without me, Alejo entertained the crowd with musings about how I had fled to Paris to become a famous poet, and he had a lot of fun making French jokes at my expense. At first, he tells me, the regulars asked about me, and once, José Antonio came alone after the show and asked as well. Gabriel has moved to Los Angeles, and Blas, who became a full-time bartender at Dos Gardenias, is preparing for his debut solo show. They miss me, Alejo says. But Miami is a city of transients, a cradle of first refuge, and the forgetting is inevitable as people move on. Everyone is replaceable. Alejo has found another groove to his days, his union with Gustavo blessed by the *orishas*, as evidenced by the photo he sent me of the striking painting of Ochún, the goddess of love, that he and Gustavo hung in my old living room, which is now theirs. Our little house is being showered with nothing but *aché*, I assure Abuela in our talks, which are long and devoid of secrets now. "*Aché pa' ti, Marisol*," she wishes me. I know Abuela likes my new life. *Aché* in Yoruba means good luck, and that spirit traveled to the island with a people uprooted and transplanted, and all of us, their heirs, the new pilgrims, carry it with us like a chant of hope.

Hope is the most valuable of emotions. Alejo refused to resign himself to performing alone and auditioned a Cuban actress who dabbled in theater in Havana and fled the island via Buenos Aires after marrying an Argentine. A divorce later, she ended up in Miami and on the doorstep of Dos Gardenias. She brings to Alejo's show a new repertoire of poetry by the Cuban greats of yesterday and today, a mélange of poets still on the island and also exiled. When I saw the photographs of their act, I knew that I had been well replaced. The woman wore her black hair tied back in a tight bun, and she had a dramatic flair about her, as if she were the very incarnation of Evita Perón, or of Abuela. I knew then that Miami had a new resident ghost, and I had Paris.

Paris is now my home, and this city fits me like no other. In this habitat of frolicking spirits and state-of-mind affairs, neither my losses nor my sins feel as heavy when I wander through neighborhoods, partake in the café culture, stroll the stately gardens like the butterfly I hope to be until I can wander no more. In this capital of the world, I feel like I belong. I am not perceived as exotic, although it is not so easy to define me, and the French, like everyone else, are always searching for definitions. But they understand passion and perfumes, ambivalence and detours, pauses and one-page loves, excesses but never regrets. *Vive la différence. Liberté.*

By French standards, my life has been well lived, and I can't help but chuckle at what my new French friends find to disapprove of in my multiple personality. When I counsel against affairs, my last ride on the elevator of the Riverfront Hotel coming back to me with all that flash of brass, they chastise me for being a prudish American. Or worse yet, they think me a slovenly American given my penchant for canvassing the city in sneakers, the quintessential fashion faux pas. On my Cuban days, when the island is the subject around the dinner table or when I am invited to recite my poetry at the cavernous American Center across the Seine, the French complain that I am too elegiac to be Cuban, as their idea of the island is that of a tropical paradise of oversexed *timba* dancers, hips in full throttle. I tell them that Cuba is like a betrayed woman nursing wounds so deep she cannot love again.

"Dramatic!" chimes in my friend Camille, a divorcée who wears a pixie haircut and designer ensembles and works three-month stints in the linen department of Galeries Lafayette to save money to travel to her next destination. Camille dreams of jetting to San Francisco, and I have not been able to talk her into escaping to Miami. I do miss Miami, and I amuse my French friends quoting my favorite epithets for my first adoptive city. "Oh, you mean the Independent Republic of Miami," I joke. Or, "Yes, I was raised in Cuba's largest metropolitan area outside of Havana." Truth is, in my heart, Cuba and Miami will always be one. Perhaps someday it can be as well for the rest of the world. Once the wounds of history are healed, Cuba will breathe the freshness of freedom and Miami will stand as what she is, a beacon of hope and refuge.

But Paris is my home now, and I love it with the passion I reserve for the most exquisite of scents. I cannot fully explain why my spirit soars here, but it does. Perhaps it is because from Paris, the world seems accessible, and my nostalgia, conjured by the faintest scent of the perfumes I've worn and the new fragrances I explore, acquires an expanded geography. Living in Paris is like finding the perfect perfume.

The most intriguing fragrances inhabit every corner of this city, but like the good Cuban that I am, sometimes I can't help but glance back. When the remembrances overwhelm me, I walk into any of the perfumeries dotting every neighborhood and I ask the salesclerk to let me try on one of my old scents: Pleasures. White Linen. Miracle. Habanita. Most of the time, they have them all, and I select one for the day. I let the salesgirl spray on me a tester dose, and I walk around for hours smelling of my past, remembering, making peace, forgiving, and sometimes forgetting again. But that is as far as my travels to the past take me. Those scents no longer fit. There is no return.

One day, while on a trek to Montparnasse, the heart of intellectual and artistic life in Paris in Picasso's time, I spot in a window a pretty yellow bottle with a bow tie around the top. The moment I hold the bottle, I can smell the gardenias, Abuela's favorite flower, and mine. Then I see the name: Essence. I spray the fragrance on my cleavage with gusto, inhale, and it is mine. I walk out into the subtle sunshine of spring with my purchase, and I am so infatuated, I lose my sense of direction. I am lost.

I am standing on a busy corner, look-alike cafés and stores around me, all of it too similar for me to decide on a direction. I see a man park his motorcycle in the tiniest spot, and when he starts to stash away his helmet, I approach him.

"*Parlez-vous anglais?*" I ask, going for my best French accent.

"Yes, I speak English," he says.

"I'm sorry to bother you, but I've managed to get myself lost. Can you help?"

"No bother," he says. "Where do you want to go?"

"It's not so much where I want to go. What I need to know is where I am, so I can place myself on my map."

"That's a new one," he says with a laugh.

"What do you mean?"

He extends his hand.

"I'm Claude," he says.

I shake his hand.

"I'm Marisol."

There is an awkward pause, and we are distracted by a group of American tourists crossing the street en masse and barreling toward us. One of their overloaded backpacks swings into me, pushing me into Claude. He catches my fall, and then breaks into one sneeze after another.

"Achoo! Achoo! Achoo!"

He cannot stop.

"It's your perfume," Claude says. "I am allergic to perfumes."

I smile the widest smile of my life and I invite Claude to sit with me and enjoy a cappuccino. "Not to worry," I quickly add. "I am going to the bathroom first to wash off my perfume."

He laughs.

"Don't," he says. "We'll work it out."

As we claim a table for two outside, I imagine Claude and I

making love in my tiny apartment, which is full of fragrant flowers and candles, and he sneezing his way to climax. He tells me I have the most mischievous smile he has ever seen, and I think about how grand love is, as grand as freedom.

With Claude and his allergies and a new life in Paris, I no longer need bottled fragrances. I prefer to buy a bouquet of sunflowers or pink tulips or blue hydrangeas and an international calling card, walk to one of the glass-enclosed telephones on a quiet stretch of the tree-lined Champs-Élysées, and call my beloved Alejo as I admire the spring scents of Paris.

"*Bonjour, monsieur,*" I tease him in a throaty delivery of my French accent, newly acquired in an immersion course at Paris Langues.

"*De que culé que sé,*" he says, pretending that the gibberish, delivered in his thick Cuban accent, is French. "*Como ta le vú?*"

It's only a greeting, and I am already laughing with the heartiest pleasure. As Alejo relishes telling me the latest gossip, I begin to mentally plot his trip to Paris. Alejo has never been to Paris, but I know one day in spring, on his birthday, he will stroll these streets with me.

I am here to stay. I no longer desire to live in the shackles of history, nor to wage the battles of lost causes. There is no forgetting the past, and perhaps I do have an obligation to remember it, but to dwell in its grip is suicide. The red earth of Matanzas, the soft sands of Varadero, the royal palms rising from the Yumurí will always be the home of my soul. And Havana, she, the pearl, the beacon, the incomparable, will forever remain in my dreams, a distant chimera of boulevards and *callejones* I don't yet know. She, waiting, like a woman who has lost in love. Me, waiting, like a woman in love. Someday, I will stroll the streets of La Habana, and at Prado and Neptuno I will conjure the glory of the republic, and salute the ghosts. Oh yes I will. I know this. Someday Havana also will stamp my soul, and I will claim her as my own. But for now I have Paris.

EPILOGUE

News Report from the Miami Standard, *picked up by the wires and published in the* International Herald Tribune, *Paris Edition:*

> MIAMI—The historic Miami Riverfront Hotel was demolished Sunday to make way for a new development of luxury high-rises on the waterfront property. As crews cleared the debris, remains of what had been a sacred Tequesta temple were found. Preservationists called a halt to the construction. Developers opposed it and offered a compromise: A monument to the Tequestas will be built at the site, the sculpture of a man and a woman in perpetual prayer to the sun and the sea.

From a letter mailed from Miami to Paris, and forwarded from address to address until it was received, the envelope stained and crumpled, at 3 rue Gît-le-Coeur, steps from the Seine:

> My dearest Marisol,
>
> *To have you was a privilege, to love you was easy, instant. To forget you will be impossible. I accept your decision to leave with a broken but grateful heart for the time we spent together. Please forgive my cowardice. It is too late for me, but for you, life is just beginning.*
>
> *Yours always,*
>
> José Antonio

*O*F TRUTH AND SPIRITS

If I were to tell the truth,
I would say that these words were written not by me
but by a spirit from beyond,
un espíritu que se encarnó,
a spirit who took flesh in my heart,
a translated spirit like me who crossed the waters.
These kinds of spirits dwell in the soul of an island's people,
even when the people have left the island never to return.
I did not write these words,
this story,
in the disciplined way that writers write,
with the first light of day, or under the quiet embrace of night.
No, not I.
These words came from another world
and in their own time.
For more than we know,
la isla arrastra,
The Island calls,
as true love always does.

ACKNOWLEDGMENTS

The production of a book is like the staging of an opera. Those who enjoy the work seldom see the cast behind the scenes, and *Reclaiming Paris* had a magical troupe: editor extraordinaire Johanna Castillo, who saw the novelist in me when I was trying to quiet her, Judith Curr, Amy Tannenbaum, Michael Selleck, Christine Duplessis, Gary Urda, Kathleen Schmidt, Sue Fleming, Elizabeth Garriga, and the rest of the team at Atria Books and Simon & Schuster. Writers only get one debut novel, and *Reclaiming Paris* couldn't have found a better home than with you. Equal amounts of gratitude go to my agent Thomas Colchie, a talent I long admired before this collaboration, and to his leading lady, Elaine, whose keen observations and encouragement made this a better book. Johanna, Tom, and Elaine, I thank you for making this an unforgettable journey.

To my family and friends on both sides of the Florida Straits and scattered around the world, my gratitude for the cariño, memories, and support. I could not have written this novel without the spirited wisdom of my cousin Amelio García, professor of literature, crooner of boleros, and soul mate. To my daughters, Tanya, Marissa, and Erica Wragg, my thanks for enduring my absences and for showering my life with joy. A special thanks to Tanya, the writer in the trio and my first reader, and her husband, Michael Wallace, photographer and website designer, for the technological and creative expertise.

Most of all, I want to thank my parents, Olga and Teodoro Santiago, who left everything they loved behind so that I could be a free woman.

RECLAIMING PARIS

FABIOLA SANTIAGO

A Readers Club Guide

Synopsis

In this debut novel, a young Cuban-American woman explores her life and relationships, each major era defined by a different perfume. From her early childhood in the midst of the Cuban revolution, through her college years in Iowa and her adult life in vibrant, changing Miami, Marisol finds passionate love and great loss, each moment leading her to a greater understanding of her culture, her family, and herself as a woman.

Questions and Topics for Discussion

1. Marisol recollects switching perfumes whenever a significant shift has occurred in her life. In what ways do you think relationships are like scents? Can you relate to associating different scents with different periods of your life?

2. Discuss the important relationships in Marisol's life. How does each romance fulfill her and fail her? How does each man help her to work out her identity as a Cuban-American?

3. How is Marisol's immigrant experience different from the experiences of Cubans from Havana? Why does she feel conflicted about her connection to Cuba? How do you think it changes Marisol's perspective to discover how her father died?

4. The narrative of *Reclaiming Paris* is organized around important eras in Marisol's life, structured nonchronologically. How does the progression of anecdotes mirror Marisol's own thoughts in the "present day"? Do you think the novel would have been different if you had known the truth of Marisol's childhood from the beginning?

5. Explore the poetry at the end of each section. What added emotional truths are revealed by the poems that cannot be expressed in prose? How do you think Marisol's life and journey of self-discovery are enhanced by her becoming a poet?

6. Why does Gabriel change so dramatically after moving to the United States? Do you think he was always self-absorbed and superficial, or did he lose something by losing his identification with Cuba?

7. In what ways is Alejo an ideal friend for Marisol? What does he provide for her that none of her romantic relationships are able to?

8. How has her mother's great betrayal unconsciously affected Marisol's life? Why does it take Marisol so long to acknowledge what happened? How is she healed by remembering?

9. Do you think that in moving from Miami to Paris, Marisol lessens her identification with her background? Why do you think she's happiest after letting go of her history? Do you think she'll truly give up perfume for Claude? What would that mean?

10. Discuss the meaning of the title, which refers both to the French capital and to Havana, the "Paris of the Caribbean." What does it mean to Marisol to be able to reclaim Paris, both in terms of romance and in terms of her love and hope for Cuba?

Tips to Enhance Your Book Club

1. Curious about the scents described in *Reclaiming Paris*? Sample each of the featured perfumes. Bring along your own favorite fragrances, too, and share what you associate with the scents in your own lives.

2. Spice up your meeting with Cuban food and dessert. The *picadillo* Marisol makes for her friends in Iowa is a staple dish and easy to prepare, as are the *merenguitos* Marisol's grandmother lovingly roasted in her kitchens in Miami and Matanzas. Find the recipes at reclaimingparis.com.

3. For more information on the author, her essays and articles, and upcoming projects, visit her website at fabiolasantiago.com.

A Conversation with Fabiola Santiago

What inspired you to write a first novel in the midst of a successful career as an essayist and journalist?

I began writing fiction in the early 1990s as a way of expanding and honing my writing skills, and of exploring the complexities of Miami, its history, and its people beyond the confines of nonfiction. The *Miami Herald*'s esteemed Sunday magazine, *Tropic*, published my first two short stories, "The Spy" and "Seatmate." I also wrote children's stories for my daughters, and *Highlights for Children* published "Citizen Carmen," the tale of a Cuban girl struggling to learn English. But my journalism career was so high-charged and motherhood so all-consuming that I couldn't devote serious and consistent time to fiction. Still, I wrote on weekends, on vacation, whenever I ended up with hours of leisure. Everywhere I went, I carried a notebook. When my home became an almost empty nest, the characters of *Reclaiming Paris* filled the empty spaces. Marisol, her men, her grandmother, and Alejo became my everyday companions.

How did you begin your career as a journalist?

Three weeks after I came to the *Miami Herald* as an intern from the University of Florida, the Mariel boat lift of 1980 began, bringing to our shores 125,000 Cubans in five months. An account of the arrival of a group of unaccompanied teenage boys who had left a party in Havana and sought refuge in the Peruvian embassy was my first front-page story. I still get goose bumps thinking about that story. While the *Herald* had great reporters, most of them could not speak Spanish or fully appreciate the nuances of Cuban culture, and so as a twenty-one-year-old I was thrust into a big story in which I was one of the few journalists who could interview the protagonists. Since then, the essence of my best stories has always come from people who lived the history—the protagonists—not from official sources or documents. I played the same role during the rafter crisis of 1994 when thousands of Cuban families were sent to refugee camps in Guantánamo.

Like Marisol, you were born in Matanzas a few months after the revolution. How closely did you identify with your protagonist? How much of her story is pulled from your own?

The novel deals with what happens privately within the framework of history. I "borrowed" from my life the historical chronology and I gave Marisol my birthplace because I longed to write about my beloved Matanzas. As a child exiled from her land and loves, I also identify with the feelings of loss and rebirth Marisol experiences, and happily so, with her wanderlust! Surely, I've had my share of interesting love affairs, but my life is defined by my marriage of twelve years to a wonderful man who was my college sweetheart and remains my friend, by being the mother of three daughters, by my career in journalism, and by the close relationship I have with my parents, my brother, and his family.

Poetry plays an important role in *Reclaiming Paris*. Have you always written poetry?

Yes, in sixth grade I wrote in my notebooks love poems to "Bruce," a teacher I adored. In adolescence, I wrote poems in my diary about Cuba and my grandmother to deal with those great losses. Although my writing language of choice is English, I pen poetry mostly in Spanish, and even poems that end up in English began as first drafts in Spanish. I love languages, and poetry is an unrestricted playground for words. Poetry, however, is still something I prefer to write only for myself, as Cubans like to say, "*para la gaveta,*" to keep in a drawer, under lock and key. You could say that when I let Marisol roam the house, she found the key.

The novel explores the new sort of identity formed by Cubans raised in the United States. Do you think it's important to remain actively connected to your background? How do you pass this heritage on to your daughters?

In Miami, Cuban culture is considered mainstream, so it's not difficult or unusual to remain connected to your roots. It happens simply by existing, and my daughters spent their after-school hours in my parents' Cuban home. Language and cultural knowledge are assets, and my parents and I made an effort to speak to my daughters in Spanish when they were little so that they would grow up to be bilingual, and they are. When asked about their background, my daughters always say they're Cuban because that's their closest cultural affinity, but they're half Cuban and, via their paternal grandparents, a quarter Japanese and a quarter English, with a dash of Irish and Welsh. I've traveled a great deal and consider myself a citizen of the world, and encourage my daughters to connect to people through our common humanity. I want them to be free to be whoever they want to be.

You mention several literary influences in *Reclaiming Paris*. Which authors and poets do you consider the most inspirational to your life and work?

The literary influences in my life and work are a mosaic, and representative of the different stages in my life, and they include those referenced in *Reclaiming Paris*, but there's a richer mosaic. The beautiful verses of José Martí were my lullabies, the slim *novelitas* of Corín Tellado in *Vanidades* magazine nursed my romantic adolescent heart, and in high school and college, I was riveted by the literature of the South, particularly Flannery O'Connor's short stories, Tom Wolfe's *Bonfire of the Vanities*, and Maya Angelou's *I Know Why the Caged Bird Sings*. I gobbled up the books of contemporary American women like Alice Walker and Anne Tyler, enthralled by how they turned intimacies into great novels. It was not until I became a journalist working in Miami that I began to read Latin American literature, seriously and in Spanish. My first love was *Boquitas pintadas* (Painted Lips) by Manuel Puig, an extraordinary Argentine storyteller who used journalistic devices, such as press releases, newspaper accounts, and letters, interlaced with narrative to tell the story of life in provincial Argentina. The epilogue of *Reclaiming Paris* is a tribute to him.

You describe the hopeful atmosphere in the Cuban-American community after the fall of the Soviet empire. Do you think those hopes have returned with the current Cuban political climate in transition?

Unfortunately, no. Although there are indications of some change in Cuba, as of this writing, it seems to be only cosmetic. This second regime by a Castro brother has not translated into freedom of speech, freedom of assembly, the release from prison of independent journalists and peaceful dissidents, or open multiparty elections. Any positive change is welcomed, of course, but the hope that real freedom would ring for Cubans, so pure and ebullient in 1989 when the Soviet empire collapsed, has not returned. There is still hope, though. Cubans always say, "*Lo último que se pierde es la esperanza.*" The last thing you lose is hope.

***Reclaiming Paris* is written in English, with Spanish phrases sprinkled throughout. Was it challenging to write a bilingual narrative for an English-speaking readership, since the two languages flow together naturally for you?**

Language is musical, and when I'm writing I'm in a trance and the words flow and find their place. When the Spanish words find their way into my English narrative and when I let them stay in my final draft, they are there for a reason, sometimes to convey a sense of place, sometimes emotion. A few remain simply because I like them an awful lot; they strike the right note to my Miami ear.

The novel is structured around different perfumes signifying new life changes and relationships. Do you also connect perfumes to certain periods of your life, or did this theme come from your imagination?

Like Marisol, I also have a penchant for collecting poetic scents, and when all else fails, I change my perfume to recharge my life with a little inspiration. I think my relationship to perfumes goes way back to when I left Cuba on a Freedom Flight in 1969. I had to leave behind people and things I loved dearly, and I carried with me only three mementos: a doll lost in the labyrinth of early exile, a set of silver bracelets that I still wear when I fly, and a tiny bottle of perfume, a gift from my best friend, Mireyita, who remained on the island until recently, when we were reunited in our forties in Miami. I don't remember the scent Mireyita gave me, but I've always kept the little bottle, made of wood and inscribed "Cuba," on a shelf in my bedroom. I remember giving it little kisses when I was still a girl.

Do you have any suggestions for first-time novelists looking to draw from their own backgrounds in their work?

Read, read, read. Write, write, write. Every day. A writing career demands passion, commitment, immersion, and solitude. Dig into your background like an archaeologist. Listen to those wonderful *viejitos*, the elders who are full of great stories. Travel as widely as you can. Your background and experiences are at the crux of what makes you unique as a writer. It's what makes your stories genuine and resonant for readers.

PERSONAL AUTHOR'S GUIDE TO PARIS

Dear Paris lover,

I could write another book on Paris alone, but here are some highlights of my favorite places (all of them reasonably priced and loaded with French charm) to launch you on a visit to the City of Light:

- When I'm not renting an apartment in the bustling Latin Quarter, I stay at Hotel Du Continent, 30 rue du Mont-Thabor, because this small hotel is all about location, location, location—and clean, comfortable beds and bathrooms. It's located in the first arrondissement, right across from the Louvre and Tuileries gardens, and a short walk away from Place de la Concorde, where Marie Antoinette was guillotined! Cross this plaza of voluptuous fountains and ornate lampposts and you'll be at the famous Champs-Élysées. Best of all is the price of a room, from $114 to $154 euros per night, and you're in the company of the most famous and expensive hotels in Paris, steps away from places like the Vendôme and the Ritz. Stroll the neighborhood and you'll run into the original Coco Chanel and Christian Dior boutiques alongside some of the city's hottest new designers. Another plus of this home base: there are two Metro stations right across from the hotel, and several others throughout the neighborhood, so you can easily travel to anywhere in Paris from here.

- French cuisine is world-famous, but knowing where to eat in a big city makes all the difference. Guidebooks are sometimes dated or some restaurants have become so well-known they're way overpriced. For dinner, my favorite spot is Ferdi, 32 rue du Mont-Thabor, just two doors down from the Hotel Du Continent. It's reasonably priced and has a friendly vibe. It looks like a cozy tavern, packed with locals who know the owner, a burly Bono look-alike who runs the bar when it gets busy. Dozens of tiny toy figurines literally climb the walls, running along the wood accents, as soft romantic Mexican boleros play in the background. The food is spectacular. I've had everything from delicate risottos to Spanish *piquillos rellenos* (stuffed peppers), fried shrimp on a stick with a Japanese sauce, and Arabic-style meatballs and pasta rice. All expertly cooked. I love the sign on the door, in three languages, that goes something like this, "Good food takes time. We have the food and we hope you have the time." When I Googled Ferdi to get you the address, I learned that it's Penélope Cruz's favorite restaurant in Paris. She likes to come eat cheeseburgers for lunch. How about that? I had no idea. Thought I had discovered it!

For breakfast, I walk to Angélina at 226 rue de Rivoli, my favorite *salon de thé*. I love the croissants, pastries, and breads, and the setting is traditional antique French, classically beautiful in worn white woods. And if you're a hot chocolate lover, this is the place for you. They make it thick and luscious.

My list of things to do in Paris would be endless, starting with every museum in sight, but I'll give you my top list of what may not be so obvious, yet you should not miss:

1. A run through my two favorite department stores, Galeries Lafayette (gorgeous glass-domed ceilings at the 40 boulevard Haussmann location) and Printemps. I especially love the linens department at both stores, but stick with buying tablecloths and pillowcases, because the sheets they call double won't fit our queen-size mattresses. I have two French tablecloths I adore. Even if you don't buy, it's a lot of fun to see French merchandise because it's all so uniquely designed, from decorative toasters to incomparably well-made baby clothes.

2. A stroll through Père-Lachaise Cemetery is a true cultural experience. Not only is Oscar Wilde buried here in a sculpted tomb scribbled with love notes by devotees, but it's a showcase of the reverence the French have for their dead. The family pantheons they erect are stunning. Some tombs are like minicastles, others are adorned with the most whimsical sculptures. The gardens are luscious, but make sure you wear comfortable shoes. The walkways are all paved with cobblestones, and wearing the wrong

shoes will hurt. Not the place to show off your fashion sense! (The cemetery is far from the city center, but the subway leaves you right at the entrance.)

3. The Sunday street market on rue Mouffetard in the Latin Quarter is my favorite. Vendors spill into the sidewalks, musicians play accordions and saxophones, and the French, carrying their straw shopping totes, stop to sing along with the musicians, especially when they break into the old standard *"La vie en rose."* The Latin Quarter also is a lively place to stroll at night, when it becomes flooded with people out to dine and play; a lot of them are tourists from all over the world.

This is but a nibble of the Paris I love. Everyone comes away from a trip to Paris with a list of favorites. The most important thing on a visit to Paris is to remain open to the possibilities of discovery. Stroll the city's streets like the quintessential flaneur, with no plans and only for the thrill of the journey. Paris is the kind of city where you can get happily lost in just about any neighborhood and discover the most charming scenes: a gorgeous white cat resting on a windowsill dressed in lacy white curtains, Parisians kissing on a park bench, a sexy French man parking his motorcycle. Take a seat at the famous Café de Flore—where many famous writers, including Jean-Paul Sartre and Simone de Beauvoir—once hung out, and practice the art of conversation, French-style. Walk, walk, walk. There's a view of the Eiffel Tower waiting for you when you least expect it. I never tire of Paris!

Bien à toi,
Fabiola Santiago